"What's going on, Brian? Where are you going?"

"To Perrysville."

Jessica's glance intensified. "Why?"

He told her about extending the cell-tower search. That he'd found a match for the messages that had been sent to her. "Bonnie Lichen is in Perrysville."

Tears sprang to her eyes. "You think...Bonnie has Brooke?"

"I'm not jumping to any conclusions at this point. I just think the tower evidence is worth a conversation."

"In person."

"I want her to look me in the eye, yes."

"You want to take her by surprise and see if my daughter is there with her. I'm coming with you."

He had no idea what he'd be walking into. "Jess..."

"I'm coming."

She was paying him. Could fire him on the spot, and go alone.

She would do it. He had no doubt about that. No matter what danger she could find herself in. If Bonnie was more involved rather than less. If she had a gun, too...

With a single nod of his head, he waited for her to get her purse and join him.

Dear Reader,

There comes a time in life when you just have to listen to your own heart, your own instincts. When, in spite of what others might say, you have to be true to what you know. This book is one of those times. The story came to me, and while it didn't fit what I was currently doing, it wouldn't leave. Jessica wouldn't leave. Her story had to be told.

Jessica is a woman who follows her own path, in spite of everyone around her advising her differently. And doing so gives her strength. It's not about whether she's right or wrong. It's about trusting herself. And being the person she feels herself to be.

And it's a story about Brian. A man who follows his own course, who uses his skills to the best of his ability to find the truth. Good or bad.

I had no idea going in where this story was going to lead me. I had to take it on faith that it would work. I'm moved by the final result and I hope you are, too!

Tara Taylor Quinn

NOT WITHOUT HER CHILD

Tara Taylor Quinn

ISBN-13: 978-1-335-59369-6

Not Without Her Child

For questions and comments about the quality of this book, please contact us at CustomerService@Harlequin.com.

Harlequin Enterprises ULC
22 Adelaide St. West, 41st Floor
Toronto, Ontario M5H 4E3, Canada
www.Harlequin.com

Printed in U.S.A.

A *USA TODAY* bestselling author of over 105 novels in twenty languages, **Tara Taylor Quinn** has sold more than seven million copies. Known for her intense emotional fiction, Ms. Quinn's novels have received critical acclaim in the UK and most recently from Harvard. She is the recipient of the Readers' Choice Award and has appeared often on local and national TV, including *CBS Sunday Morning*.

For TTQ offers, news and contests, visit www.tarataylorquinn.com!

Books by Tara Taylor Quinn

Harlequin Romantic Suspense

Sierra's Web

Tracking His Secret Child
Cold Case Sheriff
The Bounty Hunter's Baby Search
On the Run with His Bodyguard
Not Without Her Child

The Coltons of Colorado

Colton Countdown

Where Secrets are Safe

Her Detective's Secret Intent
Shielded in the Shadows
Falling for His Suspect

The Coltons of New York

Protecting Colton's Baby

Visit the Author Profile page at Harlequin.com for more titles.

For Rachel Reames Stoddard—you are my Brooke.
I love you more than life.

Chapter 1

There were balloons. Two small, helium-filled ones on sticks in a bud vase. The vase sat next to a big, happy, pink-sprinkled cupcake with two candles.

They'd made Jessica feel good as she'd purchased them, brought them home, placed them on the table. She'd been actively engaged in being a mother celebrating her two-year-old daughter's birthday.

But when she'd walked past them a few minutes later… she'd avoided looking at them. Hadn't been in the kitchen since.

Her stomach growled. Dinnertime had come and gone.

There'd been no party.

How she'd thought, even for a second, that she'd pull it off, she didn't know. Couldn't remember why she'd wanted to try.

Some idea that by celebrating Brooke's birthday, she was putting out to the universe her belief that her daugh-

ter was still alive. That there was a birthday to celebrate. Holding fate, or whatever power might be out there, responsible for her toddler's life. For ensuring that there remained a child for her to find.

And maybe she'd been showing Clint, too. Her ex-husband had succeeded in stealing her little girl, but he would not break her. He wouldn't take away the milestones. The joy in celebrating Brooke's birth. Her existence. He would not steal an ounce of the strength she needed to continue what had already been an eighteen-month search.

Presenting herself at the table, she sat right in front of the little celebration she'd laid out, peeled the paper sides from the single-serving frosted concoction. Took a bite.

One.

Nearly choked, trying to get it past the tightness in her throat.

Blinked back tears at her sad little party. The lack of brightly colored packages and bows.

Until emotion gave way to the determination that fed her soul, and she knew the gift that she had to give her daughter.

She'd read a state news piece that morning about a firm of experts in fields like psychiatry, criminal investigation, IT, finance and law. Headquartered in Phoenix, they solved crimes, puzzles and family dilemmas.

She'd been told over and over—by colleagues, a counselor, friends, the detective she'd first spoken to who checked in regularly, the FBI agent on the case, the stepmother who'd raised her—to let law enforcement do their jobs. That they had the best of the best working round the clock to find Brooke.

But that firm of experts—Sierra's Web, they were

called—had become nationally known, and one reviewer claimed they could do what the police and FBI couldn't do.

What that was, she didn't know, and how much money she could potentially waste hiring them—she didn't know that either.

Neither did she care.

She was a mom and she was going to buy her two-year-old daughter the best birthday present ever. A way home.

She'd said she'd pick him up at the airport. Brian Powers hadn't expected his new client to be waiting at the security checkpoint so early on a Friday morning as he walked from the gate to baggage claim.

Even if he hadn't recognized the attractive oval face with the big blue eyes, the searching expression she wore—one edged with a hint of desperation—would have given her away to him. The sign she held, bearing his name in bold black letters, was only confirmation.

The loose, long blond ponytail, the slim gray pants, heels and short-sleeved silky business shirt all fit with the images he'd studied during the flight—images that were all part of the portfolio he'd compiled the night before. With help from a Sierra's Web IT expert.

At first glance, Jessica Johnson, thirty-one-year-old accountant and financial trader, looked as impressive in person as she did on paper.

And how would she look if Brian couldn't bring her the answers she needed? He'd find her daughter. Or at least find evidence to give her closure, if the latter were an impossibility. Eighteen months had passed since she'd last seen her little girl. Bodies decomposed.

In terms of an alive-and-well discovery…statistics just were not in their favor.

All of which he kept to himself as, garment bag and satchel straps over one shoulder, he approached and met the determined mother's gaze. "Jessica?"

"Mr. Powers?" she returned, sounding every bit the businesswoman she was and, when he nodded, added, "Thank you so much for coming."

She met his gaze head-on. Chin up. He saw the moisture in her eyes, made a mental note, but didn't acknowledge it between them. He wasn't there to get all up in her personal drama.

Doing so could cause him to let her down. Emotions tended to cloud judgment, and he couldn't afford to miss whatever minute clue had been eluding law enforcement for so many months.

And so, when she started giving him the laydown about Fayetteville, Arkansas, the second largest town in the state and home to the University of Arkansas, he listened, noting the layout of the regional airport as they went. He'd researched the area as best he could in the limited time he'd had, but every word out of Jessica Johnson's mouth could be a clue. Knowledge of her perspective, what she knew, and how she thought, had most definitely been used by her ex-husband as he'd plotted to steal Brooke away from her.

"Thank you for getting here so quickly," she said as she led him from baggage claim out to the parking lot. "I rented a place for you through the end of next weekend, thinking we'd reassess after that. If you aren't comfortable there, or we get an idea of maybe wanting to rent for a month, or..."

Her words trailed off and he felt the void of silence with a heaviness he shoved away. He couldn't tell her that this could all be over within that first week, but he

was fairly sure that the thought had been what she'd left off the end of her sentence.

"And the vehicle you'll be driving…it was Clint's. I've started it a few times, but, other than to leave it at the apartment I rented for you, it hasn't been driven since he went to prison…"

For kidnapping their baby girl. He'd been in prison for fifteen of the eighteen months Jessica—and the Fayetteville police, the Arkansas state police, the county's sheriff's department, US Marshals Service Missing Child Program, and the FBI—had been searching for her daughter. And he still had a minimum of another twenty-one months to serve.

Twenty-one months times four—roughly eighty-four more weeks to torture his ex-wife with false leads, give or take a five-week month.

She'd sent Brian a list of the sixty-four leads Clint Johnson had already given her—one a week since he went to prison—leads he'd only give if she visited with him every week. With at least one visit a month in person, and the rest by video.

"It's actually a truck, a sports model with a back seat, short bed, blue." She'd led them through a front parking area directly outside the terminal and was heading toward another lot further back. Pulling his bag—not his regular go-bag, but the larger one that held a week's worth of clothes in addition to his other necessities—Brian just listened.

To the tone of her voice. The cadence and rapidness with which she spoke. Learning all he could as quickly as he could.

Needing to know her as Clint knew her—even as he silently acknowledged that he never would. Clint had

been married to Jessica for almost a decade. Had had a child with her…

"The truck was still in my name—after the divorce was final, my ex-husband had been given a month to get a loan of his own to buy it from me at cost." She chatted, walked briskly without any breathiness, never glanced toward him.

"I'm going to sell it," she continued, and Brian couldn't determine if she was going on about the minutia because to do more was so difficult, because she was uncomfortable with him and uneasy about having hired him, or if she was just one of those people who talked all the time, sharing whatever came to mind.

"Just…until she's found… Forensics is through with it. It was returned to me after the trial. But that backseat is her last-known whereabouts and…"

And that's why they'd been talking about his mode of transportation. Her motive became clear. She hadn't been jabbering. She'd been giving him exactly what he needed from her.

The inside scoop.

She was right on task. Not avoiding painful conversation, not feeling uncomfortable about hiring him…she'd already gone to work.

First thing on his agenda that early May morning was to go over every inch of that truck with his own forensic kit.

They'd reached a full-sized black SUV, a couple of years old he could tell by the taillights on her particular model. The unlock system activated as they approached and she lifted the tailgate, stepping back as he moved forward to load his suitcase.

He caught a whiff of lavender—from the vehicle, or from her, he couldn't be sure. He wasn't opposed to it.

The rear-facing car seat in the second row hit him with a less than pleasant punch. Reminding him of the daunting task ahead.

He'd find the child. One way or another, he'd find her.

But that didn't necessarily put a little girl back in that seat.

The only way to do that was to find little Brooke Johnson alive. An end result that was completely out of his control…

And if he didn't fill that car seat?

He'd carry around Jessica Johnson's heartache for the rest of his life.

Came with the job—that trunk of pain. But the other side of that—giving people closure so that they could get on with their lives…

At the moment, giving this grieving mother the answers that would free her from the unending nightmare of fruitless search…

That was his reason for being alive.

Chapter 2

"I'm taking you straight to the apartment," Jessica said as she pulled out of the airport. "I've paid to have the kitchen stocked with basics—eggs, milk, bread, condiments, coffee, tea, that kind of thing. And the truck is already there as well." She'd driven it over just after dawn, and walked back to her place before heading to the airport. Reaching into the plastic storage bin on the side of her door, she pulled out a large clasped envelope. "You'll find keys to the apartment and to the truck in there. As well as prepaid gas and grocery cards. I'll refill the cards as needed."

No "Good to meet you. How was your flight?" Or even "Welcome to Fayetteville." The second she'd seen the confident stride in the dark-haired man come toward her, read the compassion in his striking hazel gaze, she'd lost the ability for pleasantries.

He touched something inside her, a part of her she'd

thought dead, and that wasn't a good thing. She didn't have the time, or energy, to…feel.

Not on a personal level.

The man was not her savior.

In the first place, she didn't need one. Wouldn't accept one even if it landed from space on her doorstep.

And if he was Brooke's savior, she didn't need to be slowing down the process by making anything about his presence in their lives about herself.

"You've got a one-bedroom place, but there's a nice-sized living area, separate kitchen and private balcony. The complex doesn't normally rent by the week, but the owner is a client of mine. The furnishings are from one of the model units."

He'd opened the envelope. Had pulled out the simple O-ring upon which she'd loaded both truck and apartment keys. She could feel the second he glanced over at her.

Her peripheral vision told her he wasn't looking away.

She couldn't have that. "What?" she asked. "If there's something not to your liking, just speak up…" She'd do whatever she could to get him everything he needed.

Hell, she'd make his meals, do all of his shopping, even shine his shoes if they were things he required to be at his best.

"You're very thorough." He sounded impressed.

She didn't want him to be impressed. She wanted him to use his expert skills to pull tricks she didn't know about out of a bag she hadn't seen and find Brooke.

"I'm determined," she countered. Determined enough that she was cashing in stock to pay Sierra's Web's hefty fee on an off chance that they were as good as the article, and plethora of testimonials, had claimed them to be.

She'd just hired him—or rather, the Sierra's Web firm—the day before. "And I don't sleep much."

He nodded, went back to the envelope, but didn't pull out anything else.

"There's a complex card in there that gives you access to the outdoor gated pool area and into the fitness room."

"I would have been fine with a hotel room."

"I'm getting the apartment at half the cost of a decent hotel room where I'd have to pay by the night."

Because the real estate investor who owned the complex, and rentals all over Fayetteville, had made a lot of money due to Jessica's handling of his finances.

And maybe because he and his wife felt sorry for her.

She couldn't do anything about that.

"My place is a mile away," she told him. "The address is also in there. I'm available to you anytime, day or night, to answer questions or provide information. Since my home is the site of the abduction, I'm assuming you'll want to take a look at things at some point."

Probably not much evidence still hanging around after eighteen months and a lot of rainfall, but his private investigative expertise supposedly made him capable of finding what others had not.

"And in case you're wondering," she added as it occurred to her, again, that he and his firm might think that her pain made her vulnerable and someone who could be taken advantage of, "I know this is a long shot. That the chance that you'd be able to come here and magically find what all of the best law enforcement in the country has not, is miniscule. I'm not expecting to get my money's worth," she added, just to be clear. "But I'm not going to leave any stone unturned, any chance uninvestigated, any harebrained scheme unattempted, until I have my daughter home with me."

His silence, in light of her forthrightness, didn't sit well. Yeah, she'd been abrupt during the entire forty-five

minutes of their acquaintance, but where her case was concerned, she needed him to be open with her. "You have no response to that?"

"None that I care to make at this time."

"May I ask why?" He was on her payroll. She had a right to ask questions.

"Because you aren't going to like it." The words, the warning tone of voice, his glance to the car seat behind her, gave her an idea of what he was thinking. It wasn't like she hadn't heard the same from pretty much every source open to speak to her about it.

"My daughter is alive, Mr. Powers." Her tone brooked no argument and she felt no apology for it.

"I know you believe that."

"I don't just believe it. I know it."

His eyes shot toward her. Stopped at a light, she looked right back at him. "You have proof?" he asked, brows raised.

He knew she didn't.

And yet…that gaze, the way his eyes seemed to light up…it was as though he truly wanted to believe her.

"My ex-husband is, in my opinion, a narcissist. He needs to be pandered to at all times. He's emotionally weak and he is cruel when it gets him what he wants, but he is too afraid of the afterlife to ever kill anyone or to lie about not having done so."

"Even if lying about it keeps you coming to visit him every single week that he's locked up in prison?"

Her stomach lurched. The granola bar she'd had for breakfast wasn't soaking up enough of the acid inside her. "There is that possibility," she acknowledged through a throat gone dry. Finding Brooke meant total honesty. With herself and others. "But when Clint gets truly worried about his mortality, his gaze tends to dart around.

He looks me straight in the eye, every time, when he tells me that Brooke is alive and well."

The man swore under his breath. Something about Clint's lack of legitimate paternity, if she wasn't mistaken.

"I also know that I'd feel something if she was gone," she said. "My certainty that she's alive isn't just wishful thinking, or an inability to accept the worst. It's a peaceful sense that comes over me when I think I can't go on, when I'm exhausted, or when I wake up in a panic in the middle of the night."

His silence was so lengthy she considered the conversation over.

"I don't believe you're wrong in what you say, or feel." His words fell into that quiet like warm tea in the morning. And then he added, "But if I'm going to do the job you've hired me to do, I have to keep the possibility of her being…gone…on the table."

He was there to find her daughter. One might look for life or…not…in different places. Using different means.

He was giving her his honesty.

She wanted it. Needed it. Was grateful that he'd given it to her.

"I understand." She pulled onto the apartment property and around to the covered parking outside his door. "And I look forward to you finding out that I'm right."

Brian didn't want to prove her wrong. He couldn't try to prove her right. All he could hope to do was to prove what happened.

To do that, he needed an open mind to any and every possibility. To find and follow evidence, no matter where it led.

That was why he couldn't get emotionally involved in a job.

Or a client.

Usually, a no-brainer for him.

So why was a woman he'd just met creating a struggle within him to find his detachment? He pondered the question briefly as he took a cursory look around the bare-walled apartment and rolled his bag into the nondescript but comfortable-looking bedroom. He changed into jeans and a short-sleeved shirt, set up his mobile printer, and surge protector that traveled with all chargers plugged in, on the kitchen counter, and grabbed the key ring he'd taken from the envelope.

He'd told Jessica he'd be at her house that morning, to familiarize himself with the scene of the original crime—the kidnapping. She kept a rigid schedule. As an investment broker, she always worked from 8:30 a.m. until 3:00 p.m., Wall Street hours on central time, Monday through Friday. Using early mornings and evenings for phone calls and research for her clients as necessary. Her standing half-hour video visit with her ex-husband was on Friday at four. Once a month, she drove the two-and-a-half hours to have the meeting in person at five-thirty. And the rest of her life was compartmentalized around the false leads Clint sent her way.

Seemingly false. According to the reports he'd read, as far as Jessica, or anyone else had been able to ascertain, Clint's information had, thus far, led nowhere. Brian would be taking a look at every single one of the sixty-four supposed clues.

But, first, was the truck, and then the scene of the crime. Start at the beginning.

The bed of the truck had a liner, good quality, professionally installed. Clean. He bagged a small blade of grass

he got off the side of a ridge in the heavy black plastic. Could have landed any time in the past fifteen months. Except that she'd said the only time she'd driven was to move it to his apartment and the grass was browned with age, but still viable due to whatever substance had stuck it to the liner.

An hour passed as he made his way around the outside of the truck, the wheel wells, bumpers, tires. He'd collected thirteen samples by the time he first opened a door. And another thirty-seven in the back and passenger seats. Most, maybe all, would lead to nothing.

All he needed was one little something. If not from the truck, then from somewhere.

Authorities had already gone through glove box and console contents. With his medical gloves on, Brian emptied both receptacles into one large zip-lock bag for his later perusal. May not lead him any closer to finding Brooke, but they'd give him insight into the man who'd taken her.

Jessica Johnson had been waiting too long for answers. Even the unthinkable would allow her to get off the treadmill leading to nowhere and move forward with her life.

On his back on the front floor of the truck, he perused under the passenger seat, found an old dried-up piece of what looked to be a French fry lodged in the seat adjustment track. And slowly moved his way over to the driver's side. The carpeted interior made his job both easier and harder. There weren't a million grooves in rubber mats to get through. But he was going to have to vacuum the carpet into a clean bag and then go through what came out—before bed that night.

With tweezers and small evidence bags, he retrieved half a dozen small, dried pieces of what he suspected was food under and around the driver's seat. Assum-

ing Clint Johnson was the usual driver of the truck, the man ate in his vehicle more often than someone else ate in it with him.

Or he was a lot messier when he ate than any companion had been. There was a lot more debris under his seat than the passenger's.

Mentally logging both impressions for the notes he'd make at the end of his inspection, Brian moved his head back toward the brake pedal and stopped. The seam at the edge of the seat, out of line of normal vision, just under the edge of the seat…it was thicker in a four-inch section. Reaching out, he ran his fingers slowly along the edge, no hypotheses forming. He'd never seen a leather seat seam be perfectly symmetric but thicker in one part.

But yeah, it definitely was. As though someone had inserted something into the seam? Heart rate speeding up a bit as a pump of adrenaline shot through him, he wondered if the job could really be that easy. Had he already found the missing piece? Something just a little bit off that would lead him on the chase to the successful conclusion?

The thin rubber of his glove snagged on an edge of the seam. Brian pointed his skinny powerful light to the spot he held as he scooted his head as far under the seat as he could get it. Working in the tight spot wasn't easy. He didn't care. He'd find a way.

Half seeing, feeling the parts he couldn't see, he realized that the seam wasn't sewn tight. With a good tug, he knew why. Inserted in the four-inch section were two thin plastic sheets covered with hook and pile fasteners that, when yanked, came apart. Heart pounding harder, and flat on his back, with his head turned to the side, he slowly slid his free fingers into the opening.

And jammed them into cold hard metal.
With a butt and a barrel.
Clint Johnson had a hidden gun.

Chapter 3

"It's not like you, Jessica, throwing money away on an 'if, come, maybe.'"

"It's a nationally renowned firm, Ma." Jessica arranged folders in order of the phone calls she had yet to make before lunchtime as she spoke into her headpiece.

Calling her stepmother hadn't been on the list. And yet…there she was…talking to her.

A certified financial planner who was also licensed to buy and sell securities, Jessica loved her job. Was challenged by it, but more, got great satisfaction out of helping her clients construct secure futures. Having grown up without, she wasn't about building wealth—she believed in building financial security.

Throwing money into the wind, on a whim, an "if, come, maybe" was definitely not like her.

Her stepmother, the most pessimistic person she'd ever known, and thankfully, firmly ensconced in her

life in a retirement community in California, kept Jessica grounded.

Not that Jackie Shepherd knew that. Jessica and the woman who'd raised her from infancy, later adopting her, didn't talk about such things.

Their lives, after her father had gambled away everything they'd owned, including their home, and then split with a rich widow, had been about survival.

Even after Jackie had graduated from college at forty-five, with a nursing degree, and Jess had made some good investments for her that had turned a little bit of money into enough to let Jackie buy a small home in a nice, gated community, her stepmom still lived with a scarcity mentality.

"I still think you need to send him back, Jess. If he just got there today, he won't have racked up hours yet, you'll just be out the flights and the week's apartment rental if you can't get a refund..."

She'd given the woman too many details.

Because she'd been...off her game. Unsure.

Not about Brian Powers or Sierra's Web. Not exactly.

But the way the man had moved her...made her feel as though he was her answer to unspoken prayers...

That had scared the hell out of her.

Hence a midmorning call to her own personal scrooge. A woman she loved. A woman she knew loved her.

Even if she disagreed with Jackie ninety percent of the time.

"I've got the money, for now, without touching a single investment," she said aloud. "I got the apartment basically on trade for a week's fees," she admitted to the only person she'd tell. Her client would pay the fee, she'd reimburse every penny. And based on what rentals went for in

town, she was making out on the deal. "And honestly, Ma, isn't Brookie worth every dime of every investment?"

There. She'd put her state of mind right out there.

"Of course she is," Jackie said, easing Jess's stomach tension a bit. Until her mother added, "But, Jess, it's been eighteen months. Even without the jackass's input, surely, if a two-year-old child was out there, she'd have turned up somewhere by now."

Unless Clint had sold her. Her stomach roiled.

Or…had given her to a good family to love as their own. Lying about her having a mother who desperately wanted her home.

"She's alive, Ma."

Jackie's silence brought an end to the conversation. The same end every time.

"I love you."

"I know and I love you, too, which you know, and, Jess, it's because I love you that I can't stand to hear you talk about all of this anymore. You're killing yourself. Making yourself mentally and emotionally a wreck. You have to stop visiting with Clint. Stop grasping at straws. You're stronger than this…"

She was strong. Jackie Shepherd knew her better than anyone.

Strong in body, in mind, and in spirit. And her spirit would not let her listen to the well-intentioned poison coming from her stepmother's mouth. "I gotta go…"

The ringing of her front doorbell had nothing to do with the statement as it came immediately after she'd said it.

"Jess, wait, please…"

She held the phone to her ear as she went to see who was out front. Her newly hired private investigator wasn't

due for another half hour. "Seriously, Ma, I've got someone at the door."

"Just promise me you'll think about what I said."

She couldn't make that promise. She wasn't going to let Jackie's lack of faith bring her down. She might give a second or two to ponder why she'd called the only mother she'd ever known in the first place. But…

The living room window gave her a view of Clint's truck in the driveway. The clock on her wall, a housewarming gift from her ma many years before, confirmed that she hadn't lost track of time. She wasn't running late, their appointment wasn't for another thirty minutes. She upped her pace to the door.

"I love you, Ma," she said, the phone still held to her head, Jackie's voice droning in her ear as she opened the front door.

And saw the gun in Brian Powers's hand.

Jessica clicked off the phone, seemingly without saying goodbye, as Brian stepped into her foyer. He'd removed the medical glove from his driving hand, but still held the gun with a gloved left hand just as he'd pulled it out of her husband's truck.

"Did you know Clint had a gun?" It hadn't been what he'd meant to say, but the wide-eyed look of horror on her face as she dropped her phone hand to her thigh and stared at him, had jerked the words out of his mouth.

"I—no! We…with a baby in the house…no!"

"He had it stowed in the seat of his truck. You need to call the detective in charge of your case, to get me pulled in, if nothing else, but they have to know about this now. Get Forensics back out." Other than the gun he'd pulled from the under-the-seat enclosure, he hadn't touched any part of the secret hiding place. Hadn't wanted to mess

with the chain of command. "I don't know if it's loaded. Or if there's ammunition in the pocket I found. I didn't want to chance my gloves rubbing off any identifying evidence."

He could have one-handedly bagged it.

The fact that he'd jumped in the truck and driven straight to her wasn't good news to him. Didn't speak well of him as a professional. At least, not in his opinion.

He had no time to assess what she thought of his actions. She already had her phone to her ear and was engaging with the detective who'd answered right away.

Detective Anderson. Duane Anderson—one of the names he'd read in the file she'd sent over.

She'd pushed one button. Anderson was on her speed dial.

Just based on the questions she was answering, Brian's first impression of the detective was ranking higher than the one he was currently holding of himself.

Yeah, he might have smudged the gun further if he'd tried to get a bag and open it with only one hand. But driving like a bat out of hell straight to her door…

The evidence was huge. If there was any gun powder residue in the barrel…even a hint of it…if there was ammunition or anything else incriminating inside that pocket…

Jessica was explaining to Duane Anderson that she'd hired Brian, who he was…

Going over the vehicle after Forensics was through with it, picking up a blade of grass and small particles that were left behind…that wasn't tampering with evidence, or tainting it for future use in court. Finding a gun…

When a body was missing…

"Yes, that's right. Sierra's Web…" Jessica was say-

ing and then handed over the phone. "He wants to talk to you."

Still holding the gun away from touching anything but his two left fingers, Brian took the phone. Kept his gaze on his new client, noticing the teeth biting her lower lip, the way her gaze continued to head toward the weapon in his hand and then slide quickly away.

Felt a knot tighten in his gut.

And told the detective everything he'd done to that point.

Minus the part where he was fending off a deep, unsettling empathy for his new client.

Five minutes after the phone call, Detective Anderson and a forensic team showed up at Jessica's door.

They took the truck, would be removing the secret pocket and keeping it, anything they found within it, and the gun, in an evidence locker. After testing all for anything the articles could tell them.

While she was mollified by the respect her newly hired Sierra's Web expert was receiving, and glad to see that Brooke's absence was still worthy of immediate attention, Jessica watched the proceedings, listened to conversation, with a growing panic.

"You do understand that the gun's existence doesn't mean Clint used it to kill anyone," she blurted, standing between Brian Powers and Detective Anderson as they watched the truck be towed away. Protocol, that.

She'd driven the truck once since Clint's arrest. Brian had driven it. Any apparatus touched during the driving process had already been thoroughly tested…

When the gazes of the men met, rather than landing on her, she took a deep breath. "I understand the need to check it out," she assured them, doing her best to calm

the agitation inside her. "I just don't want the discovery to take away focus from finding my daughter."

They couldn't stop looking for a live child due to circumstances that didn't belong to the baby's case. "As much as Clint Johnson nauseates me," she heard the tremble in her voice, but continued with, "I know that he isn't a killer. I have no idea why he had that gun," she added, knowing she was going to grill the man with every bite of anger inside her during their scheduled video conference later that afternoon. "But I know he didn't use it to hurt Brooke."

"People change," the detective said, that hint of sympathy and…something more in his tone. A type of well-meaning condescension. He not only felt sorry for her. His conversation had taken on tones of pats on the head to her. He was always kind. Attentive. Always picked up her calls.

The married man of four definitely cared about the case.

He also clearly thought that Jessica's drive to find her daughter, her belief that Brooke was still alive, was… misguided. And not healthy for Jessica.

Sometimes, in the dark of the night, she laid awake in bed and mentally entertained some of the "move on" advice Duane Anderson had given her. Replayed conversations the two of them had had on the subject.

And never once, even in her lowest moments—and with memories of her stepmother's similar words adding sustenance to his message—had she been completely convinced that he was right.

She didn't argue. There was no point. "I'll ask him about it," was all she said.

Anderson shook his balding head. "Not until after I get a sit-down with him. I want to see his reaction to the

fact that we found the gun, that we're testing it," the detective said, glancing at his watch. "He's a two-and-a-half-hour drive from here…and there's no guarantee I'll make it there today at all. And I'd like to have forensic results back first, if possible." He, better than anyone, knew her visitation schedule, knew that she'd be speaking with Clint later that day. On his say-so, he was the first person she called at the end of every visit.

"In fifteen months' time, Clint has given you nothing," Jessica reminded him. "He talks to me."

"Yes, he does." Anderson's response had that compassionately humoring tone again. "But not one of his hints has led to anything…he's using you, Jessica, stringing you along for his own sadistic amusement. You're playing right into his hands. Please, just let me handle this…"

Even while she appreciated his sincere concern for her emotional well-being, Jessica bristled. "I have to—"

"If I might make a suggestion…" Brian interrupted, seeming, to her, to have shifted his weight so that he was leaning slightly in her direction. But then, she was still suffering from a bite of that "him being a savior" bug that had gotten her that morning.

"Of course." Anderson appeared grateful for the interception. The man had come to know her fairly well over the past year. He couldn't stop her from speaking to Clint about anything. And he knew she acted upon the premises in her own mind. Even in the olden days when her life had only been about spreading cheer and helping others and raising her baby, she'd been a woman who'd trusted her instincts and pretty much always chosen to follow them.

"Today's visit is by video," Brian said. "I can set it to record, and be present—outside of the camera view so that Johnson doesn't know I'm there—and position my-

self with pen and paper within Jessica's view so that if there are any questions that need to be asked, from a law enforcement standpoint, they'll get asked." He glanced at Jessica. "Assuming you're willing to go along with this and ask them."

Maybe he was testing her. Didn't matter. She'd hired him to find Brooke. Not to find the outcome she wanted, but to find Brooke. If she wasn't going to trust his process, she might as well save her money and send him home.

If she wasn't going to trust his process, she could be failing her daughter. "I'm fine with that," she said, looking between both men, meeting them eye-to-eye—equals in their quest.

"I'll get a look at his initial response," Brian continued to their little threesome in the circle on her front walk, and then turned to Anderson. "And you'll also have the tape to view, so that you get a look, since you know his tells."

Chin jutted, his tie seeming to strain against the tension in his neck, Anderson put his hands in the pockets of his gray dress pants, tipped back and forth, heel to toe, in his shiny black shoes, and then nodded.

For a second, Jessica wasn't sure what had just happened. She'd won her first ever argument with Duane Anderson. Or, Brian had won it for her. But...winning usually meant someone lost, and that hadn't happened either.

Her newly acquired expert had negotiated a compromise between two people who held polar opposite opinions. A compromise that suited Brooke best.

Maybe, just maybe, hiring Brian Powers had been the answer for which they'd all been searching.

Chapter 4

You really got a sense of a person when you stood in their past. And as Brian—staying at Jessica's home until the truck was returned—studied reports, the impression he was getting from Clint Johnson was all bad.

All of it.

The man was above-average smart, with an IQ and scholastic records to back that up, but had wasted every ounce of that gift in terms of contributing to society. Or even his own family.

Clint had had good jobs—a few of them—and, according to his own trial testimony, had had to quit every one of them through no fault of his own. In each place of employment, all in the information technology field, he'd been treated unfairly. Hadn't had enough time off. His ideas stolen by others who'd taken credit for them. People were jealous of his abilities and bullied him.

According to Clint Johnson.

How did you remove your six-month-old nursing daughter from her adoring mother, her family, her home, and show no remorse?

Even if he'd had good reason—more like a self-aggrandizement issue, according to prosecutors who'd described Clint as a man who thought he was a godlike figure who knew best—he'd feel sorry, wouldn't he? For the breakdown of the family? For a child starting life as a seeming orphan since she was no longer with either of her biological parents?

Unless he knew the child was no longer alive?

The baby's father had said, over and over, that he didn't know where Brooke was. While his mantra to Jessica was that she was in a better place.

He just didn't know where.

He swore under a lie detector that he hadn't given her to anyone, or left her with anyone.

And that he knew she was being well cared for. Loved, even.

He'd continued to proclaim that he was innocent of the kidnapping for which he'd been sent to prison.

So how could he be certain Brooke was in a better place?

Unless he'd killed the baby.

And considered her loved in a heavenly realm.

He hadn't been charged with her murder—yet—because there was no evidence of one having been committed, but that didn't mean it hadn't happened.

The evidence of the kidnapping had been overwhelmingly convincing enough to get a guilty verdict—but it had all been circumstantial. There was no definitive proof that Clint Johnson and his daughter had been together outside of their home on the morning in question.

Most of what Brian was going over, seated at the

breakfast bar in Jessica's kitchen while she worked in her home office, was a rehash of what he'd already studied.

Reading it while sitting in the man's previous home, in the room Clint Johnson had been standing in the morning of the kidnapping, brought it more to life.

Completed trial transcript in hand, Brian walked slowly through the downstairs rooms, leaving the master suite—the scene of the kidnapping—until last. He skimmed over myriad baby pictures, having no way of knowing which were present when Clint was in the house and how many had been put up as a means of coping after Brooke was kidnapped.

The baby's room, decorated in a unicorn and rainbow motif, appeared as though the child still lived there, even down to lotions and diapers on the shelves of the changing table, a sheet on the crib mattress, and the flannel blanket thrown over the arm of the solid wood rocking chair.

The chair called to him. Three different times, he looked over at it.

Suspecting that Jessica Johnson had spent many hours in that chair since her daughter's disappearance.

He could almost see here there. Feel her anguish and frustration…

And had to move on. He wasn't there for her, except in terms of her dealings with the kidnapper.

A reminder that became much more acute as he entered Jessica's bedroom.

And was hit with a gut-wrenching sense of emptiness.

Unlike Brooke's room, Jessica's space was…benign. No real character. Opposite the bed hung a large, generic, screened canvas, depicting individual squares filled with random swirls all in beiges, golds and maroons. The bed

was covered with a comforter and pillows all in the same colors. Two dressers, two nightstands, same kind of polished dark wood as the bedframe, and a whole lot of empty beige carpet finished off the room.

He glanced toward the double doors leading into the bathroom suite. No sign of the baby swing Brooke had been sleeping in at the time of the abduction. And the window Clint had climbed in…the long curtain that had been slightly torn in the process was also missing. Open wood-slatted blinds that did not appear in crime scene photos covered the space.

He couldn't see the shower from the vantage point of where the swing had been. But Brooke had been able to see the television that had been tuned to a baby music video station.

Jessica had been in the shower. At her most vulnerable when she'd come out, wet and naked, to find her daughter's swing empty.

Feeling another chink in the armor that he wore through life, and most definitely on the job, Brian stood there, amass with sensation as he imagined how she must have felt—a strong woman attacked without a chance to fight back, to defend, when her guard was most down…

When she'd least expect it.

That had been the point, of course. Clint Johnson was the only one who'd known about the faulty window clip that allowed the locked window to be shifted slightly to the left and opened. He'd been in the area at the time of the kidnapping since he'd just been in the kitchen of the home half an hour before, been given the box of things he'd asked for and then been politely shown the door. He'd known Jessica's schedule, kept down to the minute, because it was Brooke's schedule, too.

Had known she'd nurse the baby for her 7:30 a.m. feeding, then put her in her swing to snooze while she showered so they'd both be ready for the nanny to arrive at 8:15 a.m., allowing Jessica to be in her office when the Wall Street bell rang at 8:30 a.m. Arkansas time.

The twisted fiend had stolen the infant away from her loving, secure home while his ex-wife, the baby's mother, had been just feet away in the shower.

"I had the monitor in the shower with me, set up on the top bar of the door casing."

Brian's head swung toward the sound of Jessica's voice. He hadn't heard her approach on the carpeted floor. And he hadn't had water sluicing over his head, as she had eighteen months before.

Shoulders straight, gaze steady, she spoke without a hitch in her tone. But that glint in her eyes…moisture being refused the right to fall…

Emotion washed over him.

He tensed. Said, "I know." He'd read about the monitor in the police report, and in the trial transcript, too. But standing in that room, seeing her there…

He was going to find Brooke Johnson.

Find the proof that would make Clint Johnson pay for the rest of his life for the heinous thing he'd done.

"I should have had her swing in the bathroom with me."

"You testified that the video channel made her happy."

"So, she'd have cried for five minutes…"

Five minutes as opposed to losing a lifetime. Even if Brooke was alive, there was no telling what might have happened to her in the past fifteen months. No way she'd ever be able to tell them everything.

He couldn't put the thought out there. Jessica's stark expression didn't ease his tension any.

"There's no part of this that's your fault. You know that, right?"

Just like it hadn't been his detective father's fault that his cop mother had taken risks that had cost her her life.

Brian's strong mental shake chased away the cobwebby thought.

"He turned the monitor off the second he came through the window," he reminded Jessica. Getting himself back on track. She was paying for his time and it didn't come cheap.

Because he was good. Focus came then. The intense inner study that made him an expert. Facts settled themselves in his mind. He'd been drowning himself with them…

"Clint was successful because he used his single-focused intelligence, and his intimate knowledge of you, to complete his mission," he said. "Having the swing in the bathroom, or even in the bathroom doorway, wouldn't have made a difference to him. He knew your showering routine. My guess is he'd studied it as he had everything about you. If he'd had to, he'd have hidden within arm's reach of the swing, and snatched Brooke the second you closed your eyes to rinse your hair…"

He might not be able to bring her baby back to her alive, but helping with any misplaced guilt…that was a critical piece, too.

He was there to bring her whatever peace of mind he could. To give her what she needed to be able to move on.

Jessica needed facts. Truth.

He'd just given her some.

And could tell, by the way those strikingly attractive oval cheeks relaxed, that he'd helped.

So maybe, just perhaps, the emotion hitting him out of the blue wasn't such a bad thing. Maybe it was all just part of that particular job.

Jessica could hardly breathe for a second there, staring at the tall, strong-looking, jeans-clad man in a room she'd grown to hate. What he'd said, this total stranger… he was right.

Oh God. Holding on to his gaze, her only visual those unusual hazel eyes, she felt herself weaken for a second. As though something inside her had started to melt.

Deep breath. Exhale, pushing out from the diaphragm. Words from a counseling session came to her. She heeded them automatically.

Drew in a long stream of life-giving air.

And knew that the previous moment didn't matter. Whether she could have prevented Clint from taking their daughter from her or not wasn't going to bring Brooke back.

Getting Brooke home was all that mattered. The thought brought her back to her reason for making the trek down the hallway to begin with.

"If you have any questions…anything that's not in the reports that I can add to help you…"

He was there to find what others hadn't. Everything he'd read, all that had been written, recorded, documented…what she needed wasn't there. At least, not in enough entirety to lead a single one of multiple law enforcement agencies to Brooke.

"There were a couple of more things on the dresser in the crime scene photos…"

Crime scene. The words jabbed her heart every time

she heard them. A year and a half later and the pain didn't recede.

Not even a little.

"I mention them because I need to know if Clint left any of them there. Or moved them. What might seem innocuous to some could mean something to me. Anything out of place. Anything he might have touched. I know his fingerprints were on things in the room. He'd lived here. I'm asking for anything different that morning..."

She nodded. Shook her head. Nodded again.

Couldn't keep a single aspect of her life private from the man. Not and have him do his job.

"Yes," she said. "I kept a picture of Brooke on my nightstand. I noticed it missing a few days after the kidnapping. It, um, was the first time I'd been back in the room since."

"So the rest of this..." He held out a photo, showing her the bedroom she'd shared with a madman. The room she'd last nursed her baby in...

"It's all exactly as it was that day, and every other day," she told him, looking around at the current emptiness. "I...don't sleep here," she started to explain. Stopped. Forged on. "With all of the time I spend looking for Brooke, I often end up doing research for my clients late at night or early in the morning." Sometimes the two ran right into each other. "Just seemed easier to go to the spare room right next door to the office to fall into bed..." Her things had moved with her. Gradually. One by one.

No one had to know what she did in her own home alone. Though some, her stepmother mostly, had offered her a place to stay, no one had offered to stay with her. She'd have declined if they had.

Just as she'd refused to leave Brooke's home.

Brian seemed to silently compel her to tell him everything.

And she would. She'd lay her life bare, wide open, to find Brooke.

But she would not, absolutely could not, allow any form of affection toward the man himself.

Not him or any man.

She couldn't take that chance.

Because she knew, no matter what anyone thought about her being at fault for Brooke's disappearance, that she was partially to blame.

She'd married Clint. Had stayed with him in spite of her growing awareness of his emotional selfishness. She'd made excuses. Had focused on how attentive and gentle and sweet he'd been in the good times. The way he'd tried to be the best cook, the best at whatever he'd attempted to do. When it had been just the two of them and Jessica had been giving him whatever it was he'd wanted in the moment, he'd been more fun to be around than anyone else she'd ever known. She'd believed in him, believed that he'd grow up.

She'd chosen him to be the father of her child.

She couldn't go back, couldn't undo. But she could give her life over to saving her daughter. And then make damned sure that she provided the child with a safe, loving home. That meant no man in Jessica's life. She didn't trust herself to choose a father for Brooke's future.

Chapter 5

She didn't sleep in the space anymore. Brian wasn't standing in Jessica's current bedroom. The small step-back from intimacy helped him stay focused.

"Did the photo from your nightstand ever turn up?" He hadn't seen mention of it. Anywhere. Not in it being missing, or having been found.

Frowning, seeming as though she was someplace far away, Jessica blinked. He could tell when she focused on him again. And lost a bit of the emotional distance he'd just managed to reinstate between them.

"The photo from the nightstand," he repeated, ignoring the rest.

She shook her head.

"Did you tell Anderson about it?"

Another shake of the head. "Like I said, I didn't realize until later that it was even gone. And it doesn't matter to the case, other than to prove further that Clint took her. I

like to believe, and actually do think, that in his own way, he loves Brooke. He liked to hold her when we were sitting on the couch watching television. And he was worried when she had a fever. But his resentment of her was more prevalent. He hated how much of my time she took from him. Hated that I wouldn't just leave her with a sitter to take the week at the beach he'd said he needed. He'd been furious when I suggested taking her along, going as the family we'd become. And he detested the fact that when I did have a minute, I was so tired I just wanted to sleep. Needless to say, when I put that picture of her next to our bed…" She shrugged.

"But you left it there."

She nodded. "I kept hoping that he'd see that she was a part of us. A product of us. Not the wall between us he was making her out to be. And…honestly, at that point, after so many fights about taking weekends away just the two of us—even after I gave in once and had my stepmom come stay with her while I went to the boat with him—I felt like I couldn't take away that picture of her from my room for my own mental health.

"I'd begun to see who Clint really was when I started talking about having a family, but it took a long time before I saw what others, my stepmother in particular, had seen for a long time. He and I had always talked about having kids. He'd always prevaricated, with logical enough reason to have me capitulate, until I started talking about turning thirty and running out of time. He eventually pretended to be fine with the idea, but only after I agreed to buy a little houseboat, which was what he most wanted…"

Radar blaring, Brian pinned her with his gaze. "You still have the boat?" It hadn't been in any of the reports.

A boat. Means of transportation. Ability to drop anything overboard… "Where was it docked?"

"Over in San Diego, and no," she answered his second question first.

Clint and the baby had been missing four days before he'd been apprehended… The ocean, thousands of miles of dump space…

Hard lumps of dread filled his gut.

"The boat is what prompted him to take Brooke from me." Her tone, her entire countenance, seemed to have been physically drained of all emotion. One minute he'd been speaking to a grieving woman and the next, a beautiful android.

He got it. The need to push all emotion aside in order to move forward, to accomplish. The understanding started to plummet him back into the mire of her suffering. He couldn't let it.

Eyebrow raised in question, he didn't have a chance to get the associated words out before she said, "I filed for divorce when Brooke was three months old. I knew what he'd want most was the boat, and offered it as part of the settlement, with the caveat that he take over the payment and dock rent. He agreed, right up until the next week when he felt that he'd been disrespected at work and quit his job. He was certain I'd carry him until he found another job…"

"And you said no."

"For the first time in ten years, I didn't catch him when he took a dive."

"He lost the boat."

"I sold it. It was either that or bail him out by making the payments myself, and I just couldn't do it again. It was never going to end…"

The picture she was presenting came through loud

and sickeningly clear. "That original bargain you made… a baby for a boat…" He let the words trail off when he saw her nod.

The sickening man had kidnapped his daughter because, in his mind, Jessica had stolen the baby's counterpart from him. She'd been the one to break the bargain.

Brian was pretty sure it didn't get any lower than that.

And knew then and there that, no matter what, he was not going to leave until Jessica Johnson had the means to fight her way out of the hell her ex-husband was trying to drown her in.

He had to end Clint's insidious hold over her once and for all.

By three thirty that afternoon, Jessica felt like a hot mess. Sitting in her office—trading done with a day of nice profits for her clients, in spite of the monumental personal interruptions—she couldn't find even a hint of satisfaction. Instead, her meeting with Clint loomed, half an hour away, and her insides were shaking. She should never have agreed to have an expert private detective—or anyone—present for the video conference. Even in hiding.

Clint knew her so well. And if he figured out that she had anyone else, let alone another man, joining in their weekly time together…

She hated that half hour with her ex each week, dreaded it, and yet it was the highlight of her week, too. Her chance to get another lead, something else to add to the list of clues Clint had given her, another opportunity to unscramble his sick puzzle and find Brooke.

Every single Friday she awoke with the thought that, by nightfall, she could have her daughter back home. Even if her ex didn't yet mean to reveal their daughter's

whereabouts, he could inadvertently say something that would lead her to Brooke.

That morning, knowing she was picking up an expert detective who'd be working solely, and full-time, on Brooke's case, plus speaking with Clint, her hopes for her baby's return had been high for the first time in months.

But having that expert present during her private conversation…

Brian Powers was no longer just a figment out there coming in to help. He was an impressively tall, lithe, strong, and yet sensitive man who'd stood in her and Clint's bedroom and made her actually feel, for the first time, that Brooke's kidnapping wasn't because she'd been careless and left the baby's swing out of her sight. That her hurry to get her shower in while keeping Brooke happy hadn't been the determining factor.

Clint knew her. Their home. Everything. With his diabolical intelligence, he'd have found a way…

She hadn't been solely to blame.

But what if Clint knew she'd hired someone to work for her full-time to bring Brooke back? Not just someone, but an undeniably attractive man who'd been alone in her home with her all day? The way he'd grown so possessive after their marriage, and her professional success…the way he grilled her still, every week, about her free time—making sure, she knew, that she wasn't dating anyone…

He'd made sure she wasn't even getting close to girlfriends. The way he'd slowly isolated her all those years, teaching her, without her even realizing, that she wanted to avoid certain expressions on his face—the features that stiffened, denoting disapproval that would trigger his sadness, or depression, or neediness.

Expressions that appeared whenever she mentioned

other people in any way that could be construed as being grateful for them, or affectionate toward them.

He'd groomed her to keep him happy, instilling guilt in her anytime she did anything that she knew he wouldn't like. Even after she'd been living alone for fifteen months, his ability to make her feel guilty, even in her thoughts, was still there.

In the background most of the time. Fading, quite certainly.

But…

Clint wanted her to believe he was the only one who really understood her. The only one who could ever love her as much as he did. The only one who could make her truly happy.

Clint was the only one who knew where he'd taken Brooke. She couldn't lose his cooperation.

Firm on that one, she stood, shoulders back. She had to renege on that morning's agreement with Anderson. No way was anyone else going to be present, giving her hidden messages, during her half hour brain-picking session with her daughter's kidnapper.

Her daughter's father.

Headed toward her newly hired employee, she met up with Brian in the hall just a few steps outside her office door. Still in the snug-fitting jeans he'd had on that morning, satchel on his shoulder.

Of course, since he didn't have transportation back and forth, he hadn't changed. The truck had been promised by five, but hadn't yet been returned.

"I thought I should get set up plenty of time before the video conference, give us time to practice how you want to communicate," he said, and then, meeting her gaze for a long look added, "Were you coming to find me?"

"I was," she told him, silently thankful for the opening. For a second there, she'd wanted him to be present for the meeting. Not because she thought there was a chance it would be good for Brooke, but because the idea of someone else witnessing Clint's behavior after fifteen months of such meetings, had been...welcome.

Sometimes being the strong one, carrying the burden of the relationship all alone, wore her out.

More so since she'd realized how badly she'd been manipulated. Since the counseling sessions that had, after the fact, helped her understand how she'd allowed it to happen...

"You can't be there," she said baldly. She wasn't going to argue about it. He was her employee. They were in her home. And she knew it couldn't happen.

"What do you mean I can't? Who told you that? If it's prison guidelines, we can get around that. I'll make a phone call." He reached into his pocket for his phone.

"No, Brian," she said, feeling odd using his first name, but doing it firmly. "*I'm* saying it. You can't be there. If Clint sees me looking anywhere but at him, or sees my eyes move in a reading motion, even being distracted by something popping up on my computer screen...he'll cop an attitude..." She heard the worry in her tone even as she tried to make it go away.

He was shaking his head. "You were fine with it this morning," he reminded her. "Anderson agreed to let you be the first one to speak with him about the gun..."

She shook her head right back. "He really didn't have a choice." Her gut had spoken, perhaps a bit late, but she wasn't going to be swayed. "He couldn't make it over there before my phone call and he doesn't have the right

to tell me what I can and can't speak to my ex-husband about and—"

"Hey, Jessica." The soft tone, the warm look in his eyes, stopped her words as much as the interruption had done.

She stood there, looking up at him when she needed to get back to the office. To get online, open the meeting app, and be waiting the second Clint came on. It upset him if he lost even a minute of his time torturing her and, for the purpose of getting as much out of him as she could, she avoided all needless upsets.

"Detective Anderson isn't your enemy," Brian continued without any argument at all coming at her. "He wants exactly the same thing you do, to find Brooke. And he's had a lot of training in working with perpetrators, especially those who are incarcerated. He thinks the gun's going to give him leverage. Maybe Clint gets nervous that the gun was found and Anderson offers up a deal on whatever Clint might have done with the gun, or what Anderson's going to tell the prosecutor Clint did with the gun, in exchange for Brooke's whereabouts. You don't have that power..."

She didn't budge. "Right, but if Clint has something to be nervous about, me telling him about the gun just gives him time to stew about whatever it is that he might have done with the gun. To stew over whatever else the police might find out when they run ballistics, and that will just work in Anderson's favor for any deal Anderson might want to pretend to offer him. As smart as Clint is, he's like a kid, emotionally, when it comes to his own needs."

"Or it gives him time to invent a really good explanation for whatever might turn up on that gun. An excuse that has nothing to do with him, one that at least allows for the possibility that someone else might have

handled the gun. It also gives him time to concoct a believable alibi. As smart as he is, I have no doubt he'll figure something out."

The way Brian said that—*I have no doubt he'll figure something out*—hit her oddly. Made her feel as though she wasn't alone in her knowledge of Clint. Of the way he worked.

Brian was only going by what she and the reports he'd read had told him. Things that everyone else working the case also knew. There was no reason for her to feel less alone because of one statement.

And yet…she did.

But the video conference wasn't about her. It was all about pandering to Clint so he'd talk to her every week and she'd at least have a chance of finding her daughter.

Because while Clint knew her, she knew him just as well.

"I can't take a chance on setting him off," she said again. "I need whatever clue he's set to give me." She glanced at her watch. They'd already wasted five minutes. Another ten and she had to be online, ready to take Clint on.

If he got an opportunity to show up early, he would.

Finding her there ahead of time, too, would feed his ego. And make him more amenable.

"And if I don't tell him about the gun, if I let him be blindsided by Anderson, when Clint knows full well that I have his truck, so I'd be privy to knowledge of the gun before Anderson is… I'm not going to go there. It'll complicate things between him and me and he could choose just to cut me off."

And there was the rub, of course. She knew exactly what Clint Johnson was, saw how he'd spent years men-

tally and emotionally abusing her with his manipulation. And knew very well that he was still doing so.

Because he had the one thing on earth she needed above all else. Knowledge of her baby girl's whereabouts.

"I know he's playing with me, Brian. I'm no longer in love with him in any way. No longer giving up my power to him. Nor am I an unknowing victim. I'm consciously choosing to let him have his way, with my eyes wide open, so that I can get my way. I want these meetings with him as badly as he does. Because, at some point, he's going to tell me the truth. Whether wittingly or not, he's going to lead me to Brooke."

"I'll find Brooke."

She wanted to believe him.

Wasn't there yet. Wasn't sure she ever would be. Brian was a wish on a star. Clint was the holder of the truth.

Shaking her head, she turned back to her office, intending to close the door on her own personal private investigator.

"At least let me observe." Brian didn't sound like he was demanding, but rather the words hit her as suggestion. Maybe even question. Whatever, they stopped her. Swinging around, she looked at him, gave him a chance to convince her.

"I can stay behind you so that you don't see any reaction from me at any time, but out of view of the camera. I won't make a sound. It'll be like I'm not there..."

She feared there would never be a time when the disturbing man was in her vicinity but off her radar.

All day, even though they'd been in different parts of the house and her office door had been shut, she'd known he was there...

Not like when Barb, who cleaned for her, was there. Or Kyle, the handyman. They both had been in every room

of her house—Barb countless times—and yet had left fewer impressions than Brian had in just a few minutes…

"Insight into the kidnapper, into the man who's giving us the clues, will help me find your daughter."

Anderson, the others, they'd all had their time with Clint.

She was Brian's only in.

As long as he wasn't expecting her to watch him, communicate with him, she had the mental wherewithal to block him and focus fully on Clint. Because having Brian privy to Clint was in Brooke's best interest.

With a nod, she motioned him to follow her.

And felt a little bit less alone when he did so.

Chapter 6

Brian purposely chose the vantage point furthest away from his client. She signed on a full fifteen minutes before the scheduled visit, giving him ample time to test her camera range so he could be sure he wouldn't be in it. To show her how to record the session. And to give her a different headset to use: one with a noise-canceling mic so that unless sound entered directly through the mouthpiece, it couldn't be heard on the other end.

"It's made to cancel out background noise," he told her as he pulled the headset out of his satchel, along with a wipe, and cleaned it before handing it to her. Her look back at him was a little off, distracted, and he added, "In my line of work, there are times, like when I'm in a bar surveying the person I'm calling, I need...well, privacy." Just to put her at ease.

And he receded to his corner. The office was big—one of the biggest rooms in the house—and he figured,

since he could no longer smell the ocean freshness of her hair, she wouldn't be able to detect any telltale identifier he might unknowingly give out. Once her conversation started and she was focused on Clint, she wouldn't even know he was there.

Sliding down to the floor, to make certain that as the sun moved there wouldn't be any chance of even a shadow of his shoulder showing up in the camera field, he leaned back, head lodged in the corner, eyes pinned on Jessica's two-foot-wide computer screen.

She still wore the same figure-hugging gray pants, the silky shirt, she'd had on that morning at the airport.

Had it only been a matter of hours since he'd met her? That one was hard to comprehend. He knew it to be true. But didn't feel like it was. Having spent the past night and day fully immersed in her, her life—and having spent the past several hours learning so much about her through her home and mannerisms—having felt her desperation so acutely—had made his sense of knowing her…timeless.

And had also made him certain that the only way to Brooke was through her kidnapper. Not from what he'd tell them, but from all the pieces of him that had formed into one hellacious, unforgivable action. Brian had to get enough pieces of the guy's puzzle to figure out his whole picture. To know what he'd do with the daughter he'd stolen from her loving mother.

To know how he'd dispose of her.

"Hey, Jess. It's so good to see you, babe." The softly spoken, loving-sounding words hit Brian hard. Even more than the emotion pouring from the brown eyes on the screen. Other than the orange jumpsuit the guy was wearing, he could have been a movie star out to lunch. His sandy somewhat messy hair, the little bit of stubble on his

perfectly shaped jaw, shoulders that were big enough to be attractive but not overpowering…a posture that spoke of comfort in his own skin…

"Don't call me that." The small square in the corner of the screen depicting Jessica's face didn't give Brian nearly enough. But he could feel the steel emanating from her.

"Sorry. I know I promised I wouldn't do that. You just… I miss you."

"Where is she, Clint?"

"You having a bad day?"

"No. Yes. Yes, I am, which is what you wanted, isn't it?"

"Hey, Jess, seriously, what's going on? Something's happened. Tell me." Clint's tone changed, becoming not threatening and yet…not right either. Brian heard warning, but detected no hint of imminent danger—not in the man's words, tone, delivery or body language.

Brian, on the other hand, felt every nerve in his body clench. She'd said having him there would ruin things. That Clint would be able to tell…

He could slide down, get on all fours, crawl out. She'd know he was gone, Clint wouldn't see…

"Either you're more of a heartless jerk than I ever knew or…you really are so self-absorbed that you forgot your own daughter's second birthday."

Today? Brian froze. He'd read reports, knew age, but hadn't seen a birth certificate. Had had no idea… Anderson hadn't said a word that morning about it.

Clint's face softened again, into the same loving, compassionate expression he'd worn when he'd first popped into the meeting.

"Sorry, no, you're right. And I didn't forget. You can ask anyone here. At breakfast this morning, I talked about how we had to leave for the hospital in the middle of the

night. How I was so nervous and scared you actually insisted on driving..."

Taken back, Brian froze, focused. Clint Johnson didn't seem to get how off his comment was. How it made him look, being so caught up with himself that he couldn't put his wife first.

Even when she was in labor?

"I talked about it during group last night, too," Clint continued. "But...her birthday was Wednesday—"

"Well I don't get by things as quickly as you do," Jessica cut in, her tone different, too. Not as biting.

Brooke's second birthday had been the night she'd called and left the message with Sierra's Web. He'd been hired by noon on Thursday.

Her daughter's birthday had prompted the call. Brian didn't know if the news was significant, but he filed the information with everything else his brain was quickly compiling about the case.

"I know. And I'm sorry, Jess." *Seriously?* The guy was *sorry*? Had the audacity to say so when he could end Jessica's misery right then. Right there.

Incredulous, Brian stared at the screen.

"Tell me where she is, Clint." Jessica seemed unfazed.

"I don't know where she is."

"Then how do you know she's okay?"

"I know."

"How do you know?"

The man's shrug, his sympathetic expression, seemed so genuine as he replied with, "I just do."

"So how was your week?"

Blinking, Brian's gaze shot to the small square in the corner of the screen as his brain processed Jessica's question. The change in her voice, the relaxation of her shoulders.

"Okay, you know, better than some. It's warmer, so more time outside. But I think some of the guys are jealous of the way Jennifer really gets me in group."

"Dr. Owens, you mean?"

"Yeah. She's really happy with my progress, Jess. And, you know, I can see where I demanded too much of you, sometimes. But you know I didn't mean it. I've always loved you, Jess. Only you."

"If you wanted me to believe that you really care about me, you'd tell me where Brooke is."

"See, that's the thing Jennifer is helping me to figure out," he said, leaning his arms on the table, bringing himself closer to the camera so his entire face filled the screen. "My psyche, or my soul…they know, deep down, that the only way to fix us, to fix me and to win you back, is to do it with just the two of us. We have to fix us, Jess, which means I have to fix me, before we can raise a family."

Jessica didn't move. Not onscreen. And not from where Brian was sitting.

"I did what I did for all of us, Jess. For our family. The family you said you always wanted. That's what I'm trying to give you. I know it's drastic…" Clint's voice faded as he stared straight at the camera, his big brown gaze taking over the room. The man was good—maybe better than any actor out to lunch. Scary good.

"I just didn't know of any other way, Jess. I was willing to spend my time in prison, if that's what I had to do, to get us back on track. All you could see was the baby, not us. Not me."

The woman just sat. As if in stone.

"I promise you, the baby's fine, Jess. You'll see. And someday you'll understand why I had to do this. You'll thank me for sacrificing myself for the bigger picture. To save our family."

Brian's stomach contents started to back up on him.

"I need to know she's okay, Clint. I can't just take your word for it. She had her second birthday. How do I know if she even got to celebrate it?"

"You have to trust me."

"Clint."

"Don't you get it at all yet? Not even a little bit? You're smart, Jess. It's been fifteen months. I thought you'd start to get it by now. Most people would."

"This is all about me being able to trust you."

"Right!" The man smiled; an expression that seemed to exude happiness right out of the screen and into the room.

Brian wasn't buying it. But only because he knew what the man had done. What he was still doing.

"I guess I need help, then. Give me something, Clint. My heart's dying here. I spent all day Wednesday thinking about that first day in the hospital. You say you want me to think about us, to believe there could be a family. Then, please, give me something."

There was truth in Jessica's tone. And something else as well.

Maybe that same wall of resistance he'd been up against in the hallway moments before? A determination so fierce that she had the force to move mountains?

She hadn't said she'd ever believe, only repeating back to him what he'd said he wanted. Brian caught the distinction.

Had a feeling, as smart as Clint was, he had to as well. The man on the screen sat back, arms folded, and said, "Tell me about your week."

"Why did you have a gun?" Brian felt the accusatory darts in every word, watched Clint intently, but didn't see any of them land. The man actually gave a lazy grin.

"You found it."

"You know I vacuum under car seats, you have to have figured I'd run into it sooner or later." Jessica pulled off the lie perfectly as far as Brian was concerned. But then, she'd had fifteen months of these weekly meetings.

Clint's nonchalant shrug was convincing. For a man sitting in prison with a whole bunch of officials looking at him for murder, Clint Johnson seemed remarkably unconcerned. Could have been an act, but the rise and fall of his chest, slow and rhythmic, the steadiness of his stare... showed at the very least a physiological lack of turmoil.

"I'd have told you about it, but I know how you feel about firearms, having them around. Which is why I paid to have that pocket installed in the truck, and left the gun there at all times."

"Why do you have it?"

"Remember when I told you about the guy at Blueit who had it in for me because I came in brand-new and found the program glitch that had been eluding him?"

"Mitch somebody..."

"Right. He followed me out to my truck a couple of times. Made me nervous. I knew he had a gun, heard him talking about buying it from a friend. Made me think that I should get one from a guy there at Blueit that I knew had a couple for sale, you know, just to show around that I'd done it, so Mitch would know to back off. It's not like you need a license or any kind of registration for it in Arkansas when you buy it from a private individual..."

"You've owned a gun since before Brooke was born?"

"Yeah, but I swear, Jess, I put it in that pocket under the seat and never took it out again. Not once."

"You're sure? Because it's being tested to see if it's been shot..."

"I'm sure I never shot the thing. I can't say what happened with it before I bought it."

"Who'd you buy it from?"

"Guy named Blake Redmond."

"That guy who delivered all the computer components when you were outfitting the office building?"

"Yeah. I'm surprised you remember him. You only saw him like once or twice."

"Brooke threw her rattle and it hit him, remember? He picked it up and handed it back to you and said, 'This ball's in your court, Daddy.'"

"Yeah. Wow. I'd forgotten that."

She'd handled the interview as good as many cops he knew. Brian half believed the guy himself.

"Tell me about your week, Jess."

He got the rundown in exchange for random pieces of information that were supposed to be able to lead her to her Brooke. The fiend's way of making her beg.

For less than crumbs.

Brian had to force himself to relax enough to stay still, to remain unemotional as, over the next twenty minutes, he heard about stocks rising and falling, about a tech drop and a new player on the market. Interest rates were rising, digital currencies played their part, and there was value in horses.

"Why do you care about horse value?" Clint's comment came with more than casual interest. And a return of the nonthreatening yet tense tone.

"Research I'm doing for a client," Jessica responded easily, and continued with her report.

She never mentioned actual dollar amounts, or identified clients in any way. Didn't say whether it had been a good week or bad, if she was up or down financially, or even if she'd completed any projects.

The half hour was pretty much up, a minute or so left, when Clint, hands clasped on the table in front of him, sat forward.

"You asked if she celebrated her birthday," he said softly, brows raised, expression compassionate. "She likes chocolate."

The prisoner's hand moved, Clint's image was gone and the screen filled with Jessica's despair.

For a split second, Jessica thought her heart was going to drown in agony. Clint was gone without giving Brooke back to her.

And then, as had happened every single week since her ex went to prison, she took a deep breath, sucking in pure determination.

For those few seconds, she felt irrevocably alone. Reaching for the journal she kept with all of Clint's clues, she grabbed a pen, and heard shuffling behind her.

Brian.

Playback of the past half hour rushed through her mind. She'd actually been so focused on Clint, she'd completely tuned out the presence of her new employee.

Not yet ready to hear what he had to say, and needing him to come forward with an immediate plan to go out and get Brooke, she opened the purple book to the lined pages in the front where she was recording the list of Clint's clues. The second half of the book—also lined pages—was filling up with her impressions, her thoughts, anything at all that came to her regarding Clint's weekly visits.

She likes chocolate. Her pen held to the dot on the page as tears filled her eyes. *She likes chocolate.* In all of the supposed hints and clues Clint had given her, he'd never once told her anything directly about Brooke herself.

Her baby girl likes chocolate!

And… Jessica hadn't offered it to her. Hadn't seen the expression on her face the first time she'd tasted it.

What else did Brooke like? And not like? The reality of not knowing squeezed the air out of her lungs.

"Look at numbers four, eight, twelve…" Brian's warmth beside her gave her air enough to hear his voice sounding from far off. His finger turning back the page of her book to the first entries, and then pointing to the numbers.

"Here," he said, grabbing his laptop out of his satchel and pulling over a chair from the table to sit next to her. Opening his computer, he clicked twice and had some kind of workbook open in front of him.

"Read them to me," he said, turning the screen toward him as he put his fingers on the keyboard, clicking as though opening a different page. "Every fourth clue."

She stared at him. Wondering for a second what kind of game he was playing, ready to tell him she didn't need him to pander to her, and realized that he was so focused on whatever was going on in his head, he didn't even seem to notice her.

Other than as a source that could easily disseminate the information he wanted.

So she read. "'Her blankie made it. A river runs through it. Time plays a part. Within feet not miles. Birds of Paradise. Where the greenest grass grows. In plain sight. More drawers would be nice…'" She paused. "He has to have seen her if he knows she likes chocolate." Her tone changed, got stupidly high, as she blurted the words. "Or have heard from someone," she added, dropping her pen to grab her phone and push the speed dial for Anderson.

In succinct, unemotional words, she told the detective

on her daughter's case that they needed to get prison records for all of Clint's correspondence, phone calls and visitors. To find out who her ex had been talking to. And gritted her teeth as she heard his patient, almost condescending tone as he told her he'd check into it and then didn't even take a breath before asking about the gun.

With a reminder that the man was on her side—even if he didn't believe, as she did, that Brooke was alive and Clint knew where—she gave him an exact account of Clint's gun explanation and knew, when she hung up, that the information would be verified within the hour.

Was thankful for that.

And thankful that, as the day was waning on another week gone, she wasn't going into the weekend—and a search for chocolate—all by herself.

Whatever the chart on Brian Powers's computer meant, she didn't yet know, but as he turned the screen to her, revealing a long spreadsheet with all columns and rows denoted with abbreviations, she knew she'd made the right choice to hire the man.

If nothing else, he was unwittingly helping her to keep her sanity while she waited Clint out and searched for her baby girl.

Chapter 7

The woman was…intimidating. Her ability to fall apart and stand strong at the same time wouldn't even compute for him if he hadn't witnessed it on several occasions that day.

Most currently, as he listened to her professionalism with Anderson, while seeing the way her eyes were darting and her foot was bouncing.

She wouldn't be happy to know he was noticing. Would stop both if she knew. He'd bet a year's salary on that one.

He noted, too, the look of resignation on her face, and then the peace she brought to her expression as she hung up the phone.

Expecting her to get right back to the listing she'd been giving him—every fourth clue she'd been reading before she'd interrupted herself—he was surprised when she said, "He thinks Clint just made up the bit about Brooke liking chocolate."

And she clearly didn't think that.

Nor did she ask what he thought.

"Not surprising, based on the fact that none of his other tidbits have led to anything but your continued being at his beck and call, but he's still going to run a check, right?"

"Yes."

"Then what does it matter what Anderson, or anyone thinks, as long as they're following up?"

Her gaze steady, assessing, she stared at him for a few seconds. Nodded. And glanced back at the page in her open journal.

"'Butterflies are free.'"

The thirty-sixth clue. He typed. And words burped out of him. "She was six months old when he took her. Maybe he gave her some chocolate. Chocolate milk. Or a tiny piece that would melt in her mouth. A lick of chocolate ice cream." It hurt, sitting there, with her actually allowing herself to hope that her ex still had some kind of contact with her daughter, after fifteen months in prison.

Clint Johnson was a brutal man.

"Babies don't get milk until they're a year old."

The man had kidnapped a baby. Giving her some milk before she should have it didn't seem like a stretch. Brian kept that thought to himself.

And burned to find out what disgusting move in Clint's insidious game he'd just delivered. How chocolate fit in to the big play.

"'Wrinkles are good.'"

He typed.

"'It's better when it's warm.'"

She hadn't looked up from her journal. But each time he'd finished typing, she read again.

"'A good book.'"

He entered in the twelfth of the fifteen clues.

"I believe he knows that Brook likes chocolate."

Brian's gaze flew to hers. She held on with her core of steel. Bobbing her head slightly, she said, "He knew he had to give me something more today. I told him I didn't trust him and if he had any hope of getting me to continue playing his game, he had to give me something."

He hadn't heard those words but… "When he talked about you understanding someday, and thanking him…"

Her gaze softened. "Yeah. He knows me well enough to be able to play me, but he knows me well enough to know when I've had all I can take, too."

Brian believed her about that. Believed that there was some real way that chocolate had played a part in Clint's plan.

And try as he did, sitting there, meeting her look for look, he couldn't find an ounce of him that believed Clint had any way of knowing what Brooke liked or didn't like in present day.

He knew, when Jessica looked away, that he'd disappointed her.

"'The only one.'" She read, as though part of a lecture.

Back at his spreadsheet, Brian entered the next every fourth clue, wondering if he'd ever been on a more difficult job. Didn't think so.

"'Singing in the air.'"

The clacking of his typing keys reverberated in that room like firecrackers.

"'The rising star.'"

Jessica picked up a pen and wrote on the page from which she'd been reading, saying, "And she likes chocolate."

The sixty-fourth clue, the first time the words had been personal to the baby, falling on the week of Brooke's birthday.

The man's attention to detail, his plan, was diabolical.

But he had limitations. And those were Brian's tools for success. With a couple of clicks, Brian incorporated information, sent it to a new page, and turned his computer toward Jessica.

"Smart, narcissistic people—and Clint, while not clinically diagnosed, exhibits signs of being such—are largely incapable of reflective thinking. That being the case, they sometimes work in patterns. A clear A, B, C, D that makes sense to them. Gives them a sense of control over a situation, as they're the only one who knows the pattern. The only one with the complete puzzle."

Mouth open, Jessica looked at his computer screen but then straight back at him. "How do you know this?"

"I've spent years studying people, studying their actions. I have to get in their heads in order to figure out their actions," he told her. Then added, "And I made a call this afternoon to Sierra's Web's psychiatric expert, Kelly Chase."

Her attention turned to the spreadsheet on his screen.

"When I was looking for patterns, I kept coming up with the number four." Brian leaned in closer, more to get his point across than anything else. He had to prove to her that she could rely on him to get the job done.

Because he had to get the job done. Not because it was his job, but because it was eating at him. Hearing Clint Johnson, seeing the man's seemingly genuine confidence, his ability to play all the right emotions to get what he wanted… Brian couldn't walk away from it.

As he opened his mouth to begin his next sentence, a flash hit him, almost literally, like a blinding light behind his eyes. Except that he could still see information on his computer clearly. Was still in the room on the job.

And he was twelve again. *What he's doing to their*

minds, the way he controls them... I can't let him get away with it. I can get this guy...

A couple of seconds was all it took. He blinked and it was gone.

But not forgotten.

Brian's intensity captivated Jessica, maybe escalated by the warmth of his nearness as he drew closer to her, pointing to the first heading across the top of his chart.

"Look at the timing," he said, his voice vibrant. "He took her the fourth day of the week. He was missing for four days before he suddenly turned up at home, claiming to have been fishing..."

Claiming he didn't know anything about Brooke's disappearance. Crying with her those first couple of days, comforting her as they grieved, worried and waited together.

Until his alibi hadn't panned out—a fluke that the river he'd claimed to have been camping beside had been dammed up in the area due to a sewage backup five miles away.

"He insists on an in-person visit every fourth week," Brian noted.

"Why not two? Or three?" she said aloud what she'd wondered many times, nodding. Nerves on full alert, flooding with emotions, she sat forward. Skimmed other facts on the chart.

Their meetings were at four o'clock. Clint had asked four things of her. Weekly visits, one in person visit the fourth week of every month, that they meet alone, and that she share her daily life with him when they met.

When he eventually confessed to the kidnapping, he'd said the same four things over and over. Brooke was in

a better place. He didn't know where she was. He didn't know who had her. And he didn't kill her.

That column didn't feel right to her. Clint had had a lot to say, ardent in his message, eager for her to hear him. And yet, when she thought back, all he'd ever said before and during the trial, to her, to detectives, on the stand, amounted to those same four facts.

"It's possible that I'm fitting things into a pattern that doesn't really exist," Brian said as she continued to silently study the screen. "I have to start somewhere, and this feels like the place," he continued. "So what I wanted you to do was take a look at every fourth clue, in a list by themselves, and see if, by themselves, they say anything to you."

Yes, yes! Oh God, let them say something...

Her gaze glued to that last column, she read quickly. Then again, more slowly. A third, fourth and fifth time. Despair showing up again, but not completely taking over.

"Let's start with 'a good book,'" Brian read one of the more recent clues. "Did you read to Brooke?"

She nodded. Spoke through a dry throat. "Every night."

"Did she seem to have a favorite book?"

"*Bear Bellies*." She named it immediately. A story about bears with symbols on their bellies. "My stepmother read it to me as a kid," she said, trembling.

"Did Clint take it? Have you seen it since Brooke's disappearance?" The intensity in Brian's tone surged through her. Keeping hope alive.

And then reality sucked everything back out of her. "It's still here," she said, not mentioning that she'd spent innumerable nights in her baby girl's room, in the rocking chair, reading the book aloud to herself before bed in the past fifteen months.

Because it calmed her. Made her feel peaceful enough to go to her bed in the spare room and lie down.

She did what she had to do to keep going.

One of the things no one needed to know.

"I need to see it." Brian didn't seem at all deterred. "To study it. If, as I'm theorizing, these fourth clues are the ones with real significance, there could be something in that book…or about that book…"

Heart leaping, she turned to him. "He could have bought it for her after he took her," she said. "If she was fussy, he knew the book, had read it to her. He'd think it would calm her down."

She grabbed her phone. Pushed two for Anderson. Told him about the book. Asked if he could check bookstores in the areas they'd been able to trace Clint's truck through gas receipts and see if he'd purchased the book. And purposely added that Brian Powers had been instrumental in bringing up the question. With a sigh, but good cheer, the man said he would look into it.

Not that the book alone was going to do anything for them all those months later. At best, it helped to show what they already knew—that Clint had had Brooke after her disappearance. Even if only for long enough to hand her off. But if it panned out, if they found a bookstore with the book purchased during the four days after Brooke's disappearance, there was a possibility of surveillance footage in the store or the area. Maybe even a bookstore clerk they could find and question.

Someone who'd seen Clint with another adult. A woman who was keeping Brooke safe…there could be a picture of her that they could show around, find someone who knew her, who knew where she lived, knew if she had a two-year-old living with her.

Or…even if there was no surveillance, no clerk…

"If they find any evidence that Clint purchased a book during those four days…not that he'd used his credit card, of course, we already know he didn't since we have all of those records…but searching by the book's title…if there was a cash transaction for that book, when Clint's truck was in the area…"

"Then you can reasonably assume that there's some basis of reality in at least one of the clues Clint has given you," Brian finished for her, his tone, the seeming satisfaction there, drawing her eyes to him.

He didn't say anything more. Didn't move toward her. Wasn't touching her. But those hazel eyes, they seemed to be doing it all, talking to her, drawing her in, wrapping her in warmth and, for a long moment there, she let them.

Chapter 8

The gun had been fired.

Back at his temporary apartment Friday evening, eating lo mein and honey-walnut shrimp out of cartons, Brian had just settled back into full focus on his computer screen in his makeshift kitchen office when he got the call from Anderson.

"Since the weapon's been sitting for so long, there's no way to tell if it was fired before or after Brooke Johnson's disappearance," Anderson continued as soon as he'd delivered the news in lieu of hello.

Brian's expletive didn't escape his lips. "Was it loaded?"

"Yes."

"Fully?"

"There were two empty chambers."

Anyone who could shoot a…

No, he wasn't going there. He was going to find the truth. "What's the seller, Blake Redmond, say about it?"

"Can't find him. Which is why I'm calling you. Does tracking this guy down fit within the scope of your employment?"

That was up to him. He decided what would or would not lead him to Brooke. "Absolutely." Jessica wouldn't like it. She'd understand, though. "What's his last-known whereabouts?"

Anderson rattled off an address for an apartment complex in a small town an hour outside Fayetteville. And an out-of-date website for an online hunting goods store that Redmond had managed before driving a truck. Brian agreed to take it from there.

And called Jessica. He'd left her studying the sixteen clues they'd pulled out of the list Clint had given her. Her stated intention had been to spend the evening brainstorming each one, to see if anything came to mind, as the storybook had. All but the chocolate one she'd already followed up on in various ways, but seeing them separated, and together, could trigger new directions.

The objective had been to meet up again in the morning and spend the weekend ferreting out whatever they could based on what she came up with. Or he did.

"Change of plans," he told her as soon as she answered the phone, giving her the news from Anderson exactly as it had been given to him. With a clear thought in mind.

He did not want her with him when he chased down and confronted a seller of guns who appeared to be on the lam.

"What did ballistics show, other than that the gun had been fired?" she asked before he could get the part out about him going into that area of the investigation on his own. "Did it show up as involved in any other crimes?"

"No."

"So, this finding Redmond, it's to verify Clint's alibi,"

she said then. "To give credibility to what he's saying, to show that he does tell the truth..."

Most successful liars told the truth some of the time.

"Possibly," he told her. He didn't doubt that a Blake Redmond sold Clint Johnson the gun. The slimy man was too smart to lie about something that easy to confirm. Higher on Brian's list was finding out if the gun had been new when it had been sold to Clint Johnson. To ascertain whether or not Redmond knew if the pistol had been previously fired.

"While you do that, I'm going to work on our list of clues," she told him.

And as relieved as he was that his new employer wasn't going to try to insist on accompanying him on what could be a dangerous mission, he didn't feel great about leaving her to investigate alone.

Shrugging off the still lingering sense of unease, he hit the road for Redmond's last-known address at sunup on Saturday morning. Brian eased his gut with the knowledge that Blake Redmond—the seller of the hidden and now-found gun—was the surest lead anyone had had since the reemergence of Clint Johnson without his daughter eighteen months before.

Believing that the gun could be key in getting Clint to break—if nothing else, in getting the man to give up his cruel manipulation of his ex-wife and to confess to what he'd done with his daughter—Brian sped out of town. He hoped to soon have answers that would set Jessica free to get on with the rest of her life before Clint returned.

What it meant if Brian was successful—that the baby hadn't survived her father's punishment of her mother—he refused to dwell on. He'd taken the job. His goal was to give Jessica the answers she needed to be free.

By evening, his gut was telling him "I told you so." He

still hadn't found Redmond, though his investigation had led him to three other places within a fifty-mile radius where the young man had lived during the past couple of years. When he'd called his employer to report in, he'd heard that Jessica had spent the day on the road as well. Visiting a series of towns with rivers running through or along them that also had establishments that sold chocolate near green grass.

The type of thing she'd done every single other weekend since her daughter had been kidnapped. Activities that shouldn't be happening now that she'd hired him to do the searching for her.

His second full day on the job had wasted her money on all accounts.

Looking for chocolate was worse than searching for a needle in a haystack, since there was no one place to go find it. Not even one place in one town.

It came in so many forms. Was she looking for ice cream? Milk? Candy? Chocolate frosting on a donut? Cookies?

Much of which could be found in every grocery and convenience store, every gas station, in every burb in every state in the union.

Rivers and green grass narrowed things a little bit. As did her inability to travel far in the time allotted to her.

But at least, if she was out, there was a slim chance she'd hit a jackpot. If she didn't try, she was guaranteed not to succeed.

If she didn't stay busy, keep herself "doing," she'd lose her mind sitting at home worrying about guns and bullets and the guy that had sold both to her ex-husband.

While she drove, her mind worked the sixteen clues she'd memorized, searching for any familiar landing

place. And kept coming back to the conclusions she'd drawn when she'd first heard each clue and had spent an entire weekend only on it.

A good book. Though, when she'd been sitting there with Brian Powers, the clue had appeared differently to her.

She'd had a potential breakthrough. Not that she'd heard back from Anderson yet on that score.

Picking up the phone, she dialed the man. If he was with his family and she didn't text a 9-1-1 to him, he'd let the call go to voice mail as per their agreement when he'd insisted that she call him anytime she was out searching, if she thought she had something.

He didn't pick up. She left a quick message, giving him authority to release access to all of Clint's financial information, including credit card databases, to her newly hired expert so he could cross-check on the spot. Not positive she had the power to issue such a mandate, she still felt better as she ended the call.

Almost as good as she'd felt when she'd had the call from Brian an hour before, telling her he hadn't found Blake Redmond. Probably not smart, being glad about that, as it meant her private detective would be wrapped up with gun investigation yet another day. Still, she couldn't help the instant relief that had poured through her as she'd heard that there was no new evidence on Clint's gun. Nothing to put the newly found gun to bed and move on, yet, sure, but also no proof that Clint had ever used the gun, let alone shot another individual with it.

At home that night, in her office, busy plotting out the next day's road trip, Jessica jumped when her phone rang. But seeing Brian's name pop up, she answered immediately.

The slight rise in her heart rate, the tiny burst of good feeling flowing through her, was to be expected. She was still getting used to having someone on Brooke's case, exclusively, 24/7. Too bad she hadn't known about the expert firm months before…

"You ever hear of Lincoln, Arkansas?" he asked, all business as soon as she said hello.

Heart pumping faster for real, she told him, "Noooo."

"It's a two-road village on the way to one of Redmond's last-known addresses. I'm just passing through again, on my way back to Fayetteville."

"I thought you were back already."

"I was, but I got a call from someone with whom I'd left a card and made a trip back."

"Did you find Redmond?"

"No, but I found out that he's still driving a truck, just no longer for a company. He's got his own rig now. Purchased used, with money he got when his grandmother died. It came with a bed area behind the seats, has a fridge, a small counter. He lives in it. And rents himself out to any company that hires independent truckers."

Her mind jumped ahead to where he and Anderson were going to go with that one. Redmond probably wasn't just driving legal goods. He used the truck to sell and deliver guns. Maybe drugs, too. She watched television. Knew how things worked.

"I've been told I'll get a call as soon as he's back in town." It took her a second to catch up with the fact that Brian wasn't going all illegal-arms dealer on her.

"In the meantime, driving back, I'm on a different road and just passed a small sign, visible only from one direction, that's an advertisement for the Birds of Paradise café…"

Her breath caught. One of the clues.

She tried to suck in air. Dropped the pen she'd been holding.

"I followed the directions and am sitting outside a small boarded-up place—"

A café. Is that where Clint met whomever he'd given their baby to? Was it a woman he'd known? Dated? Someone who'd worked there who was loving Brooke and keeping her safe? Oh God. Did she live close by? Was Brian within a mile or two of Brooke?

"—and the sign on the building is decorated with painted butterflies."

Butterflies are free.

Tears blurred her vision. She didn't need to see what was in front of her. "She's there. In that town?" She wanted to be more firm. To state something that she suddenly knew to be true.

Her instincts weren't talking to her at the moment.

"I have no way of knowing, but I was going to suggest, since I'm waiting on a call regarding Redmond, rather than spending a day tracking hundreds, maybe thousands, of companies that use independent truckers, hoping to find anyone available to talk to on a Sunday, maybe we should take the day to explore the village of Lincoln."

Lips trembling, she smiled. Didn't bother to wipe the tears streaming down her cheeks. "Okay," she said, trying her best to maintain a calm tone in her voice at least. "I'll pick you up at dawn?"

"How about I pick you up?"

"I'm not a good passenger. Most definitely not when I'm working."

"Being in Clint's truck makes me sick to my stomach."

"I'll be there at dawn. We leave the truck in the driveway, and I drive your SUV."

Grinning from ear to ear, she didn't care that tears were dripping off her chin to her keyboard. Another compromise that left no losers…

"Or I could rent a vehicle…"

"No." She had to be able to afford him for as long as it took. "You drive my SUV. I have no problem being a passenger."

Not when she trusted the person driving her.

That meant…she hadn't trusted the man she'd married—the man who'd fathered her child—for years, but she trusted a virtual stranger?

Something she could look at in the future. Until she had Brooke home, there was no room for anything else.

Chapter 9

What Jessica hadn't counted on were the long minutes into hours spent strapped in the passenger seat of her vehicle on their way to wherever Sunday was going to take them.

Most particularly when they kept her in such close proximity to the jeans-clad man in his black short-sleeved pullover, looking…like someone you didn't want to mess with. The gun he was wearing—the first she'd seen it—added to the effect.

At least the sun was shining. And in early May, wasn't too hot yet.

Keeping her gaze peeled for any sign of her daughter—something she did every single time she was out of her house and was easier when she didn't have to pay attention to the road—she stared at miles of seemingly unending grass, trees and farmland. Having no idea what she might see that could lead her to her daughter, but

knowing if she wasn't out there, looking, nothing would present itself.

And as she sat, aware of Brian's kind of musky scent—though it didn't appear he'd shaved that morning—questions infiltrated her thoughts. One or two at first.

Then they seemed to breed.

Half an hour from their first stop, the Village of Lincoln, she allowed herself to voice one of those questions. Because it pertained to the moment.

"Are you licensed to carry a gun in every state?" He'd just flown into Arkansas on Friday. Had been with her all day. And then there was only the weekend with governmental offices all closed. She didn't doubt the gun was legal. Not solely because he was working so closely with Detective Anderson, but because…she just didn't doubt his correctness.

"All but Hawaii," he told her. "But in Arkansas, you don't have to be licensed or even have the gun registered to open carry as long as you're over eighteen and can legally own a gun."

She hadn't known that.

Had never had cause to know it.

"So Clint having that gun…there's absolutely nothing wrong with him having purchased it, just like he said."

"Right."

Based on his search for Blake Redmond, she knew he had more thoughts on the matter, but didn't push him to share them all with her. She'd already gotten the gist of it.

And almost thanked him for not pushing the matter.

The lack was…a relief. A breath of fresh air.

Because she knew Clint hadn't killed their daughter, and just wanted to move on. To focus on things that would lead them to Brooke.

And yet…there was more.

It took her a second, sitting there staring out her window, to realize why she was particularly appreciating the way the man at her side had handled the conversation.

With her question about Clint's lack of wrongdoing in owning the gun, she'd given him an opening to warn her, again, about what that hidden gun could mean. To cram his opinions and hunches and gut feelings down her throat. He hadn't done so.

Clint would still be going on with her if he'd been the one in Brian's position. He'd repeat himself, find every opening to bring up the topic again, and continue doing so for as long as it took to get Jessica to doubt herself and see that he was right.

Or at least do his best to get to that point.

That last year they'd been a couple, maybe even before that, she'd begun to fight back. Mentally, at least. To have her own internal conversations that rebutted his, to take back whatever control of her mind he'd stolen from her.

Not that she'd had any conscious realization that's what she'd been doing. Counseling from a kind and talented therapist had pointed it out to her.

She'd been helping herself before she'd even known she'd needed the help.

The man beside her drove silently. She didn't look over at him, but could feel him there, strength and ability wrapped in an overly attractive package.

Guilt sluiced instantly through her at the thought. Because of Clint. His reaction if he knew, the quick and debilitating punishment he'd shoot at her. She turned away thoughts of him. And still felt like she was failing her daughter…sitting there having pseudo sexual thoughts, awareness, for a man with Brooke lost out in the world.

Curiosity killed the cat.

But if she just asked a couple of questions, his mys-

terious aura would disappear. He'd become like any of the hundreds of good, decent men who'd been her clients over the years.

She had a plethora of healthy, business relationships with men who belonged to other women.

"You being on the road so much of the time…is your wife into investigation as well?"

Not at all what she'd meant to say. But how did a guy have a home and family if he was never there? His job with her was open-ended. He could be there for months. And…

"I'm not married."

She'd noticed the lack of wedding ring, of course.

"Girlfriend, then."

His glance seemed to touch her—her cheeks, which grew warm, and other parts of her, too. A soft, tender touch. Sexual, maybe, or appreciative, but more empathetic than anything else.

When he turned his eyes back to the road, she realized she'd been holding her breath. Took a deep one.

"As you say, with my job, me being gone so much, there's never been time for anything else."

Okay, well, so much for diminishing his mysterious aura. Shoot him a question, his answers just led to more questions.

That she most definitely was not going to utter. She might be internally vulnerable, but she was not lacking in intelligence.

"You have no cause to worry." His words, their kind but respectful tone, as though he considered her someone to reckon with, grabbed her complete attention.

Frowning, she looked at him. "No cause to worry about what?" About her curiosity? Did he know?

About Clint?

Because she most definitely had cause to worry, every single second of every day, about her baby girl.

"If I've inadvertently sent off any vibes…you know, making you uncomfortable or—" he cocked his head to the side, his gaze facing straight ahead as though glued to the road "—giving you some sense that made you hope I had a wife…"

Oh God. He knew. Had noticed she was kind of attracted to him—was trusting him too much. He felt sorry for her. And was giving her an out.

How embarrassing.

Humiliating.

Mentally scrambling for a good, strong blurtation that shut him down on any noticing of each other between them, needing to grab firm hold of the out he'd given her, Jessica was still coming up blank when Brian continued.

"I'll be honest with you. I…notice you…in a way I've never done before on a case. Added to that a guy would have to be dead not to find you attractive…"

She was trembling. But not in a bad way. Or rather, it was horribly bad because she wasn't feeling at all like she wanted him to be quiet. Or to go away. *What the hell.*

She didn't know what to say. Couldn't even think…

"I'm alive," he continued. "But I have never, ever, behaved in an inappropriate manner, at work, or not. And yeah, I know anyone can say that, but if you'd like to call Sierra's Web, have me replaced, or have them release my background check to you, feel free to do so. Hell—" he grabbed his cell phone out of his pocket "—I'll even do it for you."

"Stop." Whatever the hell was happening, she most definitely did not want to speak with anyone at Sierra's Web about him.

For the first time since he'd started talking, he gave

her a quick glance and then returned his gaze toward the road.

Unending pavement in the middle of unending nowhere. This early on a Sunday, there weren't even other vehicles about.

"This case…it's hitting me more personally than any other…" he said then, almost as if to himself. Shaking his head.

"Why is that?" The question shot up out of her before she had time to analyze or reject it. Because, heart hurting, something occurred to her. "Did you lose a child, Brian? Or a sibling?"

It made sense if he had…the connection she felt with him. Yes, that could explain it all. The attraction…that was just as he'd said, you'd have to be dead not to notice someone gorgeous in her midst.

Did not explain why she didn't have such intense physical reactions to other good-looking men she knew. It wasn't like Brian was the first heartthrob she'd met…

He hadn't answered her—allowing her mind to run away with her, while, still, she watched the barren landscape, the shoulders and ditches on the sides of the roads for any aged, weatherworn piece of cloth that resembled the onesie she'd dressed Brooke in just minutes before her disappearance. For the blanket that had been wrapped loosely around her butt and legs in the swing.

"My mother."

The two words, so out of the blue, had her mouth dropping open. What had she missed? Or…

"What?"

"It's personal because of my mother."

He'd worked hundreds of cases. His bio said that. Spent a lot of time on missing persons. What about Brooke's case reminded him, when other cases didn't?

"She was kidnapped?" she guessed, her heart aching deeply for this man she barely knew. Hoped to God his mother had been found in time.

He shook his head. Seemed to be done talking. And then, eyes facing only the road again, said, "She was a cop. Had had multiple calls to the same house—the guy was beating up his wife and, my mom was sure, had hurt his little girl, too. Mom gave the woman her personal cell number. The wife would call, Mom would go running, no matter what time of day or night, or what else she might have been doing, but the guy would scare his wife out of pressing charges. Every time."

Jessica had gone cold. And then hot. If Brian thought she was that woman…

She wasn't a victim.

But she had been. Not of physical violence. Nothing that could be seen or irrevocably proven. Clint had abused her mentally. Emotionally.

Brian knew.

She didn't want him, of all people, to know. That made no sense. Everyone involved in her case knew what Clint was doing to her, making her call him every week. And could guess what he'd been doing for years.

"My dad, a detective in another squad, warned Mom repeatedly that she couldn't solve the world's problems on her own. But she wouldn't listen. The case changed her right before our eyes and nothing was ever the same again. In her day, my mother was a great cop. But that one case…she couldn't see beyond that little girl who was too little to fight for herself. Who couldn't even talk well enough to testify…"

Like Brooke, when they'd find her.

Brian's shrug pretty clearly indicated to her that he'd said what he was going to say. She could fill in the rest.

His mother hadn't been able to save the family and the failure had destroyed her own family. *Nothing was ever the same again.* Brian's words came at her again.

With a sick feeling, Jessica figured that the little girl had ended up dead.

And it occurred to her. The connection between them…maybe she didn't just need him. Maybe he needed her and Brooke, too. Needed their happy ending.

For his sake now, as well as hers, she hoped he hung around long enough to help give that conclusion to all three of them. Brooke, her, and himself, too.

Brian had no idea what had possessed him to spill his guts to a virtual stranger. And a client at that. Spent several minutes trying to figure out how to get himself out of the muck he'd just stepped into.

Came up with a big zero. Figured any more talk would just shine a light on his ridiculous ramblings, and was glad to let it go.

Except that then he was back where he'd started—the sense that Jessica was uncomfortable around him—personally.

As silence coated the entire interior of the SUV, he glanced her way again. "You have absolutely nothing to fear from me."

There. That was all he'd needed to get out.

He'd taken way too long to get there. Traveled dark roads best untraveled. Not like him at all.

"It's not you I'm fearing."

The vehicle swerved for a brief second as his eyes shot toward her. He corrected immediately. Never came close to leaving his lane.

Still…

Could she mean…she feared herself? That she wanted

him? They'd clearly been talking about sexual attraction, there in the beginning. He'd as much as admitted to her that he found her hot.

But…

No.

She feared Clint. The man who'd abused her just like the guy in his sad tale. The one who'd killed—

"I won't let anything happen to you."

"You might be an expert at what you do, but you aren't a god, Brian." Her laconic tone made him smile. In the middle of a tense moment.

With a nod, he said, "Point taken."

"And that's not what I meant."

Oh.

So, the sex thing?

Keeping his visual attention firmly on the long expanse of flat county road stretching out in front of him, he disengaged himself from the conversation.

As best he could with the two of them sitting there confined in a quiet SUV. Alone. Together.

"I probably shouldn't say this, Brian, but what we're doing here…what you're doing here to help me…we can't let other things…distract us."

Okay. She was doubting his ability to stay focused on the job. That one he could clear up.

"I know I alluded to—"

"Please," she cut him off. "Let me say this. Because if you don't, this isn't going to work and I so desperately need it to."

She wasn't firing his ass.

He drove. Keeping his mouth firmly shut.

Something he generally did naturally.

"I just want you to know that you aren't alone in noticing something between us," she told him. "Probably

because, like you say, we have intense personal emotions involved in the outcome of our time together…"

Yeah, maybe not. The intensity had died out in him long ago. Determination to make a difference had been left in its wake.

He welcomed the change with gratitude.

But if it meant he could escape any more alluding to attraction…he'd gladly wear the intensity label. Remembered clearly how it had felt—in high school, feeling desperate, and without answers. Or anyone to turn to…

"I'm alive, too." Her voice snapped him to present day. And words he'd said moments before. *A guy would have to be dead not to find you attractive.* Followed by his *I'm alive.*

I'm alive, too. Her voice reverberated through his head.

Three soft words. Aimed at clearing the air. Letting him off the hook.

But hitting him straight in the groin.

Chapter 10

Birds of Paradise looked more dilapidated, forlorn and forgotten than it had in the photo Brian had shown her that morning. Graying wood, boarded windows and, on the backside, a small section of roof missing.

She'd told Brian she hadn't recognized the place when he'd presented her with the picture he'd taken the day before. Standing in the deserted gravel parking lot, noting the weeds that were doing a good job of taking over, she knew for certain she'd never been to the café before.

Had Brooke?

Eighteen months before? Or more recently. Was it possible that buried somewhere beneath the weeds, in the gravel, were size one or two footprints belonging to her daughter?

Had her carrier sat on one of the scarred wooden tables or red-leather booth seats she imagined inside?

"I looked up property records and this place is owned

by a woman named Harriet Lichen," Brian said, coming up beside her as she stood before the boarded-up front door.

Feeling better since they'd gotten their mutual attraction out in the open and out of the way, Jessica glanced up at him, fully in the moment. Not worried about the fact that she was glad he was there. They shared an understanding. Of the fact that adults who were alive found other adults attractive.

And more, an understanding of how a missing child made everything else in life fade in significance.

"You have an address for her?" A flash of excitement speared through her. Why hadn't they gone there first?

"Just a PO box."

Of course. She should have known he'd have been on anything that could connect them to someone who actually knew something.

"But look over there." He pointed to an old but well-kept, two-story white house set back on a mowed-grass lot across the street. The driveway was covered in gravel, like the ground upon which they were standing. And the mailbox at the road...

"H.A.L." She read the bold black letters, her gaze rushing from the box to Brian and back. "You think that's her?"

"I think it's worth finding out," he said, pulling her keys out of his pocket and heading back toward the SUV. She was in place, door shut, before he'd started the engine. Trying to remain calm as she watched them turn around, leave the café lot, cross the street and enter the drive, bringing them closer and closer to the house. The front window was large, antique-looking floral curtains open.

No sign of life inside that she could see.

"You want to stay here?" Brian asked, his hazel gaze warm as it landed on her.

"Hell, no!"

She wasn't sure, but thought she might have seen a hint of a grin on his face as, expression professionally bland, he opened his door and waited for her to reach him before heading up to the porch.

While she worried that the homeowner was not going to welcome two strangers on her porch out in the middle of not much on a Sunday morning.

There was no bell. He knocked twice, pulled a leather envelope out of his back pocket and flipped it open in front of him, revealing his private investigator credentials so they were clearly visible. Jessica straightened her shoulders, glad she'd chosen the friendly-looking—she hoped—yellow, short-sleeved button-down shirt with puffy sleeves to go with her skinny black pants and black tennis shoes.

When she'd stepped out of the shower before dawn that morning, she'd had no idea what the day might bring. Had wanted to be prepared for physical exertion, hiking if necessary, but also wanted to look feminine and kind.

In case she came face-to-face with her two-year-old who wouldn't know her.

She'd worn her hair in the loose ponytail she'd had it in every day of the six months she'd had her daughter. She'd needed it back for breastfeeding. And, later, so that little fingers didn't tangle in it and pull it.

No one was answering.

Staring straight ahead, willing the door to open, she saw Brian's fist as he knocked again. Two short raps.

Followed by the sound of a lock clicking on the other side of the heavy wood.

The door opened about two inches, enough that she

could see a floral housedress that hung down almost to two swollen ankles.

Mostly what she saw was the tip of a gun. "Yes?"

Moving slowly, Brian pushed his credentials into the crack. "I'm Brian Powers, ma'am. This is Jessica Johnson. We'd just like to ask you a couple of questions about the restaurant across the street. Property reports say that it's owned by Harriet Lichen. Is that you?"

"Yes." The door opened no further.

It didn't shut in their faces either.

"If you're looking to buy the place, I'm afraid the answer is no," the elderly woman said, her face still behind the door.

"No, we're interested in finding out about someone who might have eaten there." Brian still held his leather envelope up at shoulder height, in the small opening.

And the door pulled open, revealing a wrinkled face with assessing blue eyes accentuated by gray curly hair and pink-and-yellow earrings that matched the housedress.

Harriet's soft-sided, slip-on shoes were yellow…endearing Jessica to her. The dress, the shoes, the earrings—out in the country with no one around.

Having the thought that maybe the woman was hosting Sunday dinner, and would soon have guests, she itched to get their information and leave her to her day.

"Thank you for talking to us," she started in, meeting the woman's gaze with a smile that faded into tremoring lips. "My baby girl was kidnapped months ago, and we have reason to believe that she might have been in your restaurant."

"Oh, my!" Eyes grown wide, Harriet stared at both of them, opened the door wide and ushered them into her living room. Old, paisley-upholstered, claw-footed fur-

niture and accent tables adorned the room. Jessica sat beside Brian on a settee, as indicated, and tugged out of her back pocket the laminated photo she showed everywhere, to everyone. Brooke, in her baby carrier, partially wrapped with the blanket Clint had taken the day he'd stolen their daughter.

"Do you recognize anything about this?" she asked. Babies looked the same. She'd had the response more times than she could count over the past fifteen months. Had honed her question.

Harriet studied the photo. Hard.

Hope swirled inside Jessica.

Until the woman shook her head. "I'm so sorry, honey, but I don't."

"How about this man? Do you recognize him?"

Jessica hadn't known he was carrying a photo of Clint. Hadn't seen him pull it out.

Taking the photo, Harriet gave it the same attention she'd given Brooke's likeness. Picked up glasses off an end table by her chair. Turned on the light.

And shook her head.

With lead in her heart, Jessica wouldn't let herself sink. Dead ends only meant they hadn't found the right person to talk to yet.

"I want to say I don't recognize him." Harriet's words came slowly. Jessica's heart rate sped up enough for both of them. Open-mouthed, she stared. "I want to say that because I don't want to know that my little place was the site of anything as hideous as part of a kidnapping and you're about to tell me this man was part of it, aren't you?"

What? Oh God. Oh God. *Breathe.* What was she supposed to do next? Taking a deep breath, Jessica felt Brian's thigh press against hers.

Him telling her to let him handle things?

She was willing to give that a try. Welcomed his expertise, since she was finding it hard to curtail the rush of emotion that was threatening to overwhelm her.

Fifteen months and she finally had a yes to something? A clue that panned out?

Blinking, she refused to let herself cry. Leaned toward the older woman, hoping she exuded empathy, not desperate alarm as she heard Brian say, "Unfortunately, yes."

Aware of Jessica beside him, getting her hopes up, and maybe fears, too, Brian knew the first thing he had to do was to establish the credibility of his witness. In the Johnson case, the starting point was a no-brainer.

He asked if Harriet minded if he recorded their conversation. With her approval, and his phone mic pointed in her direction, he asked, "Have you seen him recently?"

Jessica stiffened beside him. He pushed away the awareness. Waiting for the critical answer.

"No," Harriet said as Jessica seemed to deflate beside him. And then sit up straight again.

Harriet had passed the first test.

"Can you remember the last time you saw him?"

"Yes, of course. I only saw him a handful of times." Harriet's confident tone, the concern on her face, spoke to Brian. He could only imagine what it was doing to Jessica.

"Tell us about them," he said then, realizing that he needed to know everything she had to say on the matter.

"It was all in one week," Harriet began, her hands folding in her lap as she sat, legs together, on the edge of her chair, looking back and forth between Jessica and Brian.

Intently listening, he waited to hear the one thing that would rule out the validity of her testimony. And at the

same time, to hear every single detail in the event her memory was accurate and Clint Johnson really was the man she believed she'd seen.

He'd have the recording. Could and would replay it. But Harriet wouldn't always be sitting there in front of him, ready to answer or clarify anything her memory might raise within him.

"A couple of weeks before Thanksgiving, year before this one. So…eighteen months ago or so. I know because I start cooking turkey dinners two weeks before the actual day and the first time he was in, he ordered one. And caught the attention of my granddaughter, Bonnie, who was also my only waitress, when he told her that he was ordering it because he had something to be thankful for. Bonnie's in culinary school now, but she hadn't started yet then, and didn't agree with me selling traditional holiday dinners two weeks before the holiday. That man—" she nodded toward the photo Brian still held "—changed her mind."

He waited for the tell, the thing that would prove to him that she wasn't remembering the right guy.

If he got lucky, and they made it through the interview without one, then he'd be gladder than hell that he'd noticed that dilapidated little sign along the side of the road the day before.

"You remember anything else about him?" he asked, keeping his tone calm. Warm. Just casual conversation that tended to flow more accurately than tension-laced interviews.

"That dinner, that's not what I remember most," Harriet said, her tone growing in strength as her expression sharpened. "I remember him because of the way he parked."

Expecting his tell, Brian hoped Jessica was ready.

Knew in his heart of hearts that she wasn't. And couldn't do anything to spare her.

In more than fifteen years of investigating people, an individual's parking habits had never, not once, been high on anyone's list of memory signifiers.

Feigning patience, when he was biting to get back on the road, to get back to tracking Clint Johnson's activities from eighteen months before because they'd lead him to Brooke, Brian just nodded.

"The first time I noticed him…he was in a truck. Blue. With one of those short beds. And it wasn't one of those working trucks. It was fancier. Like something one of those kids on the college baseball team would drive."

A sports edition? Exactly like the truck he'd left parked in Jessica's driveway that morning? Her thigh pressed against his. He left his leg right there, holding strong against her weight. She'd hired him to be there for her.

He didn't react otherwise. Didn't want to lead his witness. He was more eager than ever, though, for her to get her full story out.

"He pulled into the lot, drove around the front of the building and then stopped in the back of the lot and waited. I thought maybe he was meeting someone, and went about my business. Then ten minutes later, I'm waving goodbye to Conner—he's a young farmer down the road, used to be a regular at Birds—and as he pulls out from the spot in front of the big window, that blue truck pulls in. I thought the guy was long gone. And when he came in, I expected him to be looking for someone. And maybe worrying a little bit that he'd used my parking lot for some kind of pass-off and was coming in to get a bite, you know, before heading back down the road. That's when he ordered the turkey dinner."

He had a blue truck.

Appearing to wait for someone.

Then parking.

"And you didn't see any other vehicle meet up with him? Anyone passing through the lot? Or coming in to meet him?"

"No." With sad eyes, Harriet shook her head. "I was right, wasn't I? Him waiting on someone? Did he hand off...?" With a glance toward Jessica, Harriet sucked in a breath in lieu of finishing her sentence.

"We don't know that," Brian quickly assured her, needing her mind as calm and clear as the situation would allow. "You said you saw him a handful of times..."

"Yes, that's right. He came in three days in a row..."

"Did you notice if he waited out in the parking lot to meet someone?" Jessica's question blurted from beside him.

A good question.

"No. The second time, Bonnie saw his truck pulling into the lot and she nudged me. I think he kind of got to her, all lost and, she said, 'trapped inside himself,'" the grandmother disclosed with distress in her voice. "Anyway, I watched him carefully, ready to call the sheriff. Birds was my late-in-life promise to myself and no way was I letting someone conduct wrong business there..."

And yet, as it turned out, it appeared as though she had.

Possibly.

She had Brian's acute interest at any rate.

"He didn't even seem to look around the lot that second time," Harriet continued. "Just pulled right into the same spot he'd been in the day before."

Pressure from Jessica's leg came again. He couldn't look at her, let himself get distracted, even for a second.

Not while he had a witness in front of him.

"He ordered the turkey dinner again..."

"Did Bonnie visit with him at all, do you know?"

"I know she did not. After us talking about how weird it was out in the parking lot the first day, and him keeping a watch outside, she took orders, delivered food, and otherwise stayed in the kitchen the whole time he was there. Thomas, our busboy, watched over the register. Bonnie was always bugging me to let her do the cooking and, truth be told, I was getting tired a lot more quickly back there than I'd expected to..."

Harriet's sigh sounded painful, though she looked healthy. "Now, hearing that he was...oh, my... Bonnie will be horrified..."

"Did you notice this man speaking with anyone else?" Brian asked, mindful of the woman's expressed fatigue and his strong desire to know every frame stored in her brain where Clint Johnson was concerned.

"No." Harriet's response was solid. Sure. "He sat in that same booth by the window and kept looking out at his truck. Like he thought someone was going to hurt it somehow. Way out here..." She shook her head.

The second Jessica's thigh plowed into his, and her foot covered his on the floor, he was being hit mentally with the strong possibility that Clint had left Brooke sleeping in his truck when he'd gone in to eat.

A possibility.

One to look at.

After he had all the facts.

"And he came in the next day, too?" he asked, keeping his thigh pushing against Jessica's but otherwise not acknowledging her at all.

"Yeah. Ordered the turkey again. I remember because it was kind of weird. Me and Bonnie have a difference

of opinion about serving it early, and then him coming in for it three days in a row."

"Did you see him speak with anyone that third day?"

"Nope."

"Did you notice where he parked his truck?" Jessica asked.

"Right in that same place, in front of the window."

"Could you see inside the truck?"

"I'm sure I could. It was parked right in front of the window. But I don't remember anything specific about it. I'm sorry. I so wish I could be of more help. Oh, my... when I tell Bonnie..."

Brian stood, eager to get Jessica out of there, to give himself a moment to catalog and calculate while his first impressions were still fresh.

"And you're sure, that last time, he still didn't talk to anyone?" Jessica's question sounded desperate as they headed toward the front door behind their hostess, and Harriet turned to her, laying a hand on Jessica's forearm, then sliding it down to grab her hand.

"I'm positive, sweetie. I wish I could tell you different. Give you something—anything—but that last day, he picked up a newspaper from off another table on the way to his same place by that window and, other than checking on his truck regularly, like he had before, he read the paper the whole time. Took it with him when he left, too. I remember because it wasn't his to take. And that was the last time I saw him. Never knew where he came from, where he went, or why, for those three days he stopped at my little country place."

Jessica nodded, and when Brian saw tears fill her eyes, he thanked Harriet Lichen, assured the older woman that she'd helped them more than she knew, and got his new employer out of there.

Chapter 11

Harriet didn't want to give out her granddaughter's phone number without her permission, but she'd taken one of Brian's cards and said she'd ask Bonnie to call him.

As they left the property, Jessica felt pretty confident that the grandmother already had Bonnie on the phone. She wasn't nearly as certain that the younger woman would call.

She wasn't sure about a lot of things at the moment. But one stood out boldly.

"His clues mean something."

"At least one of them did."

"Two, if you count the butterflies."

"The place is out of business. I'm fairly certain he didn't expect you to ever find it. And even if you did, as has happened, we're no further to finding Brooke. Clint did nothing but eat there. There was no sign of a baby and he didn't speak to anyone. He's sitting in jail with lots of

time to think about his days on the run, he remembers the great turkey dinner, and he knows that if you ever did happen to find the place, he'd have you on the hook with that clue. While giving you nothing. He's likely playing with your head, Jessica."

The words were no surprise. Anyone who spent any time in her life, or on the case, got there eventually.

But…with Brian…

She stared over at him. "Are you saying you're just going to drop this?" Because she wasn't. He could go look for his gun seller. She'd pay to have that information, and anything else he turned up, but she was not going to let go of Birds of Paradise. Something about that café was more significant than a turkey dinner.

"I'm not dropping anything," Brian returned with obvious frustration. Over her question? Her refusal to see the sense everyone was trying to cram into her? Or his inability to find answers? "Unless you have objections, I'd like to find a place to stop for breakfast, get on our phones and map all directions heading out of Lincoln up to four-hour stretches. He made it to that village three of the four days he was gone after the kidnapping. Four hours one way would be eight hours of driving every day. Doesn't make sense that he'd do that, but it sets parameters for a search. If we find something that rings a bell with you, we can check it out today. Starting tonight, I'll map out every village, town, city within a four-hour radius of Lincoln and check out every known establishment, village name, news piece, I can find…looking for any other match to any of the clues he's given you."

He was a man with a plan. An impressive one. She nodded. So glad, once again, that she'd called his firm. "Breakfast is good."

Mouth still open, she was all set to apologize for doubt-

ing him, but he'd already dialed his phone, had it to his ear. And seconds later was leaving a message for Detective Anderson to call him. He'd like someone to pull what surveillance footage, if any, had been available in the village of Lincoln, Arkansas.

She wanted to go knock on every door in Lincoln and surrounding farms and countryside. Look up the closest daycare in the area—private or otherwise. To see if a two-year-old girl lived in the vicinity. And then, if she didn't recognize her daughter, do everything she could to compel DNA checks. Of course, the DNA samples were a stretch. No court was going to force parents to comply with such a request. And someone with something to hide wouldn't volunteer the test. There'd be others who'd refuse, too, seeing her request as an intrusion and a violation of their privacy—which it would be—so she couldn't assume that those who denied her were guilty of stealing her daughter...

But knocking on doors... If she had a reason to do so other than suspecting them of possible kidnapping...

She'd take up selling makeup if she had to. If nothing else occurred to her. And when Brian went off chasing the uninvolved gun, she'd head back to Lincoln on her own.

No stone left unturned.

No action left untaken.

If she didn't keep trying, she couldn't succeed.

After spending the majority of the day in Jessica's SUV with her, Brian was eager for an early night alone at the apartment. Had been ready to suggest as much—after a couple of completely unproductive hour-long drives to check out potential towns where Clint might have stayed during his four days away—when she beat

him to it. Indicating that she wanted time at home on her computer to better study the areas around Lincoln, to research business names, street names, anything that might click with something Clint had said to her over the past fifteen months.

She'd shown him the second half of her journal, the one with all of her impressions. Had allowed him to make copies of the pages. And knew that she'd be using those pages during her search.

Further research was a better expenditure of time than aimless driving, but he'd been relieved by her suggestion for a completely different reason.

The announced attraction between them had become like a third person in the vehicle as the afternoon wore on.

He didn't feel at all good about it.

Needed some time to regroup.

And was about to tell her so when his phone rang.

An unknown number with an exchange not immediately familiar to him. By the time he'd hung up, after a whole lot of uh-huhs and yeahs, interspersed with some thank-yous, he'd already turned on to the road to Fayetteville and let go of any further conversation regarding their early night.

"That was Bonnie Lichen," he told Jessica instead. Business was all that he should be discussing with her.

"Her father is Harriet's son. She's currently in culinary school in Perrysville, with the hope of getting together enough cash to reopen her grandmother's café. It closed last summer, after a tornado took off that portion of roof. Harriet used her life savings to buy the place, ran it on a shoestring, and had let the insurance lapse."

Nothing pursuant to the case, but information Jessica was paying him to relay. "She had nothing further to add regarding Clint. Said her grandmother asked her about

anything in his truck and she didn't remember anything either. She said that Clint was really nice, that she felt for him, eating turkey dinner all alone weeks before the holiday, but got a sense that something wasn't right with him. Most particularly, after her grandmother pointed out his behavior in the parking lot that first day. She also said that other than ordering in a kind tone, being patient when he had to wait for her attention, he had nothing to say, even when she tried to initiate conversation."

Jessica faced the road in front of them as he spoke. Made it easier for him to keep his mind on the facts of the case and off the fact that he knew every word reopened her wound.

And lessened her ability to get on with her life.

He was helping her relive the past, not put it to bed.

Somehow, he had to turn the corner on that.

Before she went to bed Sunday night, Jessica was a Brain Play Toys representative. She'd applied, paid not just for the starter kit but for the top-seller package, a satchel to load for door-to-door selling and overnight shipping. At the close of the market on Monday, she tore into the boxes that had arrived that day, set on memorizing items and prices enough to be ready to sell on Tuesday after work. Stock exchanges closed at three, she could be in Lincoln by four and still have four hours until dark.

Her phone going off at five after four, with Brian's number popping up, didn't weaken her resolve even a little bit. She picked up after the first ring.

"We expanded the search on stores that sell *Bear Bellies* to include areas south, east and west of Lincoln, as well as all the places we already were looking at here in the northern part of the state, and got nothing. A few

sales, but all traceable and none that matched our parameters." No "Hello. How was your day?"

All business.

As it needed to be.

Still, it was good to hear his voice. To recognize the intensity in it as he gave his all to finding her daughter.

And being honest with her, too.

Even when it hurt.

Weird how someone telling her something even when they knew it would hurt could be a good thing. A positive in her life. But after living with Clint's insidious lies for so many years, lies coated with the illusion of love and promises made, being taken in by them, she felt strengthened, respected, by honesty.

"Maybe he found one in a used bookstore," she said. "Or maybe there's something in the book that's a clue to where he left her."

Her. Not "Brooke that night." Not "her baby." She was all business, too.

After the day before, she had to be.

Telling a guy—the last-ditch effort to find hope—that she was attracted to him had been an eye-opener to her. A cry from her inner self to her brain for help.

Fifteen months of endless, completely unsuccessful searching—combined with birthday number two—was taking its toll.

"Maybe." She figured out what he was likely thinking. That he believed the book was a dead end. Another way for Clint to torture her. Because even if Brian thought it likely that the clue was a dead end, he didn't know for sure. Until they had the truth to rule out other suppositions, the possibility that she was right belonged on the table.

"I've been through hundreds of street names, busi-

nesses, business types, business owner names, even obituaries, located in the four-mile radius of Lincoln and have found nothing that pops with anything in your journal," he said next.

Glancing at the colorful toys, still in their plastic, strewn across her dining room table, Jessica thought about how she wanted to arrange them. Some in the satchel she'd take to the door. Some in a bin in the back of her vehicle.

"Did you have any luck?"

Not on that score. She'd left the investigative work to the expert. "No, but I'm not giving up on it," she told him. She'd have her journal with her as she traversed Lincoln and its vicinity. Paying attention to every street name, ever homeowner who shared a name, even asking for private daycare in the area for her own child, she'd already decided.

She had a whole list of get-to-know-you questions to intersperse with toy information as she started out on her new side career. Her opening line was going to be that she was new to the area.

Just thinking about getting out there…talking to real people in an area she knew Clint had been after the abduction…renewed her spirit. Invigorated motivation that had been chugging along on the fumes of desperation.

"I have word on Blake Redmond," he told her then, his tone unchanged, and all she could think in that second was that things came in threes. Except, apparently with Clint, who was on a four pattern.

"He's due back in town on Wednesday, to pick up a delivery from a warehouse east of here. I'll be meeting him there."

"Does he know that?"

"No."

Good. Not that Redmond likely had any reason to

run, but him not having a heads-up, just in case, seemed expedient.

"I know it seems as though we're getting nowhere, Jess." He'd spoken again. After the third thing.

Sinking into her dining room chair, her back to the table, Jessica stared at the polish on her toes, visible through the black dress sandals she had on with her dress pants and blouse. Things she'd worn for a business lunch with a group of clients that day. The fund they'd shared was due to mature and there were choices to make.

Business choices.

Him calling her "Jess" was not that. But her traitorous body warmed from the inside out. Even the toes hanging out in her air-conditioned home.

In the midst of pure hell, she liked Brian Powers...

"Trust me." His next words seemed to be in response to thoughts not uttered, until he continued. "I'm an expert at this because I've been successful on hundreds of jobs and what's going on here, the little pieces, the dead ends, they all get us closer to the truth. For everything we rule out, there's space for something else to appear..."

Yes.

Turning, she surveyed her newly crowded dining table.

Yes!

Moisture filled her eyes. "Thank you," she told him, meaning the words in more ways than she could even think about.

"Get some rest."

As a tear tripped down over her smile, she said, "I think maybe tonight I will."

And hung up before either of them could mess up the moment.

Chapter 12

"That gun was brand-new when I sold it to him." Blake Redmond, a bearded, skinny guy a few inches shorter than Brian's six-one, didn't run when approached.

He accepted Brian's offer of a cup of coffee in the café across the street from where dock people were loading his truck Wednesday morning and, reaching the door first, held it open for Brian.

"Clint Johnson was a strange dude," Redmond said, his coffee, black with sugar, in between his elbows on the table. "A nice enough guy, likable, until you try to talk to him about his wife. He'd be, like, 'What you asking about her for? You seeing her?'" He sipped, frowning, and shook his head. "Then I'd see him with her… the guy never seemed to look at her, he just kept watching everyone around her, making sure no one was making eyes at her."

"What about her?" The question stuck in Brian's throat.

Made him wish he hadn't had the single sip he'd taken of the coffee in his stomach. But to do right by his employer, with the new information, he had to ask.

"What? You asking me if she seemed into guys hitting on her?"

He hadn't been. But with a cock of his head, he shrugged. To understand the whole picture, to be able to decipher Clint Johnson enough to break through him, he had to know what anyone could tell him, who'd had dealings with the guy around the time of the abduction.

"Hell, no. Anytime I saw her, which was, like, twice, she stayed back with that baby. She was clearly captivated by the little girl. The kid would grin and she'd call out to Clint to come see, not wanting him to miss it." Redmond kind of grinned. "And, boy, that baby had an arm on her."

The truck driver told him about the plastic rattle Brooke had thrown. Rubbed his forearm as he mentioned the red mark it had left.

"Did Mrs. Johnson seem bothered by Clint's possessive behavior?" The question he'd originally been asking. He knew what Jessica had told him about her handling of her husband, her awareness of his shortcomings before the kidnapping, but it helped to have outside perspective. So far, everyone he'd met or spoken to directly pursuant to the case had only come into the grieving mother's life after her daughter had been stolen from her.

"I can't say for sure." Redmond was slow to answer. "The woman was, like, one of those smart types, you know? Definitely careful to not upset the dude, and not doing anything that might, you know, antagonize him."

"Like talking to you..."

"Or even looking at me."

Smart type.

Brian was most pleased by that piece of information.

Because it fit his own assessment of the woman he was there to serve.

The woman who had to be constantly on his mind in order for him to do the job he'd been hired to do.

Redmond held his cup out for a refill as the waitress came by their table carrying a pot. Brian had yet to take a second sip of his own.

"Johnson say why he wanted the gun?" he asked.

"Nope, and I didn't ask. It's all legal here, you know. A guy can sell another guy a gun."

"As long as it's not stolen."

"It's not. I got a few of them, wholesale, from the guy I used to work for online. Totally on the up-and-up, even have the paperwork to prove it. As a manager, buying wholesale was a perk of the job. Guy said it was in lieu of a bonus. I couldn't stockpile them or nothing. Just a few at a time. But I racked up a bit of a side business. The pistol I sold Johnson was one of the last I had."

"And you're absolutely certain that the gun hadn't been shot."

"It hadn't never even been loaded. And, no, I didn't sell him the ammunition for it. That's not cool, either, if he goes straight from me to commit a crime with it. I'm no angel or nothing. I like to drink when I'm not driving, and am more of a drifter than a home guy, but I don't knowingly break no laws." The guy gave a raw, humorless chuckle. "Much as I can't stand being trapped in a home, I'd be a flipping lunatic if I was ever locked up in a cell."

So maybe Redmond's wandering spirit made it difficult for him to settle down, or to locate easily, could likely make it impossible for the guy to ever have a wife or child of his own, but Brian didn't take him for a liar.

That meant that Clint Johnson's gun had been fired after he'd taken possession of it.

Jessica was not going to like that news.

The dread in Brian's gut as he thought about delivering it to her was far more acute than it should have been for an expert who was only relaying business information to his employer.

The very likely possibility that she couldn't save the little girl was growing more tangible by the day—and Jessica was going to refuse to accept it.

Just as his mother had done.

And that led nowhere good.

Jessica was already on the road to Lincoln on Wednesday when Brian called. His daily check-in generally came just minutes after the market closed and, Tuesday, she'd still been at her desk. But after Tuesday's successful-beyond-her-imagining Brain Play Toys selling experience, she'd been out the door as soon as the bell rang the next day.

And Brian's call came half an hour later than it had the previous two days.

When his name showed up on the navigation screen in her dash, she almost clicked to send the call to voice mail. He'd be able to tell she was on the vehicle's hands-free calling system.

She absolutely did not want him knowing what she was doing. Not until she had a viable lead.

He, like the rest of them, would think she was letting grief—and Clint—get the better of her. And that really was none of anyone's business but her own.

People coped in their own ways.

If knocking on doors and getting peeks inside homes, looking for signs of two-year-old girls—or better still,

getting young mothers to talk to her about her kids and kids in the area—helped her, then that was her business.

Her way was to fight back against giving up. To take action, any and all action, that was legal, that she could.

Brian would think she was going way too far, that she was out of control…

Guilt held her frozen, without decision for two cell rings.

She hadn't forsaken life. Other than the first two weeks after Brooke had been kidnapped, she hadn't missed a day of work. Her career was thriving.

By the fourth ring, she was back in sync with herself. Remembering who and what she was. A woman with her own mind. A woman who deserved her trust.

"Hello?"

"I met with Redmond. He was fully cooperative. Had no problem speaking with me, and has already met with Anderson as well. Without provocation, he relayed the same incident you remembered regarding the toy that hit him. And indicated that Clint's possessiveness where you were concerned was over the top, to the point of making Redmond uncomfortable…"

A wave of vindication swept through her. Others had seen.

And that wasn't the point. "What about the gun?"

"It was brand-new when he sold it to Clint. Had never even been loaded."

"That's what he says."

"We've verified his statements. He bought a few guns wholesale when he managed the online hunting supply company. He has all of the paperwork, including gun serial numbers, to verify his account. He did not sell ammunition with the gun."

Long stretches of growing corn blocked much of the

view on either side of her as she drove the two-lane road she'd taken.

Clint had lied to her about the gun.

Didn't make him a killer.

"My guess is, he went out for target practice, just in case he needed to prove to the guy harassing him that he could actually shoot the thing." She said what had first come to her mind. "He wouldn't have wanted to admit to me that he had to practice. Or that he wasn't sure of his ability. To him, testing it out wouldn't have been really shooting the gun. It was only practice to know how to do it." She was preaching to deaf ears. She knew that. Knew what Brian would be thinking.

But she spoke anyway, through the haze of their differing beliefs. Even though he didn't currently trust her enough to know she was of completely sound mind on the issue of her missing daughter, Brian needed to hear her side. For the time when pieces started to come together. He'd remember what she'd said and have a way in to deeper understanding when he needed it.

If he was going to get the job done, he had to understand Clint. And she was the expert on that one.

Until others got on board with what she knew, she had to continue alone, in spite of their help. In addition to their hard work on her behalf. Because Clint Johnson had taken her daughter. And the only way to find her was to figure out what Clint had done with her.

In addition to continuing to research areas around Lincoln, combing through hundreds of databases for anything that clicked with something in Jessica's journal, Brian spent Thursday tracing the ammunition in Clint's gun. Anderson and his team had other, current cases,

and Brian needed the work done immediately. His client needed it done.

So, on the road once more, he headed north of Fayetteville Thursday afternoon, on his way to question an ammunitions dealer who sold the type of bullets found in Clint's gun. His establishment was located close to a gas station where Clint's credit card had been used the day after he'd purchased the gun from Redmond.

Even when faced with evidence that Clint had lied to her about the gun, Jessica hadn't thought that her husband had likely killed their daughter. Or, at the very least, that he'd been involved in an altercation that had escalated to the gun going off.

Brian had to find the truth. And the only way he had to do that was to put the puzzle together piece by piece.

Maybe Clint had been passing the baby off and something had gone wrong. The man had been out of work, needed money. If he'd been dealing with one of the groups that paid top dollar for babies for illegal adoptions...he'd probably have wanted a gun for protection. And if he'd been as lacking in proficiency with the weapon as Jessica thought, he could foreseeably have fired the gun without meaning to do so.

Or fired it poorly.

Might be that someone shot back.

Or even that someone shot at him first.

Could be it had all been a tragic accident. That he'd never meant for the baby to get hurt.

But the fact remained. Clint Johnson had kidnapped his own child.

To get back at Jessica.

Was that why she couldn't let herself see the possibility that he'd hurt their daughter? That the baby could be dead?

Because she'd then find herself responsible? Believing, as she did, that she'd given Clint a reason to need to get back at her when she'd sold the boat?

Regardless of what demons drove his client, Brian had to stay on track. Even more so with her inability to consider all possibilities, including what appeared to him to be the most likely outcome of Brooke's case. He had to get her the answers, to release her from the hell in which she'd been existing since her daughter's abduction.

Lest she end up as his father had—spending his whole life looking for something he'd never find. Something that wasn't there.

His father had set himself impossible odds—ridding the streets of any chance of another police officer dying on duty. There'd been no peace in it. No matter how many crimes he'd solved, no matter how many people he'd sent to prison.

Because there'd always be bad guys.

And no matter how hard Jessica looked, if her daughter was gone, Jessica was never going to find her. Never find her peace.

And without definitive answers, she was likely never going to get off the merry-go-round she rode.

He couldn't let her end up as his father had.

The whole point of Brian's life, the reason he got up in the morning, did what he did, was to give people the answers their hearts needed to allow them to move forward and live their lives.

Never, since the start of his career, had he come so close to the core of his purpose as he was on Brooke's case.

Could be why Jessica was hitting him so much more personally than most jobs. Why he found himself wak-

ing up in the middle of the night in the little apartment she'd rented for him, thinking about her.

Why he wanted to know that she'd been going to run errands, to meet a client, out to dinner, or to meet friends the day before when he called and she'd picked up on her car's audio system.

He couldn't ask. Wouldn't, even if he could somehow make it part of his job. She answered to no one but herself.

But he'd been uncomfortable ever since.

His gut was telling him that she'd been out looking for her daughter. Either pursuant to meeting Harriet on Sunday. Or due to some other hunch she'd had since he'd last seen her.

The woman didn't seem to get—or maybe to care—that if she got close to what Clint had done with her baby, she could be dealing with human traffickers. That she could get herself killed.

Brian just couldn't let that happen. His life would never be the same.

And, considering that she was just a job, there was no good explanation for that either.

Chapter 13

"Let him play with it for a couple of minutes, if you'd like." Cleaning the plastic ball covered in three-dimensional shapes and numbers with an antibacterial wipe, Jessica let it dry and then handed it to the young Indian mother. The woman's two-year-old son had pulled the toy out of Jessica's satchel seconds earlier.

And when the toddler had the toy back in hand, Jessica's heart soared for a second that Thursday afternoon. She was going to leave the ball there. At her own expense. Just being able to watch a two-year-old interact with it… For a moment there, she could get a real-life idea of how Brooke might react. Of typical two-year-old behavior.

For a moment there, she felt happy.

Her phone vibrated a call, and while Charita showed her son how to more successfully roll the unusual ball, she quickly pulled the cell out of her pocket to see that Brian was calling. A little later than the day before.

With a quick text, telling him she was with a client and would call him later, she brought herself firmly back to the business at hand.

That was not living vicariously through little two-year-old Amit, or his pretty mother.

For the next minute or two, she had a chance to pose questions without coming across in a wrong way.

"Does Amit have a play group?" she asked, smiling as she watched the boy trace a five with his index finger and then try again to roll the bumpy ball.

Her long dark hair in a ponytail, Charita shook her head. "We're such a small village…and mostly spread far apart…it's just him and me most days while my husband is at work."

She already knew, from Tuesday and Wednesday visits, that there were no daycares in Lincoln.

"Does he like the park out by the church?" She'd noticed it just that afternoon, having approached the town from a different direction—as she'd done each day.

Charita, her gaze mostly on her son, a smile on her face, said, "I take him there sometimes. He's a little young yet. He's afraid of the slide."

"But he gets to interact with other kids," she pointed out, as though everyone knew that peer interaction was a major part of healthy child development.

"He watches them mostly. And runs to me if anyone talks to him."

There were other kids at the park. Good to know. It had been vacant, seeming like a ghost-town playground, when she'd driven past.

She had to get out of there. Get back to the park before everyone went home to bed.

"He loves that ball," she said then, trying to temper her haste with a reminder that she was a Brain Play Toys

saleswoman. "I'd be happy for him to keep it, on me," she said, handing Charita a pamphlet with a full array of toys. "There's a website address on the back," she added, before pointing out her own, handwritten contact information on the back.

And then she grabbed a couple more of the pamphlets specifically designed for toddlers. "Do you know of any other two- to three-year-olds in the area?" she asked. "Maybe you could pass these along to their parents."

Shaking her head, Charita said, "We only just rented this place a couple of months ago. We go into Barneysville to church and shop, and everything else we do. It's where we're from. I know some people there, though, if you'd like me to take some of these. I don't know if you want to service that area."

Not sure she'd still be in business the following week, Jessica gave Charita the go-ahead. She could always turn the sale to someone else if one came in. And it seemed the quickest way to end the visit.

She hurried to her car. Had to call Brian back.

The church playground called out to her more loudly.

Seeing cars in the parking lot, her heart started to pound as she pulled in, figuring there was some kind of church function going on. Didn't much care about the cars, or the church. Rounding the building, she had attention only for the small patch of dirt and grass that housed the play equipment.

Hoping...

Yes. The swings were moving. A body was coming down the slide.

And she parked. There were three kids. All elementary age, she figured.

No parents.

Not yet.

Maybe when they came to pick up the kids, they'd have little ones in tow…

She could wait.

Dialed Brian directly from her cell.

"Sorry about that," she told him, her gaze focused on the children playing. Glad to just sit for a minute and watch them having fun.

To remind herself that normal life existed.

"No problem. You have to work." Brian's voice came over the phone, sending another bout of warmth through her.

She was getting used to it. Her reaction to the expert's voice when he spoke to her. If nothing else, Brian Powers's presence in her life was empowering her to be better. Stronger.

Of course, if he knew the kind of "work" she'd been doing…

"I found the shop where Clint bought his ammunition," he told her. And her heart didn't sink. He was doing his job.

She was doing hers.

"Turns out, he came back twice. He was there the day after he bought the gun. And then, again, the day before he took Brooke."

Her eyes closed. Shutting out the kids. The blue sky with hints of rose foreshadowing the soon-to-be-setting sun.

"How many boxes did he buy?"

"One each time. Paid cash. The owner of the store doesn't mess around. He's got digital cameras around the place, and saves every bit of footage on memory cards filed by date. I have a copy of the ones showing Clint."

He was a good investigator, she'd give him that. And didn't need to see the images he had in his possession.

Maybe they'd be of use to Anderson. Some way to prove child endangerment—since Clint had owned the gun when he'd had possession of Brooke—and extend the fiend's prison sentence.

"How many bullets to a box?" she asked what she had to know.

"Ten rounds. Nine millimeter."

The size meant nothing to her.

"My guess is he really was afraid of whoever he thought was threatening him," she said, doing her job, making herself think like her ex-husband would to figure out what he'd been up to. "And that he practiced until he felt confident he could defend himself."

If he'd meant to do more, he'd have bought a bigger box of bullets to begin with. "Clint wouldn't waste money buying two small boxes if he could get double the amount for cheaper," she said then, her gaze once again focused on the playground. The children were all on the monkey bars and she focused on the empty swings.

"I need to confirm that I'll be present for your call with Clint again tomorrow, set up the same as we were last week."

The leap of good feeling inside her was brief.

And notable.

She hadn't seen Brian since Sunday. Had only ever been with him three days in her whole life.

And was glad to know that he'd be on her calendar in less than twenty-four hours.

"Of course," she told him as though she'd been planning all along to have him there. She might have wondered a time or two if he'd think it important. Hadn't allowed herself to attach to the idea one way or another.

He made plans to be at her place early, so they could exchange notes from the week. He hadn't asked what

she'd been up to, but he had to know she'd at least been following up on the internet. She agreed to seeing him as soon as the Wall Street bell rang.

And was still feeling a bit of a lift as she disconnected the call.

Focusing once again on the playground.

The children had left—all running back to the church building together, as though they'd been called in.

And it was time for her to get back, too.

Back to Fayetteville. To the reality of her life there.

The constant, unending search for her daughter.

With what was becoming a major difference.

Knowing she wasn't alone in her daily fight made the prospect seem a whole lot more manageable.

Whether her expert knew Brooke was alive or not.

No matter what he thought, he kept his mind open to all of the facts. He'd figure it out.

She'd known him less than a week and she had faith in him.

A strange development.

And a welcome one.

She looked good.

In blue stretch pants that highlighted shapely thin legs leading up under the blue-and-white-striped formfitting shirtdress that fell just to her thighs, with those blue and white, heeled sandals, Jessica Johnson could have posed on any red carpet anywhere. The long blond hair in a loose ponytail and light makeup gave her an air of realism. Made her seem more accessible.

And yet none of that hit him as strongly as her sense of calm, of confidence, as she greeted him at her front door.

He'd dressed up for the occasion, too, though he couldn't say why. Other than a meeting with Anderson

earlier in the day, he'd been on his own, with no one to impress. The black pants, white shirt, open at the collar, and black-leather belt and shoes were his office clothes.

And he was heading in to sit on the floor of his client's office.

"Hey." The word held warmth as she greeted him. Her gaze, meeting with his there in her foyer, held more than that.

The message he read clearly was that she was glad to see him.

He was pretty certain she read the same message back.

Wanted to freeze the moment. To stay there and bask in it for as long as he could. A lifetime, maybe, if it meant he didn't have to cross over into what was coming next.

That, of course, he did. Before the phone call coming in less than an hour.

"I just left Anderson's office." The words came deliberately. Pushed out by the man he was. The job he had to do.

She responded as he'd expected her to do—turning around so that all he could see was a long blond ponytail hanging down a stiff spine. He wouldn't let his gaze go any lower than that. "Let's head back." Her words came just after the spin as she moved toward the hallway leading to her office.

And he got it. Business happened in her office.

"I'm assuming you told him about Redmond. The ammunition," she said, arms crossed as she faced him from beside her desk.

"You gave me your permission to communicate with him," he said slowly, establishing boundaries first.

Maybe buying himself some time. She was going to hate what was coming.

He hated it for her.

In ways she probably wouldn't even be able to comprehend.

With a nod, she said, "Of course I did. I'm glad it's you and not me, frankly. It's been…nice…this week, not having to be the one to check in on every little detail."

He wanted to be surprised by the response. Wasn't. Jessica's fairness, her ability to look outside her own perspective, her own hell, to be able to understand that they were all working for her, even if the actual job brought her pain…all of it spoke to him.

Captivated him in a way no other client ever had.

She wasn't the first who'd raised empathy in him. Not even the hundredth. But his sense of her, his inability to stop tuning into her so deeply…

"I've been keeping him up to date as things happen," he told her then, forcing himself to do the job for which she'd hired him. "He knew about Redmond on Wednesday, and he knew about the ammunition yesterday."

Another nod from her, with her chin a little tighter. Her lips pursed. Pretty clear she was preparing for the more that was coming.

"With the evidence collected, he had no choice but to go see Clint."

Her first reaction, closed eyes, lasted about ten seconds. Then she sat. Straight up. Stiffly. Hands in her lap. "Clint knows that I know he lied."

"Anderson didn't say so, but that's an obvious conclusion."

With a quick, eye-to-eye look, she said, "Tell me."

Tell her quickly. Get it over with. He got the message. Struggled to make it happen.

"He doubled down on the fact that he didn't shoot the gun. Couldn't account for where the rest of the ammunition was. Suggested that perhaps whoever found the gun stole it. And spent the rest of the visit grilling Detective

Anderson about the week's activity. Wanted to know if Anderson met with Redmond personally."

"What did he tell him?" Her words came out froggy. Like her throat was so dry she was ready to choke.

"The truth. Nothing stops Clint from making a call to Redmond. An easy check."

"He knows about you."

"No." He spoke firmly. Followed the assurance, the only good-news part of his announcement, with a firm shake of his head.

"Anderson just said that someone else who's working with the department did the legwork."

"'Working with the department.' Not for them."

Yeah, he'd caught that, too. "That's what he said."

Hands in his pants' pockets, Brian did what he could. Stand there.

A minute passed. And another. Then Jessica turned her chair to her desk. Signed back on to her computer as the large monitor attached to her laptop by the docking station in the corner came to life.

"He's going to be doing everything he can to get on early today," she said calmly, as though speaking to a new client. A stranger, albeit one with whom she was planning to share an amicable relationship. "We should get ready."

She didn't want to piss Clint off.

That pissed Brian off. At Clint Johnson. Not at the stronger-than-rock ex-wife the criminal was trying to annihilate.

Without another word, he did as she asked. Repeated the headset protocol, the camera shadow tests, lowered himself to the position he'd have to maintain for however long the call took.

And left Jessica alone in the silent world she'd entered without him.

Chapter 14

"I did not lie to you, Jess." The words jumped into the silence pervading the room the second Clint's face appeared on the screen.

A full fifteen minutes early.

The sting in his tone bit into her heart. Replacing anything good trying to flower there with stone-cold fear.

She could stave him off from her mind. Had a full arsenal of mental defenses that would keep his control of her thoughts at bay for the rest of her life.

But…he knew where Brooke was.

And, conceivably, had the power to make certain that Jessica never saw her little girl again.

"I didn't say you did," she responded, drawing upon the strength being Brooke's mother gave her, to keep her tone, her expression, calm.

If he saw her fear, he'd win.

She had to stay focused.

And…she wasn't alone. Not anymore.

She had a full-time investigator who'd been instrumental in turning up more leads in a week than everyone else—including herself—had found in a year.

"That detective you sent to see me this morning—yeah, thanks for that, by the way—sure thought I did." She recognized the huge dollop of sarcasm practically drowning his words with new lead in her stomach.

"In the first place, I didn't send him. As a matter of fact, I didn't even know he saw you until I got his report after the bell rang."

If she protested too much, he'd have the upper hand.

And doubts as to her innocence.

And he, of all people, knew how she was about not being bothered while the market was open. She'd touched the open sore completely on purpose.

When her words seemed to be getting him to at least slow down and think, she leaned into the screen as she'd seen him do so many times before. "You know that Anderson and I have disagreed many times over the course of the past eighteen months, Clint. He's a cop. Working a case in which we're both involved. He doesn't work for me. And he absolutely doesn't do what I want him to do."

All true. If she told an outright lie, she could lose everything.

"You told him what I said about Redmond selling it to me, Jess." The pouty tilt to his lips gave her a second's respite. She'd managed to distract him from his anger.

For the moment anyway.

"So that he could verify your alibi and get off the whole gun thing," she said with enough honesty to fill a church. "I want Brooke, Clint. You know that. Either you tell me where to find her, or he finds her… I need our daughter home safely." Her voice broke. Not by design.

She gave herself a second, noticing that his gaze changed on the screen, becoming more the calm, sincere-looking guy she usually stared at for half an hour every week.

The guy who was confident in his game.

His return was a relief.

That was the guy who'd give her another clue. A reason to get up in the morning. Activity for her weekend.

Though, if Brian's pattern theory was right, she had three bogus clues to sit through before she got the next valid one.

Or perhaps they were all valid, in their own little twisted ways, just not paramount, like Birds of Paradise.

She hadn't decided yet whether or not to tell Clint she'd found the place. She wasn't going to give him anything unless she thought she could get something back for it.

She couldn't decipher his silence. And finally said, "My immediate response, when I heard about the gun being sold to you new, was that if it had been shot while in your possession, it was only you making certain you knew exactly how to properly use it in the event you had to." He was a guy who had information about her daughter's whereabouts. A guy who was making her play a sick game to extract that information. She'd play his game as long as it took.

When his shoulders relaxed a bit more, she allowed herself a full breath.

"You do know me, don't you, Jess?"

"Of course, I do." She kept her tone matter-of-fact. He knew she wasn't happy with him. Would be suspicious if her manner with him suddenly changed.

"You understand me."

Understood that he was a maniacal fiend. "Yes."

They'd used up the extra fifteen minutes he'd had. That left another thirty that she still had to sit through.

Praying that he got on with asking about her week—opening the door for her to tell him all the things she'd learned about direct selling as an enterprise—minus the fact that she'd done the research for herself, not a client—she waited as though she didn't give a rat's ass if he wasted his entire time allotment on staring at her, as long as, before he left the room, he gave her her clue.

"I practiced at the Timberline shooting range east of town. I shot all ten bullets. Until I was hitting the bull's-eye regularly, and then went back and bought another box in case I ever needed to use the gun."

Her eyes widened, giving him more of a reaction than she usually allowed. Before she could temper words to take away the effect, he smiled.

"Funny how my foster mother used to yell at me for playing video games so much, and yet learning to aim at the screen made me proficient enough at the range to only need ten bullets."

Taking a second easier breath, she sat back as the voice coming at her sounded exactly like the Clint she knew. Finding a way to turn the situation into him being mistreated and a brag on himself at the same time. Clint was always about his own vindication.

Even when it meant kidnapping his own daughter because he hadn't gotten his way.

The thought hardened all emotion he'd managed to rise in her. No fear left. Just the resolve to stay the course until she had Brooke safely home.

"All you had to do was ask, Jess. I'd have told you about the learning curve."

If it had suited him, he'd have done so. And in hindsight, knowing that the police were still actively on his

ass, he was now seeing that it would have suited him better to have been more forthcoming the week before when she'd given him the chance.

Of course, the fact that he hadn't been, was her fault. She hadn't asked the right question.

"Tell me about your week, Jess."

As usual, she was ready. Giving him a lot of detail concerning an enterprise she'd known little about, mentioning the most successful direct-selling products. Kitchen tools. Makeup. Laundry products. Talking about stock market movement. Company revenue and top-producer income. Listed a couple of CEOs of parent companies who were well-known names in the finance world. Names he'd heard from her before.

Also, as had been habit from call one, she watched the clock. Making certain that she left enough time at the end of their virtual meeting to get her clue.

No way she was letting him get everything out of her as he'd asked and then give her a *Sorry, we're out of time.*

Five minutes before she was due to stop, Clint suddenly burst forward, his face huge on her screen.

Shooting backward in her seat, she frowned. What did he…?

"Who is he, Jessica?"

Full name. Through gritted teeth.

Without much time to talk him down.

She froze for the split second it took her to realize that doing so made her look guilty. And then leaned forward right back at him.

"That was rude, Clint. Coming at me like that."

He didn't back up. "Who is he?"

Flashing back to countless times during their marriage, filling up with an immediate need to soothe him, reassure him, do whatever it took to prove to him that

she was not cheating on him, Jessica couldn't do any of those things.

There wasn't time.

And she…couldn't do them anymore. "I have no idea who 'he' is, but you don't get to do this anymore," she told him, words coming up from somewhere distant inside her. "You say you want us to be a family, that this time is about you and me finding what we lost… Well, right there, Clint. That's part of what lost me. I never, ever, cheated on you. And if you think I have the time or the emotional resource now to do so, you're just plain off. Or you don't know me as well as I thought you did."

He sat back. Didn't look calm or kind. But he had the good sense to keep his mouth shut.

For a second.

"Who's this guy who has the time to go talking to Redmond and chasing down ammunition dealers then?"

"Why are you asking me? He's reporting to Anderson." Truth. Just not all of it.

Eyes narrowed, he perused her. It took everything she had to withstand the assault. And the clock ticked.

"I want my clue, Clint. No clue, no call." She wasn't messing around.

He said nothing. Just watched. The guard who came in to get him at the end of the session entered. Jessica's entire body stiffened and, if it were possible for her to shoot bullets out of her eyes through the computer screen, she'd just done so.

"The blue barn."

Her screen went dead.

And Jessica's body slumped for a second as she swallowed back the tears that needed to fall.

By the time Brian got to Jessica's desk, she had pen in hand and was writing in her journal. Knowing that

her first impressions could be vital down the road, he stepped back until she was through. Waiting was hard.

On many levels.

He needed to get online. Get aerial views within a hundred miles of Lincoln. Run searches on businesses and street names. Get through the galore of tediousness he had to traverse to find that one little treasure that would guide his next steps.

He needed to take the woman sitting so stiffly into his arms, hold her until she felt warm again. She'd straightened so swiftly after her collapse that he'd almost convinced himself he'd imagined it. But the vision of her slumped in her chair kept coming at him with such force, he couldn't ignore what he'd seen.

What he knew.

Clint's torture was getting to her.

Maybe worse than anyone knew.

The direct-sales research—something about it hit him. Probably because he was stretching too far in his search, but…

He was living in Jessica Johnson's life.

Aware of the way inaction brought panic, which she fought off with action that led nowhere. Like chasing down the entire sixty-four clues Clint had given her, over a period of fifteen months, all to no avail.

Except for Birds of Paradise, he reminded himself. Whether Clint had meant to give Jessica an actual clue or not, whether Brian's pattern theory had any basis in reality or not, Birds of Paradise had been real in the kidnapper's life during the four days he'd been missing after abducting his own child.

They knew for certain Clint had been in Lincoln after taking Brooke.

What mother wouldn't want to knock on every door there to see if her missing child was inside?

She'd stopped writing. Had turned her chair and was looking at him.

"You've been selling door-to-door all week, haven't you? When I called, and you were on your cell phone, it's because you were heading to Lincoln."

"I'm guessing your deductive reasoning is part of what makes you so good at your job?"

He'd nailed it. Knew her well enough to get it right.

The realization brought no pleasure.

"What are you selling?"

"Was selling." Reaching under some folders on her desk, she pulled out a full-color, shiny booklet. "Brain Play Toys."

The bright primary colors, the happiness they represented…turned his stomach. "You do realize that if Clint sold Brooke—which isn't a stretch since he'd just lost his job and then his boat, due to a lack of money—you could have been walking into the home of a trafficker? Giving them the sense that we're on to them? Making you a target? And we'd have no way of knowing which home you were in that pushed that button."

His frustration, due in part to his own inability to find answers quickly enough, came pouring out of him.

He was not going to watch another woman lose all sense of caution to the point of walking into her own death.

She'd said, "Was selling." Was just sitting there, watching him.

"Did you find something?" he asked. He had no right to throw up on her.

But he stood by what he'd said.

"I spent a week meeting some nice people, finding

out just how much I'm not a small-town country girl, and making almost five-hundred dollars," she said. "But, no, I didn't find out a damned thing."

Seeing her forlorn expression, knowing the kind of pressure—and only being able to imagine the emotional stress—she was under, Brian wanted to pull her into his arms and hold on.

Again.

The image was repeating in his brain more frequently.

"We need to talk," he told her.

And knew, by the ashen look on her face, that he was adding to her troubles, not helping her as he was being paid to do.

Chapter 15

He was going to quit her.

She didn't regret going door-to-door in Lincoln. It was something she'd needed to do. Maybe she hadn't been wise to do so without letting someone know.

Just in case something went wrong.

She'd be no good to Brooke dead. Not unless she died rescuing the toddler.

Trying to come up with something pithy to say—so soon after her mental battle with Clint—Jessica wasn't the first to speak as Brian pulled up a chair to face hers.

"You know I think you're going off the rails sometimes, letting Clint play you."

Yeah, this wasn't going to be good. Finding no need to answer, she held his gaze steadily.

"I also know that there's nothing I can do about that."

Get on with it, already. She had to move forward, alone or not. Itched to get working on the blue barn.

Couldn't afford to use up vital emotional focus on a long drawn-out ending of employment. He wasn't the only expert investigator in the country. Maybe not even in Sierra's Web.

The last thought brought no comfort whatsoever.

She didn't want another investigator barging into her life.

She wanted Brian.

"I can't work next to a firecracker."

She blinked but then returned immediately to holding his gaze. He looked as serious as she'd seen him.

Not angry, though. As if he got that her actions were no reflection on him.

He was different…even in his displeasure with her.

She should make it easier on him to leave her. Couldn't find any words that would actually exit her mouth.

"Here's what I propose…"

Wait. What? She blinked again and hated that she'd lost that second of contact.

"You're going to do what you're going to do, and I'm going to have to find a way to be okay with that."

She loved him. Well, not *loved* loved him, but… She tried not to smile as she nodded. He wasn't leaving her!

Or trying to change her, either, as Clint would have done.

"But I need something from you."

Pulling back a little on the elation, she waited.

"I need your total honesty, Jessica. I have to know what you're doing. Where you're going, as it pertains to Brooke's disappearance."

If she'd told him about the direct selling, and had inadvertently walked into a traffickers' den, as he'd suggested was possible, he'd have known where to start on

his search for her, and would likely have found Brooke in the process.

Even if she was dead and therefore unable to free her daughter herself.

"You've got it."

This time he sat back. "Just like that?"

Her shrug wasn't feigned. "What you say makes complete sense. Beyond that, it's fair. I did you a disservice this week by not filling you in on my actions. Could maybe even have put your life in danger by opening a can of worms you didn't know was opened. It won't happen again."

The way he watched her, the way those striking hazel eyes seemed to warm right there while connected to her gaze…she'd never forget that moment.

Not in a dozen lifetimes.

The woman didn't make excuses. Didn't get defensive.

She didn't back down either. Not when it came to her doing what she believed to be the right thing for her to do.

Thinking of how she'd just taken on her insidious ex-husband, he figured she had more strength in her gaze alone than he had in his entire body.

Brian hadn't ever met anyone like her.

"We need to get working on the blue barn. It's a new clue. Let's see if it leads someplace solid." He didn't break eye contact as he spoke.

Neither did she. Even as she nodded.

"You want to go out for some dinner?" They had a weekend to plan. And he was hungry. For more than just food but was also smart enough to know which parts of himself to feed.

"While we work?"

"Of course." He was on the clock, her clock, and time

was ticking on her ability to continue holding on without getting herself hurt. He got cold all over again, thinking of her walking door-to-door, alone, in that remote area of the state all week.

There were no chances she wouldn't take for her daughter. As much as he hated what that meant, for her own safety and well-being, he also understood.

And admired her for it.

Who wouldn't want to have someone like her in their court?

Unless, of course, that tenacity got her killed and then…

"You like Indian food?" she asked, standing, reaching for her journal and a couple of folders. "One of my clients told me about this great place downtown and…"

Brian stood, too, gathered the pieces of himself that seemed to fall down around her, and took his employee/client out to a working dinner.

Promising himself, and whatever fates there were, that he would die before he let her down.

He offered to let her drive. Since Jessica truly didn't mind being a passenger, and knew he did, she was quite happy to hand him the keys. To be able to give him what he needed without abandoning herself. In those last months, Clint had only needed or wanted what was counterproductive to her. Every single second with him had been a test of her loyalty. Her service to him.

She'd felt the problem before she'd seen it.

And… Brian was only a business associate. They were not going on a date. He was not a personal item in her life.

Still, it was…nice…to be heading out for a meal with a decent, healthy man.

Maybe, once she found Brooke, there'd be opportu-

nity to have another man in her life. To have a loving companionship. Though she didn't trust herself to bring another man into her daughter's life.

She'd proven over the past fifteen months that she didn't need a man to complete her. She'd managed just fine on her own. Had preferred to be alone. Wouldn't have called Sierra's Web, or met Brian, if it hadn't been for Brooke.

But wanting…maybe there could be some of that.

Once Brooke was home.

Sitting silent beside the expert investigator, she let her thoughts flow in stream of consciousness. Giving herself a moment or two to breathe. To recover equilibrium, to remember that life encompassed so much more than Clint Johnson's diabolical head games.

A weekly process. One she'd pretty much mastered. One made oddly easier with Brian Powers sharing her space.

Until they arrived at the restaurant and she saw the crowded parking lot, the people waiting outside for their table, and heard the noise coming from within. Taking a deep breath, she braced for the onslaught her inner self did not need. She'd invited him to dinner. Had suggested the place.

"You like pizza?" Brian asked as he circled, looking for a parking spot.

"I promised you a fine dining experience."

"And I'll hold you to it, with a rain check," he said. "Unless you really want to go in there right now."

She must have looked pathetic…and he was her employee…

Sitting upright, she noticed, again, his pants and shirt, leather belt and shoes. Going-out-nice apparel more than

pizza joint. "I'm good to go in," she said, pointing to a vacant parking place.

"I didn't think you weren't up for it," he told her. "I just think it's been a long week, we only have two days in which to find a blue barn before you have to go back to work, and we aren't going to get much work done in there with all that noise."

Looking at him for a long moment, she tried to decide if he was taking pity on her. Wondered why the idea bothered her so much.

Wondered why she couldn't just let someone—a man—do something nice for her.

Another casualty of Clint's warfare?

"I'd very much like to go home, order pizza, and get to work," she told him.

Two minutes later, after fighting with herself over whether or not to speak, she added, "Thank you."

"For what?"

"I'm not sure." Total truth. "I'm just…thankful that you're here. That I'm not eating alone tonight. That we're going to get to work. That I didn't have to drive. And that…you're you."

That. The last part. So much.

Maybe too much.

He kept driving, his profile giving nothing away. And then a red light happened. He stopped. Turned to look at her.

Really look at her. Intensely.

For that second, there was only him. And her.

And the warmth flooding the SUV.

Then the light turned green.

He had a thing for his client. For the woman paying him for his service.

Halfway through the pizza they were sharing, sitting

at her dining room table with their laptops and papers and folders, her journal, his notes spread all around them, Brian glanced at Jessica and was swamped with an urge to push that stray piece of hair out of her eyes.

It had fallen from her ponytail.

He wanted to see all of that glorious blond hair falling free around her. For her to have five minutes without care.

"What?" She'd glanced up to take a bite of pizza and caught him staring at her.

"Your dad left when you were three." Her family history had been in Brooke's case file. Family members were often suspects in kidnappings.

"Yeah, so?" The bite of pizza she took dripped sauce beside her mouth. He had to look away before temptation to lick it off took more of him than he could afford to give.

"And Clint… I imagine, early on, pleasing him became part of what you did to keep the relationship together."

She'd dropped the pizza slice back onto the paper plates she'd provided for both of them. Was chewing more slowly. "You work at a relationship," she said when she'd swallowed. "It doesn't just happen."

Damn. He hadn't meant to make her defensive. Wasn't sure what he'd meant to do. Or why.

"I just… You're an incredible woman, Jessica. It pisses me off that the two men who should have honored you, crapped on you instead."

There. He sighed. Grabbed his slice of pizza. And, as she picked up her own slice, bit and chewed, he finished off his own.

They worked until after midnight. With aerial views online, they'd found half a dozen blue barns in the state. Four of them within a couple of hours from Lincoln.

Two between Fayetteville and Lincoln. Of those two, one was an older structure on private property. The other, a wholesale shoe store.

Jessica had searched children's books for blue barn images, and downloaded three in e-book form. She'd also searched children's stores. Movies, brand names and food containers showed up under searches. She made notes.

A few minutes after midnight, she was starting to think she should kick Brian out when her text app sounded the small ding notification sound she'd chosen.

Brian's gaze met hers, briefly, and then he went back to work.

He wouldn't know that she never got texts that late at night. Was probably thinking it was a romantic thing.

And… Ma.

Grabbing her phone, heart pounding, she opened the app. Who else would text that late? And only if Jackie had an emergency…

She didn't recognize the number. Pushed to read the message.

I'm watching you.

Tossing her phone out of her hand as though it was on fire, she stared at it. Shaking.

Brian was on it as it hit the table. He didn't ask questions, just read the message still on the screen. Grabbed his own phone and dialed Anderson, getting the man out of bed.

Five minutes later, moments filled with stiff chins and silent thoughts, they had a callback.

The message had come from a burner phone. And the patrol in the area had found no one lurking near her home.

"They're putting a car on the house for the rest of the

night," Brian said as he hung up. And met her gaze for the first time since she'd tossed her phone.

"You have to go. Now," she told him, trembling from the inside out. The message was from Clint. She knew it in her bones. "He's probably set up some kind of hidden camera on the house...has been watching me for fifteen months on some computer program he logs into from the prison." Stopping as she heard herself aloud, recognized the absurdity of what she was saying.

But she knew.

"We'll have the place checked for bugs first thing in the morning," Brian told her. And then, not standing and getting the hell out of there, said, "It's possible that you ruffled some feathers this week, Jessica. You had your phone number on the booklet you showed me. I'm assuming it was on all of the ones you handed out as well."

He made sense.

Too much sense.

More sense than her own suspicions.

Scared now, on two fronts, she stared at him. Trying to find her peace. Her strength. She could stay in her house alone all night. And let the professionals figure out who'd sent the obscene message.

And if her ex-husband was watching? If he knew she'd had a man spend the night?

He'd refuse to give her more clues...

Was she crossing a line...becoming irrational...allowing him to get too far into her head again?

No way Clint was going to win. To steal her from herself.

To fight off the possibility of him causing irrational thoughts in her mind, she focused again on what Brian had said.

About her week snooping around Lincoln.

The very real possibility of human traffickers.

And then, eyes wide, she looked over at Brian again. "If I ruffled feathers, that means that there's something to find, right? Something someone needs to hide badly enough to warn me off?"

It also meant that her baby could have been sold.

To a wealthy family who could pay well but couldn't adopt through normal channels?

The tightness around Brian's lips was more pronounced than she'd seen it. "It could mean that, yes."

"So we're making progress."

She couldn't keep the excitement out of her voice.

"I'm staying here tonight."

Jessica was determined. Independent. She wasn't stupid.

With a nod, she went to get him a sheet, blanket and pillow, and pulled out the sleeper bed from her sofa.

Chapter 16

If someone in Lincoln was involved in Brooke's disappearance—even, say, with the disposal of the body—they'd likely be familiar with Jessica's name.

From Clint, maybe. Definitely from the stories that had been all over the news eighteen months before. And again during Clint's trial.

She'd spread her name all over the damned village.

From there, finding her address was a no-brainer for anyone with enough smarts to do a simple people search.

Could be that Clint hadn't meant to hurt his daughter. Maybe he really had just been meaning to scare Jessica, to wake her up to his way of thinking, to make her squirm so she'd see that she was wrong to have taken his boat away from him.

After a week and two days of studying the guy, observing him in action, Brian could see all of that. And maybe he'd hurt Brooke without meaning to do so.

If, say, the gun went off accidentally. Maybe he'd had it to protect himself in case someone came after him for the kidnapping. Had had it out and ready and the baby had scooted to it without him noticing.

She'd had the strength to throw a toy with enough force to leave a mark on a grown man.

Maybe Clint Johnson had dropped the child. Or left her alone on a bed without rails and she'd rolled off, hit her head.

And another strong possibility—he'd sold her.

Not a single one of the scenarios left a happy ending in the future, where Clint and Jessica magically repaired their relationship, found each other again, he got out of prison, and they got Brooke back.

Lying fully dressed on the three-inch mattress that did little to cushion his weight, Brian stared at the ceiling. His client had excused herself to bed as soon as she'd dropped his bedding on the pulled-out bed visible from the dining table.

The fact that no one but Brian knew that she'd vacated her master suite on the far end of the house, in favor of the small guest room next to her office, gave him some comfort.

Clint—if the warning came from him and he had the wherewithal to make someone do his dirty work while he was in prison—would expect her to be at the master suite end of the house.

If someone got by the cops out front and managed to get in the house, they'd have to pass Brian before they got to Jessica.

Of course, it was possible that whoever she might have tipped off in Lincoln had found a way to get a message to Clint in jail. Possible that both scenarios were true—

Clint was behind the message *and* Jessica had tipped off traffickers or someone guilty of tampering with a corpse.

Adding to his mental list of to-dos at first light. He needed jail records to know who Clint had been communicating with.

And when. Something Jessica had asked Anderson for, but hadn't received.

And he needed a list of all of the residences Jessica had visited in Lincoln.

After a call to Anderson, he'd make a quick trip to his apartment for a shower at first light, as soon as the crew arrived to check Jessica's home for bugging devices. And be back before they left.

He'd send the list of Lincoln addresses she'd visited that week to Anderson and then he and Jessica would check out the first two blue barns—the ones between Fayetteville and Lincoln. And, by then, he should have answers from the detective who was eagerly coming back to full life on the case.

As much as the threat to Jessica angered—and scared—him, he knew, as she'd quickly deduced, that they could be getting much closer to her finding the answers she needed.

Maybe even by that night.

Or the end of the weekend.

And if that answer meant she lived the rest of her life without her daughter? Who would be there for her during the initial blast of blinding pain?

To sit with her through the grief?

He'd been there. Twice.

Knew what was likely coming her way.

And he'd be…where? Flying off to another part of the country, on to a new job?

As Brian's heart rejected that notion and his mind

warred back with its ten cents' worth of logic and hard-learned common sense, he drifted off.

Only to be jerked awake, an undetermined amount of time later, to the sound of someone moving slowly in the dining area around the corner from where he lay.

Remaining still while he quickly assessed, he allowed only the slight movement of his hand to the gun under the pillow beside his body, listening. Waiting while his eyes adjusted to the darkness.

It was Jessica.

He remained frozen. Other than his eyes.

Close them, man.

He heard the silent order.

Didn't follow it.

Dawn was arriving, and Jessica was up. He could see the floating of the calf-length, yellow, negligee-type robe she wore. She'd moved into the kitchen, out of sight, and he heard her drop a pod into the coffee maker. Saw the robe again, at the entry between the dining room and kitchen as she reached up for a cup.

And then carried it, still empty, to the dining room table where, with cup in hand, she stared at all of the notes and papers they'd left there the night before.

He could almost hear her breathe.

Could see that she was wearing some other frothy thing under the robe.

Had the ludicrous thought that she'd chosen the apparel knowing that he was in the house.

Because he was there.

When he grew to fully hard life inside his pants, he closed his eyes.

And feigned sleep.

What was proper attire for a day of real sleuthing with an expert in the field, when you had a warning out on

your head? And needed to look comforting and cheerful, familiar, in case you ended the day with your baby girl walking toward you?

It wasn't like she had a bulletproof vest.

Or that any number of layers would protect her from metal projectiles.

With temperatures in the seventies, multiple layers would make her sweat. She couldn't stink the first time she held Brooke against her heart in eighteen long months.

And if they didn't find the two-year-old that day… she didn't want to smell bad sitting next to Brian on the drive home.

Finally pulling out summer-weight black leggings and a yellow, knit, short-sleeved, thigh-length top, she spent her entire time in the shower shoving away images of her investigative expert lying on his back on her couch, with a noticeable bulge beneath his fly.

She'd promised herself she wouldn't look over at him. Had waited a full half hour upon waking before going for her coffee, hoping she'd hear him moving around.

Had thought about getting dressed before she showered for her foray into the kitchen, but having to explain that, yes, she was dressed, but then needed to go take a shower…it had all seemed so messy.

As had the realization that her robe was still hanging in the master suite with other clothes she hadn't had need of since moving into the spare bedroom.

When you lived alone, you traipsed to the kitchen in whatever you slept in to get coffee.

The negligee and wrap had been a gift to herself after a counseling session…she wore them whenever she was struggling to get Clint's power out of her system.

And…there'd been no mistaking Brian's hardness when she'd passed back by him on the way to her room.

Why she'd been looking at his crotch was a conversation she was choosing not to have with herself.

At least she hadn't been afraid of Clint watching her.

Though, until the crew arrived to sweep her house, she should have been.

Just in case he'd been responsible for the warning message after all.

The fact that she hadn't been…felt good.

Maybe she really was as free as she believed she was from her ex-husband's ability to control her.

And maybe, just maybe, her investigator was finding her as much of an enigma as she did him.

It wasn't like it would ever go anywhere. Even if they did the deed. Ships in the night and all that. But the thought of them having mutual hots for each other gave her a lift as she faced a new kind of day.

One where a threat hung over her, weighed on her, but was not about to slow her down one bit.

Because she was getting closer.

"You seem more tense than usual."

Jessica's voice filtered into the array of facts Brian had been mentally reviewing, rearranging, and reviewing some more as he headed from the second of the two blue barns they'd seen between Fayetteville and Lincoln that morning.

Eight o'clock in the morning on a Saturday, and he felt as though he'd put in a full day already.

"With the gun, last night's threat, all indications point to this investigation getting more dangerous, which is fine for me, but I'm not accustomed to having a client at my side while I face the risk."

He tried to temper his tone. Didn't need any reaction from her to know he hadn't succeeded.

And wasn't giving anywhere near the whole truth. The hours he was spending, driving around looking at blue buildings, even gaining access to both of them, could be so much better spent. Following up with Anderson on Clint Johnson's email, snail mail and phone communications. Interviewing everyone at the shooting range where Johnson supposedly hit the bull's-eye multiple times with his first ten rounds. Reading background checks on everyone in Lincoln…

Except that the woman who'd hired him had been threatened and he couldn't leave her to investigate her "leads" on her own. No matter how bogus he considered so many of them to be.

Her ex-husband was a liar. And he was clearly playing her.

"I can follow up on the blue barns on my own." Jessica's voice didn't sit well.

They were on their way to one west of Fayetteville. Taking the investigation into an entirely new direction—literally. The town of Bountyville showed up absolutely nowhere in any case file—the official one, his or Jessica's.

And the glances he sent her, a quick one-two, dared her to push that issue.

Seriously? With the previous night's threat still completely unidentified? And most likely stemming from her solitary forage through Lincoln during the week…

That's where he needed to be. Knocking on every single door she'd approached over the three-day span she'd been putting herself in danger. Investigation behind his back.

"I, um, have been doing this…exactly what we're doing today, in one form or another, for the past sixty-six or so Saturdays, Brian."

Her tone wasn't quite droll. But it bordered on it.

"And now you're paying me to do what I do because what you were doing didn't work," he nearly snapped back. Not fully. But there'd been bite to his words.

Propelled by far more than he was saying.

By far more than he was willing to consciously acknowledge. Was too busy pushing it all away so he could focus on getting the job done as soon as possible and getting the hell out of Fayetteville, Arkansas.

Pulling off to the shoulder of the road along a seemingly unending expanse of cornfield, he faced the windshield in front of him. "I apologize."

"What for? You spoke the truth."

"Yeah, key words…'you're paying me.' I have no right to take my frustration out on you."

Whether she was needlessly, recklessly, risking her life or not. If whoever sent the previous night's threat was someone she'd visited in Lincoln…

Her visit could have ended so much differently.

Could still see her to that end.

Human traffickers didn't just sell babies.

Beautiful women brought high prices, too.

I'm watching you. The words had been haunting him all morning.

Along with his own unprofessional bit of voyeurism. Only difference was, she'd walked out of her bedroom knowing he was there.

She hadn't turned on any lights. Thought him asleep. But she'd known he was there.

And had still come out in a flowing negligee robe…

The thought intruded again. Clouding his issues.

"This has to do with your mother, doesn't it?"

Talk about a head spin. And yet…

She'd hit on the other demon he'd been fighting all

morning. One that seemed less risky to admit at that moment than his personal interest in Jessica.

Putting the vehicle in drive, he pulled back out onto the road. He was wasting time they didn't have.

"Brian?"

"Yeah," he said, finding a calmer tone in spite of the topic. "Yeah, some."

And felt better, her explanation for his boorish behavior acknowledged, felt forgiven, as his phone, currently connected to her SUV's audio system, rang and Anderson's name popped up on the dash.

Brooke had been missing a year and a half. Taking two days out of his hunt for the child to keep his client safe while she looked wasn't going to make a huge difference. Not in the long run.

Losing Jessica would.

Chapter 17

Detective Anderson had been at the shooting range Clint had mentioned the day before, when it opened that morning. No one there remembered seeing Clint. Anderson had acquired security footage from the dates in question and had a guy looking through it all.

He also had a report of all communications to and from, and visitations with, Clint.

Sitting in the passenger seat of her SUV, Jessica listened as the detective gave the expert investigator she'd hired a rundown on Brooke's case. Overwhelmed, treading water, she refused to drown.

The father of her child had had his prison cell searched and they'd found a contraband burner phone with no visible call or text message history. Clint had also been on an inmate computer in the library that, upon a deep-dive search, had shown evidence of hacking into some message app she'd never heard of.

It was all so surreal. Two years before, she'd been a new mother, trying to breastfeed every two hours, changing diapers, learning to bathe a new baby and keeping her husband happy. And she'd thought that was hard.

With her ex being an information technology specialist, and the computer hack, the professionals were all adding up facts to arrive at the same conclusion.

Clint was dirty.

No kidding.

But the news also meant that he could have been behind the previous night's threat, just as she'd first assumed.

I'm watching you.

Finding it difficult to draw in air, she listened to the two investigators discussing next moves, hearing Brian telling Anderson their plans for the day, but seeing red haze.

What if Clint decided that he was done with her? With having them be a family again? What if playing Jessica wasn't satisfying him anymore? What if he told whoever had Brooke to take her away so that Jessica could never find her?

What if Clint quit talking to her, giving her a chance to figure out his game and beat him at it?

She wasn't blind or lacking in intelligence. Clint said Brooke was being loved. Whoever had been loving the baby for the past eighteen months was going to have a hard time giving her back. Already a criminal for harboring a stolen child, that person might be more than willing to take the toddler and run. Start a new life, with new identities, somewhere else.

Making it impossible for Jessica, Anderson, or even Brian, to ever find her.

He'd ended the call.

And she needed to focus outside of herself to get her equilibrium back. To care about someone else's struggles. She'd learned clearly over the past eighteen months that having someone truly understand was a rare gift.

"Tell me about your mother."

She'd never have brought the subject up if Brian hadn't admitted to her that he was struggling with the memories her case had raised with him. His shortness with her that morning had drawn her attention to just how much it had been bothering him.

His silence could have been daunting. But the glance he sent her felt more like he was assessing why she was asking than reprimanding her for digging into his personal ghosts.

"Is she still a cop?" He'd said "was" when he'd relayed the old case Brooke's situation was making him relive. But that could have just been the telling of a story in past tense.

He shook his head. Didn't look her way.

She was staring at the white knuckles clutching her steering wheel.

The case had ruined his family life.

Causing a divorce between his parents?

She could see it…his detective father seeing her take such risks…

Coming up against her refusal, or even inability, to stand down.

Mouth open, she stared at him. "This case…it's not so much the little girl involved that's bringing it back for you now, is it?"

His hands squeaked against the leather of the wheel as he rolled them back and forth once.

"It's me, isn't it? Because I won't give up on search-

ing for Brooke, regardless of whether or not I'm walking into danger."

The night before…when he'd mentioned that she could have stirred up something sinister in Lincoln and now they were after her…she'd been scared, of course. But excited, too, because it would mean that they were finally getting close to finding Brooke.

Bringing her home.

"This isn't anything like that, Brian." Her words came softly as her heart settled into place. "I'm not trying to change someone who isn't going to change. And I'm not fighting a losing battle either. No matter what condition Brooke is in when she's found, it's not a mistake to look for her. You wouldn't be here if it was."

Her gaze glued to him as it was, she saw the nerves in his chin moving. Knew the second he was going to start speaking.

"My mother got herself killed."

The words blindsided her. She had no idea… Had…

He drove as though the sky hadn't fallen into the SUV with them. Steady. On course. Slowing slightly when a car passed, allowing the guy to get in front of them before oncoming traffic made that an impossibility.

"I'm sorry." She didn't know what else to say. Watched him, saw his muscles clench and unclench. Looked out her side window. And then back at him, her heart aching for him.

"How old were you?"

More clenching. White knuckles shining bright. "Twelve."

Oh. God, no. When he'd said nothing had ever been the same again, she'd thought he meant between his parents…

He'd been a kid. Lost his mother…

She'd lost her father, but she'd only been three at the time. Could hardly remember him. Had only felt the loss in the lack of having one.

Nothing like loving, needing, and having your rock snatched away when you were still figuring out how to be a person in the world.

"I'm sorry," she said again. For pushing him. For calling him in the first place. For…she didn't even know all what.

She needed to keep her mouth shut. Give him his space. Quit trying to make more of their relationship than was there.

It wasn't like she had anything to offer at this point in her life.

She had to let the man do his job and stay out of his life.

"She got a call." He settled back in the seat, slouched down a bit, only one hand on the wheel. The other lay on his thigh, as though just hanging out.

She wondered what the position cost him. His jaw was clenched as tight as ever.

"Just after dinner one night…the woman was desperate, begging my mother to come get her. Dad was out, working on a case, and Mom said she didn't have time to call for help or wait for it to arrive. She grabbed her gun and took off. I called my dad right away. He sent help, but it was too late. When Mom got there, the guy was waiting outside. Ambushed her. She'd pulled her gun, but he shot her first…"

Blinking back tears, all she was aware of was the shock and pain of a kid going through such a thing. Gradually, though, the man that kid had grown into started to seep into her thoughts. Her feelings.

"Oh God, Brian. I'm just… I never should have…

I'm…there's no way to…" She stumbled along, watching him, the road, him again. Thought about the previous night's threat. The fact that she'd been possibly traipsing around Lincoln all by herself in the midst of a human trafficker. And finished with, "Thank you for telling me."

It didn't change who she was, or what she had to do. But she understood his struggle. She cared. And would think smarter when it came to conferring with him, including him, every step of her way.

She didn't get it. Not from his perspective. Brian understood that. She wasn't going to stop looking for Brooke. Or risking everything to find her daughter.

Just as his mother hadn't been willing to stop answering her private cell every time that abused wife and mother had called.

That meant Brian had to help Jessica find her daughter before Jessica got herself hurt. Or worse.

Pulling up the road toward the blue barn set back on a property in the distance, Brian itched to be in Fayetteville, going over the shooting surveillance footage if Anderson's team had finished with it. Sending the computer-hack evidence to one of his Sierra's Web team members who specialized in all things IT. Running names of homeowners in Lincoln against people-search databases.

He needed to be working toward finding Brooke Johnson, not babysitting her mother while she chased meaningless clues dispensed by the most despicable man Brian had ever come up against.

He'd set out to get to know Jessica and Clint Johnson, as a couple and separately, as much as he could, to find the nuances that others had missed, in the hope of get-

ting the case solved. After only witnessing two calls between Jessica and her ex, he'd had enough.

Clint was going to play Jessica until one of two things happened.

He got out of jail.

Or she cracked.

Brian wasn't sure it even mattered anymore which came first.

The man wasn't out to heal his family, or even to get Jessica back. He was going to make her pay for ruining his life. Plain and simple.

Pathetic and sick.

The barn wasn't off the main road. Taking the dirt road that led to it, albeit one with a street sign designating it as Blossom Avenue, he wondered how many properties were located back in the wooded area behind the barn.

"The aerial view didn't show how thick the trees are." It was the first time Jessica had spoken in over half an hour.

As much as he'd welcomed her silence, he'd missed her conversation, too. Had been more than just curious to know what she was thinking.

About him. His mom. Her daughter. Her next moves. Life in general.

"Probably taken in the wintertime. And seen from above, it would look different." The woods didn't surprise him. But the barn…in the midst of older farm homes, showing need of paint…looked new. Nothing odd about that…a farmer putting another barn on his property. To store equipment. Or hay. It just…didn't seem attached to anything except the short little drive he turned into. There were no other barns close, no house, no field for farming.

"There's no fencing and it's not marked private property," Jessica said as he stopped the SUV at the end of

the drive, just far enough off the street to keep them from getting hit if another vehicle came up the deserted road. Opening her door, she got out and took a step toward the structure just as Brian saw a slight movement at the middle of the barn doors—where the two came together for a secure close.

"Get back in here," he ordered, already diving over the console to get to her.

"What?" Jessica spun, surprised when he jumped out next to her. He shoved her back behind him, using his body as a shield between her and that barn door.

"Get down on the floor," he said, his gaze remaining fully focused on the blue building as he pushed her the rest of the way in and slapped the door closed.

He saw the glint of metal. Ducked and ran to the front end of the SUV. Heard the shot ring out. Ding against the vehicle in almost the same loud crack.

Jessica, draped partially on the seat from the floor, slung open his door for him, and he jumped in. Keeping down, he shoved the vehicle in Reverse, gunning the gas, his eyes firmly focused on the backup camera that was the only way he was going to see to get them out of there.

Another shot rang. Glass shattered.

And he pushed the pedal to the floor.

Shaking, ready to cry, and to fight back all at once, Jessica held on to the seat and watched Brian's face as he concentrated on the video in her dash and got them back out onto the road. He didn't stop there, didn't even put on the brake as he hit pavement, slid up in the seat as he jerked the vehicle into Drive and floored the gas pedal.

"You okay?" His tone was all-business.

"Yeah." She tried to instill the same, wasn't sure her trembling response fit the bill.

It took her another second or two to move from the floor, and when she got her butt to the seat, she stayed low.

Brian was on the phone by then. The ringing of his call seemed to blast through the SUV. Air was coming at her from behind, too. That made her straighten enough to look back to assess the damage to her vehicle. Passenger window, right behind her head. Back seat—car seat—covered in glass.

Tears sprang to her eyes. She couldn't stop them. Didn't even care to try.

"We've just taken fire," Brian snapped out when Anderson identified himself on the line. He then gave their coordinates in official terms she hadn't known. "At this point, I see no way this could be connected to the case..."

Relief flooded her. Mental capacity returned in spits and spurts. Wrong blue barn.

"Either the guy had something to hide, and it's our damned bad luck we stumbled on it, or he has serious issues with trespassers," Brian continued.

Jessica studied him as he drove and spoke. There she was, a nervous wreck who kept wanting to duck and hide her head, and he didn't even seem to have a twitch.

"The sweep of Jessica's house came up clean," Anderson relayed. "Johnson says he has no idea how that phone got in his cell. Insists that he didn't use it, and we can't find any evidence that a call or text was actually sent from it. The ID number traces back to a series of phones that were stolen brand-new a couple of years ago from a delivery truck in Texas. En route to various retail outlets. Nearly five hundred of them. Case was never solved. But another one of them showed up in a completely unrelated crime. Guy busted for illegal arms dealing in Missouri had one on him. Unfortunately, he

resisted arrest, came out firing and got himself killed before he could be questioned."

"And no one knows where or how he got the phone."

"Nope. The only other one that we know of turned up at a crime scene in Mexico, during a drug bust. No one claimed it and there were no prints on it."

Jessica heard the words being spoken, both in the vehicle and coming over the audio system. Logically, she understood them. But couldn't take them in. Own them as any part of her life.

Drug busts? Arms dealers? And Clint?

"The phone must have been planted in his cell for some reason." She blurted the only thing that made sense to her. As, even to her, her words just sounded like someone in denial, refusing to believe what was right in front of her.

Problem was, she wasn't refusing to believe anything about her ex. She'd think the worst of him in a hot second if it rang true.

Clint robbing her blind through some kind of high-tech scam—she'd believe it in a second. But drugs, illegal guns...?

"If he'd been involved with illegal arms, why go buy his own gun? Why not just use one that couldn't be traced to him? It doesn't make sense," she continued when neither man immediately responded to her.

"No, it doesn't." Anderson's voice came over the speakers.

"And it won't until we get more answers," Brian added, sending her a glance that seemed like he was trying to reassure her.

She didn't want reassurance. She wanted answers.

As did both of the men in the conversation. She got that.

But drugs? And guns?

It couldn't have anything to do with Brooke.

Because if it did…

"I've got someone looking at cell records, mostly just tower activity between Lincoln and the tower closest to Jessica's residence," Anderson was saying. "It's a long shot at this point, except that we know the time the text message was sent to Jessica last night, so that'll at least narrow down what phones were pinging the tower at that time and, if we can eliminate other legitimate calls, we can possibly see what area the message originated from. And I'll make calls now, sending someone out to look into the shooting…"

The detective was on fire, much like he'd been when Brooke first went missing. Jessica was grateful to the point of more tears.

And scared to death, too. She'd been shot at. Had received a threatening text with origin unknown—all leading out from Brian's Birds of Paradise discovery the week before.

That did not bode well—at all—for Brooke's well-being.

"I can't promise it's going to get any better." Brian was off the phone, had glanced over at her.

She nodded. She knew. Brooke was alive. She still felt the truth to her core. And wouldn't stop looking for her, no matter what.

But what she found, when she finally located her daughter, might not be a happy, loved, well-adjusted toddler.

"If Clint's wrapped up in something sinister, and it has to do with Brooke, then it only makes sense that he sold her," she said aloud, forcing herself to find the strength to continue her quest. "He needed money and most defi-

nitely didn't have any to spend to pay people to do anything for him."

Another glance from Brian got her attention. She looked at him, really took him in, for the first time since they'd been shot at.

Was grateful to him.

"The big question is, if he did sell her...was it to some illegal adoption ring targeting rich want-to-be parents?"

Or... She didn't verbalize the unthinkable.

But she figured he was already considering the other possibilities. And left them to him for the moment.

"Right now, we need to get this vehicle in for service," he told her, his tone even. Taking command.

"Right. We can grab something to eat and then head out to check the other blue barns on the list," she stated just as emphatically. She was shaken up. She wasn't quitting. "I'll rent a vehicle until I get this one back."

She had to keep moving forward.

Every day, one small step at a time.

He opened his mouth, as though he had something to say, but glanced her way and closed it again.

If, in light of the shooting, he'd been going to try to change their plans for the day, he'd decided not to do so.

"You even said that what just happened likely has nothing to do with Clint and Brooke," she reminded him. There was no reason to stop ferreting out possible sources of Clint's latest clue.

He didn't argue with her.

But Jessica felt like she'd disappointed him.

And was sorry about that.

Chapter 18

There was nothing obvious in any of the remaining blue barns. But as they headed back to Fayetteville—in their rented white SUV, same make and model as Jessica's—late Saturday afternoon, Brian wasn't sorry he'd accompanied Jessica. Anderson and his team were making the first pass at all of the information Brian would go over that night.

And, in the meantime, he was getting more of a look into the dynamic between Jessica and Clint over the past fifteen months. Observing the behavior the imprisoned man was igniting within his wife. Getting glimpses of the life she'd been living.

He even started to wonder if perhaps there was more in his supposed clues for them to find. Maybe not to lead them to Brooke. But something that would show him why Clint was choosing the words he was choosing. What prompted him to choose the clues?

Brian wasn't ready to let go of his pattern of fours yet.

But what if the insignificant hints were more than just wasters of Jessica's energy, tiring her out so that she'd be more amenable to Clint. More dependent on what he knew that she didn't? What if he was trying to make her life even more miserable through them?

That thought in mind, he turned to her as they got close to town. "Did you and Clint have a special song?" he asked. "A favorite vacation spot?"

"No to the song. And while Clint loved to travel, he always wanted to try out someplace new. He liked beaches."

A river runs through it. One of the possible legitimate fourth clues came to him. The boat Clint had gotten in his baby trade-off with Jessica. The man loved water.

Flashes of pieces of the puzzle ran through his mind.

And hung in obscurity.

"Tonight, can you make me a list of all of his favorites?" he asked. "And another of anything that could have special significance to the two of you as a couple?"

"Of course. And…we need to talk about your accommodations, Brian."

Right. The apartment was paid up through the next day. He was fine to stay there. Hated to be running up the expense of a luxury apartment when he was hardly there. And only needed a few yards of space. Besides, while she was living nicely, she wasn't a millionaire. She'd mentioned bargaining for the price of the rental.

And imagined, based on what he'd learned over the past week, that while she made really good money, Clint had been better at spending it all than earning any for himself. Their divorce had to have cleaned her out of at least half of what she'd managed to save over their eight-year marriage.

Yet he hadn't had enough money to make his boat payment…

"I'm going to try to negotiate a monthly rental fee, rather than the weekly rate, if you're good with the apartment," she said, her gaze serious as she watched the traffic-filled road in front of them.

He couldn't afford for her to not be able to pay his fee. Well, financially, he could do so all day long. But she wouldn't let him work for free.

He had no idea how long it was going to take him to find Brooke.

And he couldn't leave until he did.

There were no cheap hotels within a few miles of her place.

He'd already checked.

"I'd like to cover the living expense," he told her and added, in all truthfulness, "I often do when I'm on the road."

"From what I was told, that was when living expenses were included in the fee. I opted to pay them separately."

Telling himself that her finances were absolutely none of his business, or concern, Brian was about to give her the go-ahead when her phone dinged a text.

A look of stark fear covered her face she turned toward him before taking her phone out of her pocket and glancing at it as he pulled over.

With an obviously trembling hand, she gave it to him.

Still watching.

All thoughts of his next week's accommodation vanished as he dialed Anderson.

Her home wasn't bugged. She wasn't in her own vehicle anymore—though it would be checked for tracking devices before it was returned to her.

"I've got location off on my phone," she told Brian as they sat in her dining room half an hour later, waiting for the Chinese food they'd just ordered to be delivered. "I really needed to get some groceries in," she said, trying for a chuckle that didn't quite make it through the tension holding her in its grasp.

She should have more than just the yogurt and granola bars that were normally all she wanted when she was home, preferring to eat out or order in, rather than cook for one.

"So, I was thinking you might want me to clean out the apartment cupboards and refrigerator." Brian's words could have been as innocuous as her comment had been. A time filler.

An attempt at a fear breaker.

The way he was staring at her, she didn't think so.

"Then what would you eat?" she asked him. She knew of at least three meals he'd eaten in the apartment the past week, based on check-in calls. He'd either been in the process of preparing them, or was planning to do so.

"I want you to agree to let me stay here. That means I'd still be eating the food purchased on my behalf, I'd just be doing it here."

Her heart leapt. With relief. Gratitude.

And then slid back down to earth.

"What?" she asked him. His suggestion, while welcome in the sense that she wasn't feeling at all fond of spending the night alone in the house at the moment, was highly inappropriate. Dangerous, even, in an entirely different-than-being-shot-at or threatened sense.

"Until we can at least narrow down the source of these test messages, it would be better if you weren't here alone. Clint already broke into this home once, and while he couldn't very well do so now, we have no idea at this

point what kind of ties he might have, and who might be willing to make a second try at it to either slow you down or stop you."

As in kill her?

For searching for her daughter? "Clint's the one giving me the clues," she reminded him. "Why would he want to stop me from following them? That's his goal, to keep me on his hook, right?" It was a point they'd all three agreed on—her, Anderson and Brian. Her response to Clint was the only thing she saw differently from the two investigators.

"Maybe he didn't know what he was getting into," Brian offered softly. "Or maybe, as we said, you stumbled on to something in Lincoln."

"Or we did when we visited Harriet Lichen last week. It's possible she knows more than she said. And that her granddaughter coached her in what to say if anyone came looking for what happened at the Birds of Paradise eighteen months ago." She'd been having the thought on and off all day. What if Harriet had seen Clint pass Brooke off in that parking lot, and was afraid to say so? But was equally afraid to deny that he'd been there in case there was some proof that he had been?

"In either case, I don't need to be in that apartment to do my job. Frankly, I could work better from here where we've got everything organized and spread out with not just my notes but yours, too. Adding to them daily. It makes sense to have just one caseboard, so to speak. This is all based on the fact that I'm assuming you aren't willing to move out for a few days..."

Shaking her head, she said, "My office, all of my files..." and stopped when he nodded.

He'd already figured her job into the equation. She had to be at her desk when the bell rang Monday morn-

ing. No way she could afford a private investigation if she wasn't working…

She had a big house. Way more room than she used. But would all the space be big enough to handle the two of them together?

A small thrill passed through her—residual of the high level of emotion she'd experienced that day. She wanted to believe that.

"It would save you the cost of the apartment rental," he said then, not meeting her gaze at all.

He had to know, as practical as he was being, as much sense as he was making, that the issue wasn't just her safety.

Or even her money.

Was he going to bring it up or did she have to do so?

Watching him, she waited.

It took a good full minute, but he finally looked over at her. Met her gaze.

"And if we end up in bed together?" she asked him. Because there was nothing she could think of at that moment that would be a better antidote to the fear and worry threatening to strangle the lifeblood out of her.

"I meant what I said last week," he told her, his gaze unshaking. "You have nothing to fear from me."

The loud half grown, half huff that came out of her shocked Jessica as she said, "I'm afraid of my own shadow at the moment, Brian, but you don't scare me one bit. The truth is, I'm not averse to going to bed with you. This…whatever it is between us…is a welcome distraction…and it's not like it would ever go anywhere."

She wasn't open to another relationship at the moment and, after the past week of Clint revelations, she wasn't sure how soon she would ever be.

And he clearly wasn't.

He wasn't responding. At all. Just sitting there, a blank look on his face.

"I'm not saying I'm going to hit on you, or come crawling under your covers," she said, all business in that moment. "It would be mutual. But if you're going to be staying here, I just need the possibility clearly acknowledged, and dealt with, before something happens that we might regret."

"'Dealt with'?" His head cocked a little with the question. And there was an odd light in his eyes. An interesting light.

"Brought out into the open," she clarified, though she wasn't sure what she'd really meant by that remark.

He watched her for another minute or so. Then, with a shrug, said, "It's there. A possibility of something that could take place over the course of this investigation. It would be mutual. And mean nothing beyond the moment."

She didn't know what to do with that. Was he agreeing? Propositioning her? Playing with her?

Clint would lose his mind if he found out. Guilt clouded all good feeling for the instant it took her to step away from it. Whoever was watching her already knew Brian had spent the night.

And her ex-husband had always seen breaking her down as a challenge. Would he walk away from her, from telling her about Brooke, if he knew she'd had sex with another man?

He'd accused her of doing so many times.

He'd never left.

Things were different, though, since the kidnapping. Since he had the upper hand.

She was going to find Brooke. With Clint or without him. She needed his clues. He was her surest way to get

to her daughter when he chose to finally really help her. But she had herself, too.

And she'd made the choice to hire an expert investigator who'd moved the case along more in one week than anyone had in eighteen long months.

And when Clint got out of jail...he'd need money. She'd always been his money source. She had her own power.

"You change your mind?"

Brian's question pulled her from the fog just as she was finding her way out by herself.

"No." Her response was emphatic.

"You want to call and postpone the dinner order until we get the apartment cleared out? I'd rather be back here before dark."

She'd rather that, too.

And wondered, as she made the restaurant call, whether or not she'd be finding a small bit of ecstasy that night to help get her through hell.

He wasn't going to rush into bed with her. Sex couldn't even be on his radar, as much as his body might want it to be.

Brian hadn't been just giving her words when he'd assured Jessica that no matter what he wanted, or how attracted he might be to her, there was no worry of him losing sight of his reason for being there. He'd get the job done.

After he'd settled his things into the fourth bedroom in the house—on the other side of her office from her room, he was back at the dining room table. She had taken charge of the grocery bags she'd helped him pack and carry in from his place. And had shown him where

to find towels for the hall bathroom, which he'd be using. She'd offered the master suite.

With the possibility of someone watching her, he didn't want to be across the house from her at night.

Thankfully, her room had an en suite bath attached. And anyone coming from the rest of the house would have to pass his room first.

He'd be sleeping with the door open.

Anderson had police crew driving by frequently, keeping a watch on the house, too. Until they knew more about what they were up against, Brian wasn't going to let up on his protection of Jessica. Whether she'd hired him to offer it or not.

If things got tough—if he had to go recover a body—he could call in a Sierra's Web expert bodyguard, but for the moment, considering Jessica's finances, and how long the case could take, he was going to give her double duty.

They'd had dinner. He'd sent the prison computer-hack information to Hudson Warner, the Sierra's Web IT partner, and had settled in with his search databases, looking for anything he could find out about Harriet Lichen, her granddaughter Bonnie, and all of the other known residents in Lincoln.

Paying particular attention to the preacher of the little church where Jessica had told him she'd watched the playground. Churches were notorious for drawing people who needed sanctuary. Perhaps that was where she'd been seen. Wayne Bennet, the church's minister, had graduated from an online seminary course, but other than that, Brian had found little on the man.

Anderson had called to say that he'd personally made a trip out to the blue barn in Bountyville, where Brian and Jessica had been shot at. He'd found shell casings, was having them analyzed, but no one was there and the

place was locked. He'd been trying to get in touch with the owner of the property, but so far with no luck.

"It's possible that whoever is trying to scare me either has Brooke, or knows who does, and that person has fallen so much in love with her, they aren't going to willingly give her back. They just want me to give up." Jessica had been going through the cell tower records Anderson had been able to legally give her, just looking to see if there was anything she recognized.

There'd been too many signals bouncing off of multiple places for them to pinpoint enough specifics to even have a good guess as to where the text message the night before had come from. Brian wasn't hopeful for any better success with that day's message.

Whether the sender was savvy enough to know how to bounce off several towers, or just lucky enough to get lost in the shuffle, they had no way of knowing. Their best hope was to find a similar pattern, but they'd need more messages to be able to do that.

He wasn't hoping for more messages.

"We have to consider the possibility that Clint has made friends in prison." He broached the subject carefully, wanting her to be able to consider the idea before believing she'd know whether or not he was right because she knew Clint so well. He needed her to see that she might not have known Clint as well as she thought she did.

That he wasn't the man she thought he was.

Disappointment settled over him as she immediately shook her head. "I know he hasn't," she said, glancing at him but looking away just as quickly.

Odd, the way her eyes skittered from his. Granted, he hadn't known her long, but they'd been through some extraordinary circumstances in a very short time, had

been on the opposite side of some very electric fences, and she'd never once shied away from meeting his gaze.

"How do you know that?" Gut clenching, he waited, pretty sure he wasn't going to like what was coming.

When she didn't answer right away, he tried again. "He had a phone in his cell. Unless a guard planted it there when he was out, which is highly unlikely though not impossible, he had to get it from someone inside. Or… the text messages are coming from someone inside who's sending them for him. Or he has someone on the outside doing it for him. Since we now know by his communication report from the prison that he's had no known communication with anyone on the outside, other than you, not even his lawyer, we could only assume that someone who was recently released is doing it for him."

Anderson was already checking on that. Looking for any recent releases who might have had contact with Clint on the inside. Who could be taunting Jessica with the texts on Clint's behalf.

She'd turned back to him, looking him straight in the eye, a strange look on her face. As though she was resolved about something.

He didn't like the look. Braced himself.

And was in no way prepared for the words that came out of her mouth.

Chapter 19

"I know he doesn't have friends in prison because I've been sending money every month to his commissary account, which he then somehow lets others use. It's ransom money so that he'll be left alone."

Jessica felt sick, just saying the words. What she'd been doing was perfectly legal. The State of Arkansas made provisions for people to deposit money in inmates' accounts electronically. She could put money in every account in the prison if she so chose.

Inside, the prisoner's access of the account was supposed to be monitored. How Clint used the money to buy his safety, she didn't want to know.

Maybe she didn't even care anymore.

She just couldn't have Brian and Anderson off on another wild-goose chase while Brooke was still out in the world somewhere. Possibly not even being loved. They'd spent days on the gun and it had come to nothing.

Other than the Timberline shooting range where no one remembered Clint. They'd yet to hear on the surveillance footage there, but she was sure it wouldn't pan out.

Brian had ceased looking at her after her words "sending money." He appeared to be studying the small strip of wood visible through the papers, folders and electronics strewn across her dining room table. His thumb was working that strip of furniture pretty hard. Back and forth. Back and forth.

She waited. Knowing how it sounded—like she was some kind of road kill lying on the pavement being run over again and again. A woman letting herself be used up by a selfish jerk.

She wasn't either of those things. "He showed up on a Friday call with a black eye and split lip," she said softly. Owing him nothing. But wanting him to know. "Clint doesn't attract friends in the stronger sector," she continued. "He gloms onto nurturers. Not many of those in prison, from what I hear."

Maybe she shouldn't be sending money. She had her reasons.

"His whole block was behind it. Ganging up on him. He said that they told him that if he paid the ransom, they'd see that no one bothered him again. And they haven't. They won't be seen hanging with him because he's not respected in there, but they leave him alone."

"'They'?" He glanced over at her. "Obviously not every one of them beat him up or he'd have had more than a black eye and a split lip."

She shrugged.

"How long ago was this?"

"A couple of weeks shy of fifteen months."

"You've been paying him the entire time he's been

there." Paying him to do his time for kidnapping her baby girl.

She got his message.

It wasn't like that. Though she understood that was how it looked. That was why she'd never said anything about the money to anyone. "I need him alive, Brian. He's the only one who knows what he did with my daughter."

"How much?"

"Four hundred a month. It's the maximum the state allows."

He'd told her the amount "they" were requiring. She'd found out about it being the state-allowed maximum when she'd looked up the process, making damned sure she wasn't breaking any laws.

"I don't doubt that Clint would love to make me desperate enough to do something so off the wall that I get locked up myself. That would be his kind of justice. But I'm no good to my daughter—either finding her or mothering her when she finally makes it home—if I'm in prison."

His jaw was clenching again.

"If I break the law, I no longer have a career," she added, though for what purpose she couldn't say. Maybe a reminder to herself of the successful life she'd built, in spite of the hardships that choosing Clint had brought to her world.

Maybe Brian Powers was just making her feel defensive and she had to fight back. He had no right to judge her.

"Did it occur to you that any one of these guys could be working for Clint? On his payroll?"

It hadn't. Not once. "He can't put anyone else first enough to know how to figure out what others need. Without that, how could he possibly manage to keep an

entire wing full of prisoners happy? He's not a big man, or an imposing one."

"Maybe he's promising them all more when he gets out. He's only got another twenty-one months, right? He's proving to them that you're his gravy train."

No.

Guns. Drugs. Clint with an entire prison block in his pocket? It didn't fit.

"And maybe he's a scaredy-cat who pays to be left alone while he demonizes the person giving him the money to do so," she said softly and gathered up her laptop, her journal, and went to bed.

Or at least to her bedroom.

Far too het up to sleep, she was scared, confused… desperate to find Brooke.

And alone.

She'd been sending Clint Johnson four hundred bucks a month. Brian didn't even want to imagine what kind of contraband that amount of money could have purchased over the past fifteen months.

Texting Anderson the news that there'd been a glitch in the initial report Brian had had on Clint's prison reports, that Jessica had been sending her ex money, he had an unending pit of dread in his gut. He'd come to town to find a little girl and instead he'd found a hidden gun, connections to drug and arms dealing, they'd been shot at, his client was being threatened, or at least harassed in a very creepy manner…

And now he knew the kidnapper had had funds at his disposal the entire time he'd been in prison.

Even before Anderson responded, Brian had a new theory. Quickly texted it.

What if Johnson was using the money Jessica had been

sending to pay off whoever had Brooke? Was he sending money for his daughter's care?

Or simply paying off whoever had helped him dispose of the child? Either by arranging some kind of pass-off to someone who had Brooke, or by getting rid of the body.

Was Clint paying for silence?

Could explain the guy's cocky attitude.

Anderson's two messages popped up one right after the other. The detective said he'd get in touch with the prison warden first thing in the morning, find out what he could. Put a trace on the money if necessary.

Sending a thumbs-up, Brian went back to his databases. Cross-checking lists of names of recently released inmates for associations in Lincoln.

Sometime after midnight, he sat up straight, wide awake, as he happened on a small piece of information that might mean absolutely nothing.

The owner of the blue barn property in Bountyville had a son. An adult son who'd done time in the same prison housing Clint. He'd been in for three years for aggravated assault—his second offense. Brian only found the guy by doing an internet search of the name: Jim Brandywine. Father and son shared it.

Jim Brandywine had been released from the Arkansas prison five weeks after Clint's incarceration, so his name hadn't come up on the list they had of recent releases. And son, Jim, had just been arrested for assault in Missouri a couple of weeks before Brian had been called to Fayetteville.

Could be nothing. Not even big enough to call a coincidence, but Brian's heart was pumping a bit less sluggishly.

In the next second, it started to pound. Had Jessica just cried out? Jumping up, he grabbed his gun off his waist and, keeping himself along the wall, weapon raised,

headed down the hall to Jessica's bedroom. He couldn't be sure if he'd heard a dog yelping in the distance or his client making a distress sound, but all senses on alert, he was damned well going to find out.

"Ahhhllllaaa!" The gargled, painful cry sounded again. Definitely coming from Jessica's room. Passing the office, he got down there as soon as he could. She'd shut the door.

Holding back an urge to slam his shoulder into the wood and get inside, he turned the knob slowly. If anyone was in there, hurting her, he'd serve her better if he took them by surprise.

The restraint made him sweat. Beads of it popped on his forehead. Trickled down his spine.

Without a creak, the door slid slowly open, showing him a room filled with shadows, broken only by the night-light plugged into the wall. Curtains were drawn.

No one stood…anywhere. Not by the quilt-covered shape in the bed or anyplace else in the room.

"Ack!"

Brian jerked back when Jessica's shriek rent through the room as she flew upright off the pillows. And then his gaze met her wide-open, unfocused eyes, mere pinpricks in the near darkness. The glaze of moisture in them grasped the light, catching him, and he moved slowly toward her.

He wasn't all read up on nightmares, but common sense told him he didn't want to terrify her any more than her subconscious was already doing.

She'd been shot at. And they'd barely talked about it afterward. Not as big a deal for him. But then, it hadn't been his first time.

Or even his tenth.

Her gaze didn't follow him as he approached. Her breathing ragged, she continued to face straight ahead.

He sat on the very edge of the queen-sized bed, on the side opposite of where she'd been sleeping.

Touching her didn't seem like a good idea.

"Jessica?" He spoke in his least-threatening tone—a whisper.

She didn't jerk or turn, but her face crumbled, piece by piece, starting with her chin, and she began to sob.

"Jessica?" Soft voice that time. More than a whisper. He needed to reach her.

But gently.

Her body stilled and her head came up. She blinked. Quietly turned toward the wall on her side of the bed. And then swung slowly toward him.

Bracing himself, feeling awkward as much as anything else, he sat there in the jeans and T-shirt he'd been wearing when the bullets had been flying around them earlier that day. Not sure if he should speak or not. Warn her that he was there.

Her gaze, focused now, found him before he came up with anything to say.

Her lashes were wet, as was the skin beneath her eyes. Brows drawing together, she looked as though she might start crying again.

"It was just a bad dream," he told her, still in his softest voice.

She nodded. "Brooke was in the barn, but it was red not blue." She sounded hoarse. Swallowed. "I tried to reach her, but he had a gun…"

She was with him. And still sounded lost, too. As though she existed in some middle ground between nightmare and reality.

"Clint was there, but I knew he wouldn't risk his life for her. Or me either. He was safe inside his truck. I was going to have to do it on my own…"

That time he was the one who swallowed. Hard.

She started to shiver and he realized she wasn't wearing the negligee he'd seen her in that morning. She had on a beige tank top.

No bra.

Not his best moment, noticing something like that right then.

"You're cold," he told her, reaching for the edges of the quilt with his hand and piling a couple of pillows directly behind her. "Lie back and I'll cover you up."

She did as he directed, gently lowering herself, but as he lifted his arms to cover her, she grabbed him. One hand, clutching his forearm.

"Did you find out anything after I went to bed? No, I don't want to know. Not tonight. Not yet."

Acting like he had a hand hanging from him all the time, he continued to cover her. She was cold. And it was best overall if her body wasn't in view.

Made it easier for him to distance himself. To focus only on a person having a nightmare, not on the individual woman he'd grown to know so well in such a short time.

Even in her dreams, Jessica was alone. Fought alone.

Expected to be alone.

She closed her eyes and he didn't move. Just sat there, a resting place for her hand—and maybe enough of a warm body to coax her back to a more peaceful sleep.

Minutes passed. He had no idea how many. Enough to conjure up something pretty close to hatred for the man who'd been robbing her blind for almost a decade. And not just of money.

What kind of man took a woman's child and then conned her out of four hundred dollars a month while he paid for the crime he'd committed?

Far worse, what kind of man kidnapped his own child

and held her mother hostage in a sea of desperate grief? Feeding her with hope that her little girl was still alive and she'd see her again someday.

A man who couldn't afford to have her give up hope.

If Jessica knew that Brooke wasn't coming home, she'd be free of Clint Johnson once and for all.

More than anything, save for finding Brooke alive, Brian wanted that for her.

When he was pretty sure her breathing had been even for several minutes, he slowly inched his arm from beneath her grasp. An eighth of an inch, then…

Fingernails digging into his bare skin. "Don't go."

He couldn't stay. He was tired. Riding an emotional roller coaster watching her suffer and knowing that she wanted to sleep with him, too.

That she'd made a point of letting him know when they'd both been in business mode, not in the throes of passion.

He wouldn't disgrace himself by staying. Couldn't jeopardize his professional reputation, and his sense of responsibility to his client, for a very demanding personal want.

But he stopped pulling away from her. He just needed to sit it out a while longer. He'd tried to leave too soon.

"Please, Brian. Hold me?"

Her eyes opened, and the woman gazing up at him didn't look like she was coming from a nightmare at all. She looked to him as though she'd found a source of healthy distraction from hell.

In his eyes, Jessica could read the battle going on inside him. And guessed that it wasn't for himself he was fighting.

But for her.

He'd been loving them and leaving them his entire life. By his own account it was the only type of relationship he knew.

A conscious choice.

She also knew he wanted her. The hard-on she'd witnessed when he'd been watching her get coffee only that morning was evidence of that. If she'd needed any more than the confession he'd already made to her regarding his attraction to her.

That meant his struggle had to do with her. The fact that she was the woman he'd love and leave.

Or sex and leave.

"I'm fully aware of what I'm doing," she said then, finding the ability to draw up a semblance of her professional voice. A tone she'd been using almost one hundred percent of the time that Brooke had been missing. "I'm not leaning on you so much as using what's between us to get from this place to the next. To gain strength to take the step after that."

His striking hazel eyes never left hers. And even though the color wasn't apparent in the near darkness, she felt like she could see their golden glint shining on her.

And that gaze, the way he pulled everything from her and seemed to give it back in better shape than he'd found it, forced honesty from her. "I haven't wanted a man, really been turned on and ready, since long before I got pregnant," she told him. "I don't know what it is about you, but you make me yearn…" She licked her lips because they were suddenly so dry. "In a way I've never yearned before."

One second he was sitting there with her clutching at his arm and the next he was pulling back her quilt and sliding down beside her, his jeans-clad legs mingling with her bare ones.

She'd worn gym shorts to bed. Because…he'd been there and it had seemed proper in the event of an emergency need to fly out of bed. But…they'd ridden up.

And in that state, were far less coverage than underwear would have been.

If he noticed, he was too gentlemanly to say so.

His extra largeness against her thigh had already been apparent before he'd known about her bottom half situation.

With his face inches from hers on her pillow, she reached a hand up to palm his cheek. To caress it, nose to nose with him, staring him in the eye. "Thank you," she whispered and, moving slightly, melded her lips with his.

Chapter 20

Brian made himself hold back. The show was all hers. His body's urges pushed at him, but he didn't give in. Didn't roll her over or climb on top of her.

His hands got free reign. They moved over her slowly, softly, and then more aggressively. Taking pleasure—how could he not; she was a shapely woman—but giving as much pleasure as he received. Trying to give more. He just wasn't certain such a feat was attainable. Not with the exquisite sensations lying there with Jessica was giving to him.

More than he'd ever known, and he hadn't even had sex with her.

Hadn't had a release.

Was still wearing his jeans…

Even as he had the somewhat clear thought in the midst of sexual haze, he felt her hand on his zipper, pulling it down.

Was slightly distracted as her already bared nipples brushed against his naked chest.

His penis sprang free and, for a second there, he thought he was going to fail. Himself. And her. But shut his eyes tight, thought of her hand clutching his arm, and managed to hold on.

Movements were a blur after that, his only conscious thought about holding himself down, leaving all the pacing, the taking, the control, to her.

It turned him on, watching her gain momentum, confidence, as she played his body. Any frustration he felt as he denied himself the same pleasure she was taking was well worth the saucy look on her face as she sat over him, straddled him, held his hands to her breasts, and said, "You ready?"

How did he express, "Oh God, *yes*!" in a subservient way?

Finding none, Brian nodded. Once. With very clear intent in the gaze that bore into her.

He needed her to do it.

And when she did, when, somehow, with complete gentleness, finesse and glorious mastery, she slid down on him, he knew she'd changed him.

That he'd never be the same.

And that was before they found release at exactly the same time.

Twice that night.

Jessica woke up with regret. Lying alone in her bed, looking at the curtains covering the window she'd normally be looking out, saying her prayers to the sky that she shared with her little girl no matter where Brooke might be, she took a deep breath, let go of the night, and let the day begin.

She didn't regret the sex. Would do it again. As many times as opportunity presented itself.

She regretted waking alone.

And knew that getting up with Brian after the sex, her heading to her bathroom, him to his, calling good-night to him before she closed her door, had been the right thing to do all the way around.

For him. For the case. And for her, too.

Didn't stop her from having a moment where she wished she could have woken in his arms. Just for that one morning after their first time.

After those few seconds of self-pity, she was over it. Up, showered, bed made, and dressed in light yellow capris, a white shirt and sandals—happy attire, she'd dubbed it—she headed out to the kitchen to make her coffee.

And found it already made. Brian stood there in another pair of jeans, a lighter blue short-sleeved shirt and tennis shoes, sipping from his own cup as he handed her another. "I heard the water stop after your shower," he told her. Sipped again, watching her over the rim of his cup.

She smiled. Maybe it wasn't the most professional way to start the day. But it was real and, lord knew, she'd had so little to smile about over the past months.

"Thank you," she said. For the coffee, and more.

The way his eyes warmed and slid one very personal glance-over, she figured he fully understood. "You're very welcome."

He didn't smile, but the almost sexy tone in his voice told her all she needed to know. It had been good for him, too.

That left the door open for them to maybe do it again sometime.

When he straightened, in stature and expression, her being changed, too. They had a child to find. And a table filled with evidence that pointed to missing pieces.

"Anderson called twenty minutes ago."

The tone of his voice prepared for no great news. She just didn't know its level of not-goodness.

"He went back to the prison. Left at four this morning. Has already gone over, and has copies of, Clint's commissary account, which is where—"

"I sent the money," she interrupted. "I know." The detective would not have been pleased to hear that Jessica had been sending money to her ex-husband without telling him.

She wasn't sure why she hadn't, except that she hadn't wanted anyone to get involved, have something go wrong in the block and Clint ending up dead.

Everyone knew that that kind of stuff really did happen sometimes.

"According to the books, none of the money left the prison," he said as though that was the key point, and she frowned.

"Of course not. He's buying protection on the block, you know, like gangs make people do…"

She stopped as he looked over at her. "What?" she asked. "Who would he be…?"

And she got it. Sitting down, her cup thunking against the table with enough force to spill her coffee, she looked up at him. "You thought he was sending it to whoever has Brooke, didn't you?"

His shrug wasn't so much a lack of denial as a confirmation that he really didn't know.

Or…he suspected that Clint was paying off whoever had helped him dispose of her…one way or another.

Just like the gun. They'd all assumed it had some sinister part in Brooke's kidnapping. She'd known it hadn't.

Because she understood Clint. Probably better than he got himself.

That's what happened when you'd lived under someone's manipulative control for so many years and then fought your way out of it.

"How do the *books*..." she began, emphasizing the word and then feeling small for having done so. They were all working their butts off to help her find her daughter.

If she didn't like what they found, that was not at all their fault. And still a favor to her, too. She needed the truth. No matter what it brought her.

She started again. "How do the books say the money was spent?"

"Every dime, at the commissary, every month. He bought far more than any one man would use in a thirty-day span, with nothing left over in his cell."

The payoff.

"And?" she asked as his tone left more hanging out there.

"He claims that he uses everything himself. Every month."

"Because he does use it. To buy his safety and protection." What did it say about her that her mind immediately knew how Clint's head would spin that statement into complete truth?

"Still no word on the gun casings from yesterday, other than it was some kind of rifle."

She shuddered.

"Anderson's team is still looking for the owner of the blue barn where we were shot at," he said, taking a

seat perpendicular to her rather than the one he'd chosen across from her the night before.

Meaning he didn't intend to work at home that day?

Or that he just hadn't brought out his computer yet so didn't need the plug on the opposite wall.

Could it mean he wanted to sit closer to her?

Could she get any more high school ridiculous?

She didn't have a crush on the guy. Or want him to like her.

It was just that…the money, Anderson visiting Clint again; he wasn't going to like that at all. And gun casings… bullets being fired at her…even just for trespassing—what was her life becoming?

It was all spinning out of control and… Brooke.

She took a deep breath. Knew that she was getting exactly what she'd asked for. What Brooke needed. Every haystack was being searched for one little needle. Every rock overturned.

It was all for her baby girl.

And she needed to be out there, helping to overturn those rocks.

Based on the way Jessica's heel was bouncing on the floor, Brian figured he only had a second or two before she announced someplace she was going to go—a long-shot search for Brooke based on a new blue barn idea, or some other clue Clint had sent.

"I have a favor to ask," he said. A plan that had a better chance to produce real answers.

Looking wary, she asked, "What?"

"The database I've been building? I'd like to send it to you and have you start a new sheet. Show all of Clint's clues up against that list of favorites, of lyrics from songs you sang to Brooke, of Clint's passwords… Anything you

can think of that might give us an idea of how he's coming up with the stuff he gives you every week."

"You don't think he's just making it up as he goes."

He might have. Before the Birds of Paradise café sign had shown up in his peripheral vision. He shook his head. And then said, "I'd like to see just the sixteen we've pulled out as part of the pattern of fours. And then, again, with all sixty-six clues."

"What are you looking for?"

He shrugged, took a sip of coffee like that was more important than their discussion. "Any similarities, anything that rings a bell with you. You're the one who has the most chance of catching something. You know him."

That was what she'd been saying all along. "Why now? What's up?"

He hadn't wanted to tell her. He hadn't wanted to muddy her already-far-too-murky waters with information that probably meant nothing. But he told her about Jim Brandywine Junior anyway.

And might have fallen in love a little bit, if he was capable of such a thing, when she immediately collected her laptop and got to work.

"I don't know that Brandywine Junior being in the same prison as Clint means anything at all." Brian's warning came even before Jessica had uploaded the program he'd sent her to get to work.

"Or it could mean we found the right blue barn, but came up with the wrong Jim Brandywine," she shot back at him. "I assume Anderson's checking into the guy? Has someone talking to him in the jail in Missouri?"

"He's got a young detective on his team, a guy who shows extraordinary promise, who asked to make the drive over."

She almost wept with the news. So many people were taking up her fight all of a sudden. The support was overwhelming.

And frightening.

What if Anderson and Brian were right?

What if Brooke…?

No.

In all the months since her daughter's kidnapping, she hadn't let Clint break her. She certainly wasn't going to let fear do so.

As if to be the period on that mental sentence, her phone dinged a text.

Before nine on a Sunday morning?

Stomach tight, she grabbed the device off the table. Read the screen. Handed the phone to Brian. And sat there, feeling her heart pound in her chest, while he called Anderson to report another text.

I'm watching and you're not making me happy.

While messages were angering him where Jessica was concerned, and making him tense for her safety, they weren't all bad for the investigation.

"We've poked into a lot of unconnected things, but somewhere along the way we've gotten someone's attention," Brian told Jessica after hanging up from Anderson. The man had been on another call, took the information and said he'd get someone back out on the towers ASAP.

"But why me?" she asked. "Why not gun for the guys who can take him down? It's not like I can stop Anderson from investigating a kidnapping."

She didn't really seem to be asking the question as much as thinking the answer was obvious.

Like asking, Why would someone put a gun to their head? When the obvious answer—to kill themselves—was right there.

"You're still certain it's Clint sending the texts."

"It's the only thing that makes sense," she said. "Why would anyone else target me? And every time we find out something new that involves Clint being questioned, or his cell searched, or whatever… I get another text."

He'd already drawn the correlation as well.

Didn't get the end game. Let alone the fact that there was no way for the man to be texting from prison.

Not unless he'd already purchased another phone with some of that wad of money Jessica had been sending him.

The pinched look on her face told him she'd probably reached the same conclusion. A hunch that was verified when she said, "My money might be paying for food, or articles of clothing, but the food and clothing could be buying him contraband phones."

It was a reach. But not a big one.

"Anderson's going to order a search of the whole cell block," he predicted. That could make Clint a very hated guy in his neighborhood.

She nodded.

"So what's his endgame? Just to take pleasure out of tormenting you every time you make his life uncomfortable?"

"My guess is he wants me to get scared and stop looking for Brooke. He knows that someone else is on the case. He's probably figured out by now that I hired a private investigator. He knew that Anderson and his team had reached an impasse on all leads."

"He wants you to fire me."

"That's my guess."

And as much time as she'd wasted over the past fifteen months chasing down baseless leads at her ex-husband's maniacal bidding, she'd been right a lot of the time when it came to Clint's motivations.

And Brian had to be straight with her. He'd held the woman naked in his arms. Had, in some ways, given her more of himself than he'd ever given another human being.

"You do know that he doesn't want you happy."

"Of course."

"And that, if you find Brooke, he's going to go ballistic."

Another nod.

"So what do you think is going to happen when he gets out of prison, Jess?" He hadn't meant to use the shortened version of her name. Froze as he did so. "I'm sorry," he apologized. Clint called her Jess. He'd seen her flinch when it happened.

"It's okay." Her face softened for a second. "I like it, coming from you."

Well, then. There was that.

But…

"In answer to your question, I don't know what's going to happen when Clint's released," she told him.

"Are you seriously considering being a family with him again as an option?"

"No." Not *Hell, no.* Or *God, no!*

She had to see there was no good end to complying with her ex…

Or maybe she didn't.

Maybe he had to keep his distance from a woman who had the right to make her own choices and seemed to be unable to.

What?

What would he have her do differently? Quit playing Clint's game and lose her chance to figure him out?

One of the man's clues had led her to the Birds of Paradise.

Probably hadn't figured, with the place being closed, that she'd ever find the little cafe, or ever figure out what the phrase meant in terms of significance to Brooke's disappearance, but the bottom line was—that one clue had been real.

And that led to the possibility that more were.

Yeah, and what about the blue barn? She'd have been dead if he hadn't been there. There was no guarantee that the next time she wouldn't be.

What if she'd been shot at in Lincoln the previous week?

With his heart in his throat, he wanted to make her promise that she wouldn't do anything reckless, or take any chances, based on things Clint told her, but knew he had no right. She'd promised not to head out investigating without clueing him in.

That was the most he, her hired private investigator, could ask. Or even should ask.

Teeth gritting, the muscles in his neck as tight as they got, he faced her down. Needing more than she could give.

"Where does his game end?"

"Truthfully, Brian, I haven't let myself think a lot about the time when Brooke is back home with me. I can't afford the distraction. Or answer the questions that arise when thoughts creep in. Even easy thoughts such as, Will she like me? Will ripping her away from wherever she's been traumatize her? Will I understand her two-year-old words? Or even, What will I do about babysit-

ting? Will I still want to work a job that chains me to a desk from eight thirty to three thirty, five days a week? Thinking about Clint, out of jail… It's too much. I just don't know."

He nodded. Understanding. Even as he found her answers insufficient for his own emotional well-being.

He didn't matter. He got that, too. Wanted it that way.

But thinking of her, with Clint still tormenting her, somehow, some way…

"Maybe I'll change my name and move away," she said then. "Start a new life in a world that's brand-new for both Brooke and me."

A world where he wouldn't know her. Couldn't find her.

But a world where she'd be free from Clint Johnson.

Where she'd be happy.

He nodded again. Felt…satisfied.

And went to get his laptop.

Chapter 21

Jessica couldn't think about Clint's release from jail. Other than working, to provide herself and others with financial security, she couldn't think about the next week. Her life was a void. One excruciatingly long day with every free moment consumed by finding her daughter.

Every thought she gave to something else was one less thought that might lead her closer to Brooke. She got the absurdity of that. Knew that she was losing parts of herself, parts of healthy living. Yeah, in a normal world, she needed more. But her universe spun on a different axis. She had the right to determine her own personal actions, ones that didn't hurt anyone but possibly herself. And, for her, committing her life to finding her baby girl was the best decision.

The right choice.

The only one.

And Brian?

Well, maybe some time lost in his arms, without thoughts barraging her, was good, too. If he was the gasoline that kept her engine running for an extra day, and he was willing to fill her up, wanted to fill her up, enjoyed filling her up…then her choice to be with him was a good one.

She was a quarter of the way through the spreadsheet Brian had asked her to do, and already starting to see pieces coming together in different ways, spurring new possibilities. "Look at this," she blurted, turning her screen so Brian could see how, when she did a particular sort, a whole line of things came together.

"The church in Lincoln," she said as he read. "And the fourth clues… 'A good book' could be the Bible. You commonly hear people refer to it as *the* Good Book. And 'where the greenest grass grows.' Churches, cemeteries and, well, golf courses, are known for that. 'Singing in the air,'" she pointed out another phrase on their list from Clint. "Churches have choirs. 'The rising star.' That one's obvious in terms of the Bible, the star that announced the birth of Jesus…"

Maybe she was stretching things, reaching too far, but…

Brian wasn't nodding like he was humoring her. He was studying the list. "'Time plays a part' could work, too, considering that churches only have services at set times."

"And it's less than a mile from Birds of Paradise," she added. Not sure what she was thinking, yet. What part that church played in Brooke's disappearance. But concrete thoughts, pulling things together, pushed her to keep working.

Brian's fingers flew on his keyboard and she pulled hers back.

"There are all kinds of biblical references to a 'river runs through it,'" he said. "Water is the symbol of life." He was scrolling, reading. "The movie by that name? There's an entire article given to biblical references in the film..."

"You said Clint wouldn't be good at critical thinking," she said slowly. "That's why the patterns. So, it stands to reason that he's got some basis for his clues. He wouldn't just be spitting them out randomly. Even the ones that might not be legitimate leads to Brooke's whereabouts..."

"Maybe they're biblical," Brian continued where she left off.

"Because there's something pertinent about the church in Lincoln?" It took everything she had not to just jump up right then, get the keys to her rental and head back to that church. Something had kept Clint going back to Lincoln during his time on the run with Brooke.

It was Sunday morning...there'd be services. The place would be filled with people. She could show around Clint's picture. Look for two-year-old little girls...

Would Brooke's hair still be blond? Like her mama's? Or would it have darkened?

Standing, she reached for her purse, planning to invite him, but head out on her own if need be, when Brian's phone rang.

He listened for a moment while she watched him for any reactions that could tell her what was going on—if it was big, or good or bad—and then heard him say, "Okay, hold on."

Tapping the screen of his phone, he set it in the middle of the table and looked at her. "It's Detective Anderson. He wanted it on speakerphone."

Fear striking through her, she sat. Couldn't look at Brian, couldn't risk feeling too much. She stared at the device in the center of their mess.

"First, another search of Clint's cell block turned up no contraband. Period. Either they have a place they're stashing it, or the block is clean. I'll be sending over last night's tower usage if you want to take a look, Brian. My people here aren't finding as much time as we'd like to look for patterns in transmissions during Jessica's receipt of messages. She lives right next to one of the busiest towers in Fayetteville."

She heard about the towers. Heard Brian agreeing to take over the cell tower usage investigation, data he'd already been looking at, albeit secondhand. She heard it all, but glommed on the first part of Anderson's message. No other phone turned up in Clint's cell? She'd been so certain he'd just go buy another.

So that meant Clint wasn't sending the warning messages?

That just did not ring true to her. They sounded so much like him. Both in word, but in tone and timing, too.

"I heard back on Jim Junior." The detective foraged along. He sounded different than in days past, more like he'd been during the first couple of weeks of Brooke's disappearance. Like there was urgent energy about him.

That both excited and terrified her.

"He was shown a picture of Clint, asked who he was, said he'd never seen him before. Even when prompted with the prison reference, he still claimed he didn't know him. My guy believed him. Jim Junior says he hasn't seen his dad since before he did his stint in prison. Has no idea what he's up to or where he is, but said that shooting a gun at a trespasser sounds just like him. He said his old man hit him upside the head with the barrel of a rifle for burning toast."

None of which was more important than her getting to Lincoln before Sunday services ended.

Although, knowing that the minor connection between Clint and the guy who'd shot at them was no connection at all, did interest her.

"We got forensics back on the bullets fired at you two and there were hits to another crime scene. A bar fight a decade ago in Oklahoma, shots fired, people hurt, but no one killed. The shooter never caught and the gun never recovered. Based on that and shots being fired yesterday at your vehicle, which was stopped in the easement between road and private property, I managed to get a warrant on the barn," Anderson continued. "Members of my team found a whole cache of illegal guns. And about fifty of the burner phones from that stolen batch."

Everything inside her sank. Supported solely by the weight of dread. All thoughts of heading to Lincoln faded away.

Oh, Clint, what in the *hell* have you done?

"So what are we really saying here?" Brian asked. "Clint's only possible interaction with this Brandywine Junior, his only tie to Bountyville, is that the two of them served time in the same prison at the same time. And Clint had a burner phone in his cell that came from a batch found in the guy's father's barn..."

She stared at him. Yeah and...?

"Right," Anderson said.

"All of which, you've told me, took place after he turned up without Brooke."

Ah. She should have seen that. Would have if she hadn't been consumed by the fear that she didn't know her ex-husband at all, which meant that she might never figure out where he'd left their daughter...

That could still very well be true.

The Clint she'd known would have been eaten up by a guy like Jim Brandywine. Junior or senior.

Hence, the ransom.

It was all starting to make sense.

Except that, his newest clue—'the blue barn'—had Clint meant for them to get shot at?

Made no sense. What possible pull could Clint have on a guy like Brandywine? Enough to get the guy to attempt murder on his behalf?

She shook her head.

"And on that note, I have a favor to ask," Anderson was saying while her thoughts flew all over the table. "My people have been through all of the surveillance video from the shooting range and didn't find any images of Clint. But they say there are several instances where people are on screen and you can't make out their faces. Some appear to be around Clint's height and build. I'd like it if you, Jessica, could take a look at for me, today, please, to see if you recognize Clint in any of the footage. I need to know if he was lying to us about those missing bullets."

The gun again. As tiring as revisiting that damned gun had grown to her, she needed the issue put to rest. More than ever before. She needed to know that Clint hadn't lied to her about the gun. Because if he had… Brandywine, guns and phones, and maybe even drugs, human traffickers…they'd all be seriously on the table.

That did not bode well for her baby girl at all.

While Jessica perused the digital video footage Anderson sent over, Brian fired off a quick text to Hudson, asking for any updates on the prison computer hack, no matter how small.

There was more to Clint Johnson than anyone was seeing. Maybe way more than a kidnapping. Something was telling Brian he had to find that *more* if he was going to find Brooke.

And with the text messages, the shooting, a computer hack, contraband phones that turned up in the worst of illegal activities…he made an educated guess that *more* than just Clint wanted to stop their investigation.

What logically followed was that whoever was out there would be getting more desperate to prevent them from continuing.

That meant he was in a very real battle with ghosts and his client could end up dead if he didn't figure it all out before their desperation reached do-or-die status.

His client.

Jessica Johnson was far more than that. No point in kidding himself on that one.

His whole career—maybe his whole life from the time his mother had been shot in cold blood—had brought him to his current point.

A culmination.

Either he'd given his life to a cause that mattered or he'd wasted half of it trying to give people something he didn't have to give.

Maybe answers didn't free you to move on. Move forward.

Maybe all they did was wrap you in barbed wire and poke at you for the rest of your life…

Not job thoughts.

Definitely not the work Jessica was paying a hefty fee for him to do.

He'd downloaded the tower data. Started a spreadsheet filled with colored lines denoting various connections from various places all within the time frame of messages received on Jessica's phone—and for the second or two duration of a text message as opposed to phone calls.

After he finished one sheet, he'd need to do the same for the other times messages had come in.

Only then would he be able to find what he was looking for. If it was there. Answers would come in the sameness of design on all the charts. And even then, would only give him an approximate area from which the text could likely have been sent.

It was a long shot.

He couldn't even count the number of times a long shot had solved a case for him.

So far, his people search in Lincoln had turned up nothing connected to finding Brooke.

The clue spreadsheet was the most promising evidence at the moment, and he itched to get back to leads on their list that aligned with biblical references.

According to Clint Johnson's criminal profile, he hadn't been a churchgoer. But he could have gotten religion in prison.

A preacher or priest was a likely host for the leech to attach to. Since he only got to suck from Jessica once a week…

"I've got it!" Jessica's screech sent his purple line up to the edge of the screen rather than the dot he'd been connecting it to. "It's him," she said as Brian vacated his workspace and rounded the table to join her in hers.

She'd frozen the video on her screen and was pointing to a figure walking toward the camera, his face obscured by the large-billed baseball cap he wore.

As he leaned in to get a better look—to see if he saw any resemblance in the photo on her screen to the many images of Clint Johnson he'd been studying over the past ten days—he caught a whiff of Jessica's neck and felt a kick in the groin.

Not so much turn-on, as recognition.

He should take a step back. Have her send him the

segment and he could run facial recognition software between it and various other photos.

Trouble was, he didn't want to take a step back.

He wanted to have her back.

Knowing he couldn't stop her from following the clues of a man who was bad to the bone.

Like his father hadn't been able to stop his mother.

The thought froze him cold for a second, as Jessica showed him a couple more images of the same capped person.

Like his father…

The old man had been fighting impossible odds…

Like Brian's need to not only find Jessica's daughter, but to free her from the man who'd fathered that child?

He wouldn't be his father.

Thus determined, he focused on the case he was there to solve.

And not on the woman for whom he was solving it.

Memories came flooding back.

"I know that cap," she said as she scrolled through image after image of the video she'd been perusing a single screen at a time. And was flung backward almost a decade.

"I bought it for him." Back when she'd thought she'd found the love her life. When the Clint she'd seen had been the man of her dreams. Emotionally aware, unlike the coldhearted father who would run off and leave his three-year-old motherless daughter behind. Clint had needed her. Had been jazzed by the idea that she'd needed him, too. In her eyes, he'd been the epitome of a man who'd stay with her, raise their family with her.

Grow old with her.

She couldn't believe he'd worn it as recently as…weeks

before Brooke's disappearance? She hadn't seen it in… she couldn't remember when.

Had assumed it was in a box on a shelf someplace.

"It was the weekend he asked me to marry him. We were in California. He'd just met my ma, and we'd left for two days at the beach. We were at a pier where there were all kinds of shops. He wanted to get a tattoo with our names together on it, his engagement ring, he said. But the wait was hours long, and I knew he was afraid of needles, so even though the sentiment was cool, that was probably one of the times he'd spoken without really thinking things through."

She stopped, glanced up at Brian. Hadn't realized he was quite so close until her lips almost ran into his. That mouth…captivated her attention for a second. The world and all its ugliness, disillusionment and disappointments faded away.

For a second. "It's like you said," she continued then, turning back to her computer with a new awareness of his heat, of his body.

And in that moment, feeling conflicted about that. Needing to know what it meant. That it meant nothing.

"He's not great at cognitive thinking." She forced herself to continue.

If Brian noticed her digression from professional focus, he was kind enough not to indicate as much to her. "Anyway, in lieu of the tattoo, I suggested a hat. Because there was a shop where they did embroidery while you waited." The last two sentences were said so quickly, words practically stumbled over her tongue. "My name is on one side of the hat. His is on the other."

She pointed to an image, enlarged it so the *Jessica* showed up clearly.

And then to another image, with the hat wearer walk-

ing in the opposite direction, also enlarged to show the matching *Clint*.

The fact that Clint was wearing that hat—right before he'd taken Brooke, before he'd begun to torture Jessica—he really had been thinking back to "them." Needing "them." Not just getting even with her for selling his boat.

Did that mean that he'd left Brooke in a safe place, too, like he kept implying?

He'd told the truth about the gun.

The Brandywines of Bountyville seemed to have no known connection to the case.

The cell phone—maybe it had been a plant. Or, maybe he'd actually purchased it, in case he'd needed to make an emergency call—with some of the money she'd sent him to pay his ransom. Maybe one of the guys protecting him sold the phones and tossed it to him as a pat on the head for money rendered.

"Anyone can wear a hat," Brian said after reaching over to scroll back through the images again. But he didn't sound all that convincing. "Maybe Clint gave it away, lost it..."

Right there at the shooting range he'd named as having visited? He'd gone all the way to the range to have someone wear his hat and pose as him? And a guy would do it? Why?

But she got it...investigators went on facts...they needed proof. She had that, too. Scrolling ahead to the capped man shooting, she showed the images of bull's-eyes he made first, and then zeroed in on the shooter. "See that scar?" Her cursor pointed to a small line on her ex-husband's chin. "He got that trying to ski on a snowboard when he was in college."

With a "Send it to Anderson," Brian straightened, left

her chair, moved around the table. Took his seat. And went back to work. Leaving Jessica feeling…empty.

Alone.

Bereft.

And more afraid than she could ever remember being.

Chapter 22

By midafternoon, Brian had a list of things he wanted to check out, possible leads, but still had no clear vision of how any of the myriad pieces of Clint Johnson's puzzle were going to come together. Everything was so scattered, from Lincoln to Bountyville, a prison two hours away, and a jail in Missouri. There were things in common. And nothing solid drawing any of them together.

After finishing with the shooting range data, Jessica had put together a light lunch for them—tuna sandwiches, not his favorite—and then gone back to work on his spreadsheets. Something that only she could do as she was the only one close enough to Clint, with enough history of Clint, to see things that were reminiscent of him.

Like the baseball cap.

That incident was still rankling, giving him indigestion. The memory she'd relayed… It hadn't been so much her tone of voice, as though she'd still been in love with

the guy, but the way he could feel her in the story, tending to Clint, the way the future kidnapper had played right to her abandoned heart—getting a tattoo with both of their names as his own engagement ring…

Who did that?

Not any guy he knew.

It was the sappiest thing he'd ever heard.

And…he could almost see it. With Jessica.

What was it about the woman that drew a man to the point of him not being himself?

That drew him so strongly?

He wanted to take a drive back to Lincoln. To see where the cell tower was located and check addresses in the closest vicinity to it. He wanted to know how close it was to the church.

They'd been on to something that morning, with Clint's clues. And Lincoln seemed to be the place with the most promising leads.

His phone dinged a text. And almost simultaneously, so did Jessica's.

Thinking they were from Anderson, he glanced at his phone while she did hers.

His was from Hudson Warner, Sierra Web's IT partner. Telling him that he'd had to follow a trail of log-ins, through several encryptions, to the dark web and back, to find a user on a message app. The messages were encrypted. He only had so many tries on passwords and didn't want to get locked out.

Asked if the client could be of any help.

Said he'd try other ways in in the meantime.

"If Clint were going to use a password in a secret place, what do you think it would be?" Brian asked Jessica as he read the last of the message and then glanced up.

Jessica, tight-lipped, looking peaked, handed him her phone.

I am not happy with you.

"His cell block was searched again today," she told him, her voice unsteady. "A text happens every time he's bothered in prison."

He got that. Texted Anderson for another pull on data from cell towers.

And suggested that they go for a drive.

It was either that or take her into her room and obliterate everything from her world except the passion she'd found in his arms.

The first half hour that they were on the road, Jessica texted with Brian's associate, Hudson Warner. An actual partner in the firm. And a man who seemed to know way more about technical coding in terms she'd never heard Clint mention.

And Clint had been considered one of the tops in his field. She'd heard that from a boss or two before they'd grown disillusioned by her ex's lack of common people skills.

With Hudson's prompting of what types of things a person might use as passwords, based on various characters, letters and numbers, she gave suggestions. Good ones.

None of them worked and he stopped short of using his last chance, not wanting to be locked out of any opportunity to access whatever messages were there.

Could be from anyone in the prison. To anyone in the world.

The fact that none of her suggested passwords worked

gave her less hope that they were actually on a real trail to Clint's activities.

Hudson said he'd keep trying to find another way in.

She'd find a way to pay him.

The church in Lincoln had an evening service of some kind. A Bible study according to its website. Brian and Jessica observed from their parked vehicle across the street, where they could see the door of the church as well as the playground.

She didn't see a single toddler-aged girl.

They did confirm that Lincoln's cell tower was less than half a mile from the church.

An interesting piece of information that could mean something. They just had no way of knowing what.

They stopped for dinner on the way home. A barbecue place. With its high roof and tables full of families, the place was loud. Cracked peanut shells littered the red-cement floors and the wood-slatted benches in the red-checkered-tableclothed booth they'd been shown were hard as a rock. The food…she ate more than she'd expected to. More than she had in a while.

And being out with Brian, in an atmosphere that was the complete opposite of professional, with a noise level that precluded business conversation, was something she had a feeling she was never going to forget.

For a little bit there she felt…normal.

A woman out with a guy she genuinely liked.

And had the hots for.

The feeling lasted up until a young child's cry sounded and a man stood up from a booth down from them, walking by with an unhappy little girl…

They left soon after that, didn't talk much on the way home, and with every mile that took them closer to her house, she grew more morose.

It was late enough, especially with her having to work in the morning, that they wouldn't do any more work that night. He'd go to his room. She'd go to hers.

That was as it should be.

The weekend was over. Another one gone with her not any closer, tangibly at least, to finding Brooke.

And her mind and body in a war unlike anything she'd ever known. Clint had told the truth. He'd lied. He was playing her. He wanted her dead.

She wanted him permanently out of her future.

He was the only one who knew where he'd left Brooke. And there was the crux. The one line that was her stopping place. Over and over. Every single time.

But…

There was Brian. Not a future thing. Just a now thing.

And…

Her garage door shot up at his push of the button. He parked. Turned off the SUV. They got out. Walked in from the garage to the kitchen together.

She turned to say good-night. To thank him for all of the work he was doing. He had logical, evidence-based theories, and a whole list of things he was going to be checking out over the next days culminating from their work that day. Planned to have traffic camera footage pulled in the area of the shooting range to see where Clint might have gone before and after.

And while Lincoln didn't have anything as fancy as traffic cameras he'd taken them by gas stations on the busiest road in and out of town and had seen cameras there, too, which he planned to check out.

He was getting closer to narrowing down and exposing Clint's movements during the time immediately before and after the kidnapping.

That meant he was getting closer to Brooke.

He was doing exactly what she'd hired him to do.

And he was doing so much more.

"Thank you." Her face inches from his, she stared him right in the eye. Long after her words had been uttered.

He looked back, his gaze seeming to be on fire, but not with any one clearly definable message. He wasn't moving.

Wasn't breaking eye contact.

"I'm paying you to work for me." Were her words for her own benefit, or his? Even she didn't know.

He gave a head tilt, but still didn't look away. "For some things."

"And…others?"

"Freely given, from both sides."

Thank God. She didn't really smile. She was way too far into what she now knew was coming for anything that lighthearted. But her lips invited. As did her eyes.

"You want me to come to bed with you?" He was serious, and yet that glint that had just appeared in his gaze… he was teasing her, too.

"Yes, please."

Other than Brooke home safe and sound, there was nothing she wanted more.

Hours turned into days with a flow Brian had never before noticed on a job. He wasn't just working. He was living his life.

Only for the moment, he fully accepted that. Wanted it that way.

The future, for him, was already planned out. Continuing to live the life into which he'd been born. For which he'd been born.

As long as there were unsolved cases, hardships, questions without clear answers, he'd be out there, search-

ing, bringing people the peace they needed to move forward. He'd been gifted with an ability to find what others couldn't. His job was far more than a way to make money. Far more than work. Finding answers to ease pain was his calling.

By day, while Jess worked, he continued to delve deeper into all of the pieces that were scattered over her dining room table. And by night…he was half of a dynamic sexual partnership. There were no stolen kisses in the kitchen. No afternoon quickies, or even shared showers. They were who they were. Two completely separate individuals with vastly different goals and futures. They just happened to be sharing bodies, and a bed, at night.

Monday was spent taking every piece of evidence they'd uncovered and starting in on discovering where each piece led with further unearthing. From a blue barn filled with illegal goods to a closed café that'd served a kidnapper for three days, unknown text message threats, lies and truths, clues that might be valid if Brian could figure out where they led, computer hacking, even a missing photo of a baby off her mother's nightstand… To human traffickers? He scoured what he could find about any suspects in the police databases to which he had access.

Bible references…he was compiling a much longer list there. Residents of Lincoln, and Bountyville, too. Known associates of the Brandywines. He even made another drive to Lincoln to talk to Harriet Lichen again, hoping to discover what she could give him that he didn't know she had.

He found out what newspaper she'd carried in her café—the one Clint had taken with him. The fact that he'd had his turkey dinner hot twice and once had ordered the cold turkey sandwich with cranberry sauce.

And came away believing that she wasn't hiding anything from him. That she'd been completely open and honest the first time they'd talked to her.

Hudson, who was already on a job, had another expert on his team helping with the computer hack, but the encryptions were deep and well protected. In order to avoid disintegrated coding, she had to proceed with extreme care.

No new text messages came Monday or Tuesday, but their source was bothering Brian more than a lot of the other pieces of the case. Those messages had been directed specifically to Jess. If they were coming from Clint, her ex was getting more ballsy, not less. And showing not only his determination to manipulate her, but his belief that he could still do so.

Maybe he could. Maybe he couldn't. Clint had what Jess most needed in the world—knowledge of where he'd left her daughter—but the more Brian was around her, the more he had to respect her strength. And her ability to uphold her right to her own thoughts.

Like his mother—she would not be swayed when she believed something.

And yet, every time those messages came in, she'd been rocked to the core. He got it. Who wouldn't be? But she believed they were from Clint.

Meaning, her ex-husband still had more power over her than she knew?

Needing that piece gone, he expanded his search of cell tower grids to beyond Fayetteville, Lincoln, Bountyville, and stretching to the prison, areas.

Opened up signals coming in from the entire state of Arkansas, and added Oklahoma and Missouri as well, since they'd had evidence hits from both states. One through the bar fight involving the same gun that had

been fired at him and Jess, the other with Brandywine in a Missouri jail.

And while he was waiting for the downloads to populate his spreadsheets, he read an online version of the newspaper Clint had been reading at the café that last morning in Lincoln. Every word.

Someplace, he was going to find something. One little piece of information that would bring everything together for him.

He had to trust the process.

When his programmed colored lines started to show up in the little windows he'd minimized, Brian abandoned the news and focused on data. While there were signals crossing into Fayetteville on all searches, which he'd expected, what he hadn't thought he'd see was the same signal, at all times there'd been text message deliveries, for the few-second duration text messages took.

One tower in Perrysville, Arkansas, to the tower pinging to Jess's cell phone. And it was the only times the two towers were connected. Always just the one way. No calls from Jess's tower to Perrysville.

Adrenaline flowing now, he typed in a request for driving distance between the two cities. Nearly three hours.

It was just before three, he could be there by six.

Thinking he'd text Jess once he was on the road, he was already in the kitchen on the way out the door when he heard her call from the hall. "Brian?"

Turning, he saw her at the entrance to the dining room. "Here," he said, glad to see her. And yet…not. He had no idea what he'd be walking into in Perrysville…

What he might find out.

If it turned out to be good, she'd be just as happy at

six, or nine, when he got back, without any of the roller-coaster in between…

"What?" she asked, joining him in the kitchen, studying his face.

"I have something I want to check out," he told her. "Just a cell tower thing. I'm heading out to see where it leads and will keep you posted. And don't worry about holding dinner, I'll grab something on the road."

He had to go. Every moving part of his system—blood, nerves, brain waves—were throttled up to full gear.

"Let me get my bag. I'll go with you," she said, as he'd feared she would. The woman was not going to be left out.

Or left behind.

"It's a long drive, Jess. And maybe for nothing at all. You have to work in the morning, and with your research…" She'd left the bed at four that morning to do client research before the bell rang.

He wanted to pull the sex card. Wanted to suggest that she get her work done so they could spend more time making sparks that night while still allowing her to get the sleep she needed. But didn't. First thing to give up would be them doing the deed.

Rather than going to get her purse, she came closer. Studied him more intently. "What's going on, Brian? Where are you going?"

"To Perrysville."

Her glance intensified, every feature on her face sharpening. "Why?"

He told her about extending the cell tower search. That he'd found a match for the messages that had been sent to her.

"Bonnie Lichen is in Perrysville."

Studying culinary arts at a community college there. He knew.

She looked sick to her stomach for a moment. Drained of color and slightly hunched, then her face turned red, her mouth fell open.

Tears sprang to her eyes. "You think… Bonnie has Brooke?"

He'd had the thought. "I'm not jumping to any conclusions at this point," he told her. "I just think the tower evidence is worth a conversation."

"In person."

"I want her to look me in the eye, yes."

"You want to take her by surprise and see if my daughter is there with her." Her voice wobbled, her tears continued to well, but she stood straight, head high. "I'm coming with you."

Again, he had no idea what he'd be walking into. Could just as likely be that Bonnie had seen more than she should have and wanted Jessica to stop her search so that she wouldn't be implicated down the road.

"Jess…"

"I'm coming."

She was paying him. Could fire him on the spot and go alone.

She would do it. He had no doubt about that. No matter what danger she could find herself in. If Bonnie was more involved rather than less… If she had a gun, too…

With a single nod of his head, he waited for her to make a quick stop in the bathroom, get her purse and join him.

The drive to Perrysville was the longest three hours of her life. Jessica couldn't get comfortable. Couldn't find a streaming music station that played songs she wanted to hear. Couldn't concentrate enough to do any of the financial research she'd been planning to do after the bell rang.

And she didn't want to talk.

Couldn't analyze or even care about technicalities.

Was she about to see Brooke? After so many months.

She cried a few times along the way. Quietly. Wiping away tears.

What if Brooke was afraid of her? She'd be a stranger to the toddler now.

Would she recognize her? How could she not recognize her own daughter? But…would she?

When her hands shook, she sat on them. When her thoughts were overwhelming her to the point of making her dizzy, she laid her head back and closed her eyes.

Brian…she was glad he was there. Driving.

Glad that they'd gotten her SUV back the night before. That Brooke's car seat had been thoroughly cleaned and was firmly belted just as it needed to be to transport the little girl home.

Home.

She hadn't had time to change the sheets on Brooke's crib.

Was she sleeping in a big-girl bed now instead? Jessica had debated making the switch, but hadn't been able to bring herself to do it.

"I bought one of those baby beds…you know, that convert from crib to trundle on the floor with a safety bar, for toddlers…"

"Jess…"

"… I know." He didn't want her to get her hopes up. She didn't want to hear about that.

And could hardly sit in the vehicle when they pulled up to the apartment complex Brian had found as Bonnie's last-known address.

He'd confirmed that the cell phone he'd called her on was registered to that address.

Oh, pleeeaassseee…

She got out, stiffened her legs when they almost gave out on her. Took a deep breath. Brooke's first sight of her had to be as a happy, friendly-looking woman.

She should have changed out of the navy pants and silk, sleeveless blouse and blue pumps she'd worn to the office that morning. Put on something bumblebee…

Pulling the ponytail holder out, she shook her hair free, saw Brian looking at her with a mixture of worry and compassion and put her hair back up again.

She'd always worn it in a ponytail around the baby.

They found the door.

She knocked before Brian had a chance.

And nearly fell, with joints to rubber, leaning back against her expert detective, when the door opened.

Chapter 23

There was no young child living in the apartment.

Brian had determined that the second he'd seen the cat litter box in a far corner of the studio rental. Another few seconds of observation showed him the entire space, including the bathroom visible through an open door at the far end of the living space.

Another clue had been the way Bonnie had invited them in the second Jess had introduced herself.

The younger woman was trying to be friendly.

Overly so. He didn't share the sense of camaraderie. Whether she'd sent the text messages, or suspected who did, or not, he knew the second she'd glanced his way that she'd lied to him over the phone.

Whatever she did know was making her nervous. Skittish. Unwilling to meet his gaze—or keep her hands still.

They didn't have a warrant to be there. She didn't have to speak to them. He had to start with full barrels, lest he was asked to leave before he got what he was after.

"Multiple text messages have been sent from here to my client's phone," he said, walking into the living area as though he had every right to be there. He was tall, broad-shouldered. Bonnie wasn't. He wanted to be intimidating. And he didn't want to be standing next to a woman who oozed compassion.

"Here" could be defined as in that room or in that town. He left that up to Bonnie.

"If I search this place, I'm guessing I'm going to find the burner phone from which they were sent."

"It's not a burner phone!" Bonnie blurted the words fast. Based on the worried look on her face, Brian assumed that, if she'd had the chance to think before she'd spoken, she wouldn't have given him the information. "I bought it legally off the internet," she finished, dropping down to the edge of her worn but clean-looking couch. Her body slumped, head bent, she looked at her clasped hands. Brian looked at her. Couldn't afford to be distracted by the woman somewhere behind him.

Not until he'd finished with Bonnie. He wasn't going away with another dead end. He'd promised Jess answers and as yet had only managed to give her an overwhelming number of worrisome questions.

"When did you buy it?" He had her on the hook, didn't want to panic her to the point of clamming up. He'd ease into the rest of it.

"After you called me," she said. "I have the receipt, if you want to see it. It's an unregistered phone, and came with sixty minutes on it." Leaning over to a scarred end table, she opened the drawer, produced the phone and handed it him. "Check it out."

"May I keep this?" Anderson would want it. And might need it. That remained to be seen.

She shrugged. "I don't need it."

With a quick glance at the cheap flip model, he accessed all of the messages that had come into Jessica's phone. And determined that no other visible calls or messages had gone out from that device.

Then pinned Bonnie with a look that had cowered more than one hardened criminal. "Why?"

She looked at the window. At something behind him—Jessica, he guessed—and then toward his feet.

"After you called…all that talk about a baby… Gram was super upset and… I'm almost through with school. I graduate next month and I've already started financing to be able to open up the café again. No way I can do that if you guys keep trying to prove that it was used for some criminal purpose or that Gram and I are involved."

She looked up at him then, square in the eye, and said, "I just wanted her to leave us alone." She looked beyond his shoulder again.

"I'm the one asking the questions." Brian's tone was meant to draw her gaze back at him. And succeeded.

"Yeah, but she pays you," Bonnie said, somewhat sheepishly, but looking at him. "Gram said you said you were her private detective."

He'd told Harriet as much. The first visit and the second.

"I just didn't want some PI snooping around the place, trying to make it look as though something horrible went down there. This loan, if I get it, the café…it might be my only chance to make my dreams come true."

He remembered Harriet saying something about Bonnie's dream of owning a restaurant.

The younger woman didn't give him any warm fuzzies. He didn't trust her as he had Harriet—but then, she'd been harassing, striking terror in the woman he…

His thoughts stopped short.

The woman he what?

Worked for. He answered the question emphatically enough to get the thoughts out of his head as he told Bonnie he'd be back if he had any further questions.

He wouldn't be. He'd be turning the whole thing over to Anderson, but she didn't need to know that.

"It's not like I did anything wrong," Bonnie said, looking between the two of them as they headed to the door.

"You sent text messages with the intent to terrorize," he said, pretty sure that no court was going to charge the woman.

"I didn't threaten anything," she said. "I only meant to scare her..."

He wasn't going to argue the point. Didn't much care what happened to Bonnie Lichen.

He cared about Jess's silence. The emptiness of her expression.

He'd known it would be better for her if she hadn't come along. Not that he'd tell her so.

But *damn*.

His specialty was finding the truth.

Not doing damage control.

Jessica slept on the way home. Overwhelmed by the crushing disappointment coursing through her, she'd welcomed the escape. And when they arrived home, she entered the house ahead of Brian, turning to say, "I'm sorry for conking out on you. Leaving you to make the drive alone."

"I'd planned on doing the whole thing alone," he said, his tone kind, if distant, and she nodded. Her bag still on her shoulder, she hugged her arms around her middle and moved toward the dining room. She had work waiting there for her. More data to peruse in search of anything

that carried any hint of familiarity to her—and work in her office, too.

And just didn't have the energy right then to do any of it.

"I'm heading in," she announced to the house in general, not looking at him, or even glancing to see what he was doing. If he was settled back at the table.

And in she went. To her room. Brushed her teeth. Thought about a bath. Needing to clean herself of the grayness enveloping her, but not finding the will to do that either.

Instead, longing for more oblivion, she stripped down to panties, pulled on an old tank top and slid beneath the covers. She never even turned on the light.

She didn't fall asleep either. She laid there, alone, listening to silence. Wondering if Brian would join her as he'd done the past two nights. Or if he was done with her.

At least for a night or two.

He'd wanted to go to Perrysville alone. Had been trying to spare her.

She'd had to go. And would do so again and again.

However many times it took.

He didn't get that her own let-downs didn't matter to her. She'd been through a ton of them. And would face a million more if that's what it took.

But maybe, going through them with her was too much for someone else to take on. There was no fault in that.

Half an hour after she went to bed, she heard him in the hall. Heard his bathroom door shut. Then reopen. Pictured him heading to the bed she'd made up for him. Reaching for the covers.

And heard him at her doorway, too. He'd knocked softly, but hadn't waited for a response. His feet like muffled shadows on the carpet, he moved to his side of

the bed, he lowered himself, held his arms open to her, and she slid into them.

Not to kiss.

Or explore. She just wrapped her own arms around his middle, laid her head on his chest and continued to breathe.

It's how she got through. She just continued to breathe.

"I don't know what's happening."

The rumble of his words vibrated against her cheek.

"Nothing's happening." Not true. So much was. She just didn't have the wherewithal to deal with it that night.

"You…me…it's not making sense to me."

But he was there. Holding her. When she'd let him completely off the hook.

And she knew he wasn't talking about her. Maybe wasn't even thinking about her feelings at the moment.

That was what she should have been doing.

Wallowing in self…that was how she crashed.

Her strength was in thinking of others.

Or maybe it was in thinking of those she cared about.

She cared about Brian. Not in the sense of building rainbows, or happy endings, but just…one spirit meeting another along the way and…caring.

"What's not making sense?" she asked him, her mind needing to know how he was feeling, not even considering how his feelings would affect hers. It was who she was. Who she'd always been.

Nurturing was her strength and she'd be damned if she'd let Clint Johnson's misuse of her make her feel afraid of that.

"It's getting mixed up," he said, his voice thick. Soft in the darkness. His hand running slowly up and down her side where he held her, he continued. "Business… and you. Working, doing my job…and you. Everywhere I

look, everywhere I turn…whether you're around or not… there's…you. In ways that don't fit client…or lover. I can't find a definition. Don't know where or how to file it."

As esoteric and unclear as his words were, in any practical logical sense, she understood them. "Maybe it doesn't need defining," she said, but knew her words fell short. His struggle was beyond putting a name to their relationship.

To talking about boundaries.

"What's bothering you the most?" Made sense to start there.

Laying flat on his back, he had one arm under her neck, around her shoulders, his hand on her upper arm, and the other—he clung to the covers on his opposite side.

"After my mother died, my father became consumed with avenging her death by getting every single criminal, no matter how two-bit, off the streets. He lay in wait. He entrapped. It was like he couldn't rest, couldn't find his peace, until there wasn't a single bad guy left."

That kind of pain spoke to her. She recognized it.

"He set himself an impossible task—making sure no other cop died on duty ever again by ridding the world of bad guys. Because there'd always be more coming up."

Couldn't have been easy, growing up that way. Her heart cried for the child he'd been. And opened up wide to the man he'd become.

"What happened?" She had to know. It was a part of him. And the minutes in life they were sharing together… called for everything.

"When arrests failed to bring any kind of peace or satisfaction, he started drinking. Coupled with taking most of his meals in his car on his way to some watch or another, he had a fatal heart attack the year I graduated from college."

She hugged him. She couldn't help it. And didn't get to her tears in time to stop them from dripping to his chest.

"Just like my mom, he wouldn't listen to anyone else," he said. "Not from me, naturally, I was a kid for much of the time, but not from his chief or from mandatory counseling either. He didn't seem to care if his behavior was reckless..."

Her breathing slowed. Her heart rate slowed.

"Like me," she said.

"Maybe."

She wanted to reassure him. Her first instinct was to tell him she understood. To promise to try to change her behavior for him. Because that was what working relationships required.

But more, she didn't want to. And knew she couldn't.

They weren't building a lasting relationship.

She already had one of those to which she was fully committed and there would be nothing of her left to give to him if she didn't do everything she could to rescue Brooke.

Her flesh and blood. The child she'd grown inside her and brought into the world.

"I'm like them," he said then.

And maybe it wasn't about her at all.

"How so?"

"My ability to figure out how the pieces fit together, the way I can stick with something, ferreting out even the most minute detail until it all makes sense. My passion for doing so."

"That's all good stuff, Brian. Great stuff."

He knew that.

"It's why I do what I do. But with a difference. I don't get emotional about it all. And my goals are realistic. I'm not out to save the world. I'm just out to give as many

people as I can the peace that my father couldn't find. And hopefully save some innocent lives, as my mother was trying to do."

When tears sprang to her eyes again, she blinked them away. Didn't want him to know they'd appeared.

They weren't for him to know.

The feelings behind them weren't anything he could ever find out.

For both their sakes.

Because she was falling in love with the man and didn't have a free heart, or a free life, to give to him.

And he wouldn't want it even if she did.

Loving her, staying in one place to be part of a family, having a real home, would require giving up his life's purpose, and she'd never ask him to do that.

Brian felt her tears fall to his chest. They'd started slowly, but came with full honesty after a time. He got the sadness behind them. Related to it. She didn't speak. He had nothing more to say.

He'd figured out the answer to his problem. Still had no place to file it, but he knew. Brooke's case was different, the job was unlike any other, and his senses on the job were different because of it.

From the minute he'd seen her in the airport, Jessica had been different.

He'd done kidnappings. A few of them.

Involving young children, too.

He just hadn't gotten emotional about it all. He'd cared. He always did. On all of his cases, he cared deeply.

But not personally.

And with Jess, from those very first minutes, long before the sex, it had been personal.

He lay awake long after her even breathing told him

she'd fallen asleep. He thought about her, about her little girl.

He thought about the case.

He made his plans.

Now that he knew what was going on with him, he could deal with it, handle it. File it away. And when the job was done, maybe he'd take a vacation before jumping right into the next one.

He'd been getting more and more like his father without realizing it. Failing to take time to rejuvenate. To rest.

He'd go away someplace. Lie on a beach or veg out in a suite in a five-star hotel, maybe sip mojitos at a rooftop pool bar.

Plan in place, he slept.

And the next day, he hit the ground running with renewed energy and enough determination to satisfy even him. He had a long interview with the preacher from the church in Lincoln. Left feeling satisfied that if there was any illegal activity going on around him, the man honestly didn't know any details.

Wayne Bennet certainly had seen no evidence of any human traffickers, nor was he aware of any little children in the area who hadn't been born to their parents, though he wasn't nearly as hopeful when it came to drug trafficking.

Brian wasn't much concerned about a drug connection. As deeply as he was looking into the kidnapping and Clint Johnson's life, there'd been no evidence, other than a phone out of a batch of five hundred, that told him he should be.

No longer having to worry about Jess's immediate safety with a possible lurker on the loose ready to hurt her, he found it immensely easier to keep his emotions

in check where she was concerned. Until bed Wednesday night.

But there they just had incredible sex, and those emotions he'd already approved.

Thursday wasn't quite as free from distraction for him. All day long, as he worked, he was aware that if he didn't find the missing pieces within the next twenty-four hours, Jess would be meeting virtually with Clint again.

And have some whatever clue to go running after.

A hint that could likely lead to more danger for her.

He couldn't prove that Clint had deliberately sent Jess to a place he knew to be housing illegal arms, one that was owned by a suspected madman.

But based on her ex's behavior, over their entire marriage, he just didn't see Clint giving Jess up. The man knew she'd hired someone to help her, which, he saw clearly now, would only escalate Clint's narcissistic need to be the one who controlled her.

The one she felt she needed most.

He'd do whatever he could to remind her that he was the only one who had her answers. And to scare her into staying in line with his wants and needs.

The four hundred dollars she'd been depositing each month in his commissary account was proof enough to him of what the man could make her do.

He wanted to believe that Clint was the only source of his tension. Tried not to think about the tender way he and Jess had come together the night before, as though something about their joining was brand-new. He mostly succeeded.

He ordered in her favorite Chinese chicken salad for lunch, enough for two, and took hers in to her. She'd been on the phone and typing on her computer at the same time.

The look of concentration on her face, the confident, somewhat excited tone of her voice, had him turned on all over again.

He was still in recovery mode half an hour later when his own phone rang.

Hudson Warner.

The IT expert had managed to uncover the IP address where messages sent from the prison through a dark web app had landed—outside the prison. Hudson couldn't prove, as of yet, who had sent them. Only that they'd come from the IP address of a computer in the prison library that was there for inmate use.

But he knew the IP address where they finally landed—and were opened.

The expert who'd been working the case was using the same technical in to decode messages and would be sending them along as soon as she had anything readable.

Madder than hell, at himself first and foremost, for not seeing it, Brian hung up and dialed Anderson.

Chapter 24

The bell signaling the end of Brooke's business day had barely rung when Brian appeared at her office door. That fact alone alerted her. Other than bringing her food, and sitting on her floor during her calls with Clint, the man never stepped foot inside her office.

Showing her a respect Clint hadn't been able to do.

The way Brian's nose was flaring, in conjunction with the visible tension in his jaw, had her standing slowly. Heart pounding.

"What?"

"We need to get to the police station," he said, and she grabbed her bag, followed him out the door and down the hall as he continued. "Hudson found where the prison messages were being sent. He uploaded several of the messages to Anderson's secure server..."

She was dying there, hardly breathing as she hurried after him. Needing to know everything at once, hardly able to take in what he was saying.

"Do we know where Brooke is?" That was all that really mattered.

"No."

She nodded, still slightly behind him, looking at the side of his face. Keeping her gaze on him as though he could pull her through whatever came next.

"The messages were being sent to Bonnie Lichen."

One foot followed the other on the floor, but her knee, more jelly than joint, buckled. Brian's hand under her elbow grabbed her, supported her, all without slowing them down.

"Turns out she was visiting her grandmother in Lincoln today and Anderson has her in custody. He's going to allow you to watch the interview."

"He is?" Shocked, she found her own strength to hurry out to her SUV. "I can't believe he'd do that. I'm grateful but…" She glanced at Brian. "You asked him for the favor, didn't you?"

He shrugged, pulled the handle on the driver's door and sank down. "I would have," he admitted as he pushed the button to open the garage door and started the engine. "But he said he thought you needed to hear what she had to say."

"What?" New fear filled her. Stabbing at her stomach. Her chest. "What's she going to say?"

"I honestly don't know." Brian kept his gaze on the backup camera, and then the road as they sped away from her house. She couldn't get him to look at her. "He's seen the messages. I haven't yet," he finished.

He'd talked to Anderson, though, and clearly the news wasn't joyous. No way Brian wouldn't have caught on to that just by talking to the detective.

"We know she didn't have Brooke at her apartment." He dropped the words softly. Trying to prepare her?

Didn't he get yet that she wouldn't let her mind see a picture of her baby girl being anything but loved?

Using every ounce of determination and strength she had, pulling from reserves deep inside herself, she managed to keep hope alive as she went to find the answers she'd been seeking for eighteen agonizing months.

They had the small viewing room to themselves, door closed to shut out anything going on in the hallway. Standing at the one-way window, waiting for the audio to be turned on so they could hear the interview that was about to start in the room they could see but from which they could not be seen, Brian felt Jessica's fingers slide into his.

It wasn't a business thing, standing there with hands interlocked. And it wasn't a sex thing either. He didn't pull away from her, though.

The case would end. Maybe even yet that night.

Releasing her from the void that prevented her from living.

And he'd be released, too, from the hold her need had on him. He'd move on to the next case. And pray that he never ran into another Jessica Johnson.

He didn't ever want to have to say goodbye to someone like her again.

Her body pushed into his, not so much leaning on him as holding them together. He could only imagine how painful the passing seconds were on her.

"He's reading her her rights," he said in case knowing what was going on made it any easier.

She nodded. So did Anderson, at the officer standing in the corner of the room.

The woman reached for a switch on the wall and An-

derson's voice filled the room. "You lied to the private investigator who came to see you earlier this week, Bonnie."

The young woman was in clothes similar to the day they'd seen her. Gym shorts, a short, tight T-shirt and tennis shoes. Her hair, blond and long, like Jessica's, hung in her eyes.

"No, I didn't."

"We know that you've been messaging with Clint Johnson as recently as last week."

"So? Clint didn't know I was sending those text messages to his ex-wife. And he didn't have nothing to do with me buying the phone either. He didn't even know I had it."

Brian's circulation was nearly cut off as Jessica's fingers squeezed so tightly he half expected a bone to break.

"This isn't about the text messages you sent to Jessica Johnson, Bonnie."

"Then what is it?" she asked. "It's not illegal for someone to message with a person in prison. Clint told me, and I looked it up, too."

"It is when the prisoner isn't following the laws for prisoner communication."

She looked down. Bit her lip.

"Clint said he was the only one who could get in trouble for that. I wasn't doing nothing wrong."

Other than the stinging she was creating in his hand, Jessica hadn't moved. He wasn't even sure if she'd blinked.

Listening intently, he wasn't sure he had. What in the hell had been in those messages? And why wasn't Anderson grilling her about Brooke?

Where was Jessica's baby?

Had the detective forgotten they were working a kidnapping case?

Anderson had said he'd thought it best for Jessica to hear firsthand what Bonnie had to say…

He had to remember…yeah, he was Jess's personally hired detective, but Brooke…and Jessica…had been Anderson's case for a whole lot longer than Brian had been around. He suspected Jessica had become personal to the city detective, too. He'd bowed to the other man's wishes.

"Where's the baby, Bonnie?"

There. Right there. That's what they needed. Brian stared down the woman in custody as though he was the one interrogating her. Didn't matter that Bonnie Lichen couldn't see him through the glass.

"I don't know anything about a baby!" The young woman's eyes opened wide. Imploringly. "I told that private detective. Clint never said nothing to me about having a baby."

Clint. Like she knew him well. Personally.

Not like she was a mere accomplice in a human trafficking or disposal deal.

He should have caught the nuance immediately. Would have if he hadn't been so busy seeing Clint from his ex-wife's point of view. From the feelings Jessica portrayed toward Clint.

"The man kidnaps his own child. He comes to you in Lincoln that very first day. Eats in your restaurant. You saw him at least three times after that…"

Three times? He glanced at Jessica. Stone-faced, she stared through the glass. They knew of two other times, three total, in the diner…

"…and yet you know nothing about the baby. Tell me, how does that work?"

Bonnie's expression broke down. Her lips trembled and she started to cry. To sob.

The truth was coming. Brian wasn't ready to hear it.

He knew Jess wasn't ready. Just like he knew he couldn't do a thing to change any of it. Not his mom. His dad. Not Brooke. Or the fact that he and Jess were on different paths in life and soon to say goodbye.

The news was coming and he'd have to leave her to the people in her life to console her shattered heart.

Because to stay would bring her more heartache in the long run. He wasn't a "have kids" family kind of guy.

But he put his arm around her, pulling her close, half holding her up, as Bonnie gathered herself enough to be able to speak.

"I swear to you." She looked straight at Anderson, her tone strong in spite of the thickness due to tears. "I had no idea he even had a kid, let alone that he'd kidnapped her. I just found out when that detective and… Clint's ex… went to my gram's house. On my grandmother's life, I did not know. That first day, in the café, he just… I don't know, something about him got to me. He was so…lost. Kind and polite and…needy. He was so grateful for every little thing I did to tend to him…"

Jessica's body leaned further into his. A glance at her face told him that if her emotions had been in cold freeze seconds before, they no longer were.

"I don't know… I just felt for him. So I slipped him my phone number. He called that night and we talked for hours."

"Where was he?"

"In some motel…in Barneysville. He said he was from Missouri and was in Barneysville on business. Doing a job. He's an IT guru."

Jessica started. He glanced over at her. "Charita…one of the women I talked to when I was selling Brain Play Toys…she's from there…"

"That night when he called, what did you talk about, Bonnie?" Anderson's next question came sternly.

"His ex-wife. That Jessica woman that the detective brought to my house. Clint gave her everything he had, worked multiple jobs, spent his whole life trying to please her, but she became like this workaholic. She's a stockbroker or something, and hoarded her money. Clint told me how money meant more to her than anything—even him—and when he lost his job, she divorced him. He was just so…lost…and so I told him to come back to the café the next day, and he did, and he called me again that night, and came the next day, too. I stayed in the back, mostly, when he was at the café, so that Gram didn't get suspicious. I knew she didn't like him, because he was kind of off, but I knew why and…"

"The baby, Bonnie. Get to the baby."

"I…don't…know…anything…about…no…baby." The young woman grit her teeth on that one. Then hiccupped and shook her head. "I swear to God. If I'd known he'd kidnapped a kid, no way would I have—"

Her abrupt stop grabbed Brian.

And Jessica, too, based on the way she was clenching his arm with her free hand.

"Would have what? What did you do?"

"I invited him to my room. I was renting a little one-room cottage like place behind a farmhouse down the street from Gram's. We…he…spent the night, okay? I slept with him. And… I thought we fell in love. But then he left the next day and I didn't hear from him for, like, a year. I tried to call him a couple of times, but the number he'd called me on didn't work no more. Then, out of the blue, he texted me. Said that he hadn't been in touch because he was in prison. He said that his ex had claimed

that he stole from her, that she framed him, but that he didn't do it."

"And you didn't see the news? The baby's face was plastered on the nightly news all over the state for the first week of her disappearance."

"I don't watch the news. It's all bad and they just try to scare you. And, besides, that cottage didn't have no hook-ups. I wouldn't have paid for internet anyways. I was saving for culinary school."

"And he didn't tell you what he stole from Jessica?"

Bonnie looked him straight in the eye as she shook her head. "That one call from prison…it's the only time we actually got to talk, and mostly we talked about how he was faring, you know, in there. I figured she was claiming he stole money, since that's all she cared about. He swore that he didn't do it, and that's all I needed. I wasn't going to be like her and grill him and accuse him or nothing. He said that she was just trying to get out of paying him spousal support. He said that he'd been going to Bible study classes in prison, and thinking about me all the time, and wanted to know if there was a chance for us. He said that when he gets out of prison, he's going to help me with the café. We're going to run it together and he's going to get it online so that we can ship pies and things, too…"

Brian's shoulders dropped. His gut felt sick.

And Jessica slumped against him.

Jessica had to get out of there. To walk away from something that wasn't going to lead her any closer to Brooke.

Clint had slept with another woman the night before he'd come over, swearing that he'd been out fishing, fig-

uring out his life, and wanted to recommit to her and Brooke, only to find their daughter had been kidnapped.

After everything she'd done, even after the divorce, to try and keep him happy, to tend to his so many needs, he'd taken her daughter, and then he'd been unfaithful to her.

Her mind couldn't accept what it had just heard.

And yet it did, too. In the recesses. She knew Bonnie wasn't lying. She just didn't want to know. She'd wanted to believe that, in some way, Clint still needed her enough to be telling the truth when he'd said Brooke was safe and being loved. Knowing that he still needed Jess had helped her believe that Brooke was okay, too.

Not only was the fiend exhibiting signs of a true narcissist, he'd been systematically lying to her, playing her mind, ever since. Every week—for sixty-seven weeks—telling her loved her and was helping them get their family back...

She'd known he'd been manipulating her. She'd known he was enjoying his little game. But even as she'd known there'd been no way, ever, that she'd have taken him back, ever let him around Brooke or her again, she'd still thought his sick actions were motivated by the fact that he really thought, deep down, he needed her.

And all along, he'd been carrying on an affair with Bonnie, planning a new life with her.

She couldn't...didn't...

"I have to go," she said, stepping away from Brian and stumbling on her path to the door. Brian's hand reached out to the knob—not to her, thank goodness. She had to go. No one was going to hold her back—not even him.

He didn't touch her as they left the station. She heard him tell someone to have Detective Anderson call him when he was free, as she pushed out the door and felt the

hot afternoon sun hit her face. Turning her skin up to the blinding rays, she took a breath.

And another. Liked that she couldn't open her eyes. That if she did, she wouldn't see anything but shining light.

Wanted to just float right up to it.

And heard a car door slam.

She was in a parking lot. At the police station. She took a step. Her heel caught on a rock and she started to trip, but Brian was right there. Catching her.

And she let him.

Just for that one trip-up.

She let him catch her.

Chapter 25

Brian spent the drive home trying to come up with something to say. Somehow promising Jess that he'd find Brooke just didn't seem to fit the bill.

He was going to uncover what happened to that baby girl. He wouldn't stop until he did. But anything he'd tell her at that point rang in his brain like more of the empty promises Clint had been feeding her.

The way she sat, all straight-backed and stone-faced, he wasn't sure she'd even hear him. It was like she was trapped in a world that didn't include him, or anything normal like Thursday after-work traffic, stoplights, or even what they might have for dinner.

All he could do was watch her in torment.

Unable to help.

"I need to be alone," she said as she let them in the kitchen door and then just kept walking, through the dining room and down the hall that led to her office.

He watched her go, knew he had to let her go, and ached like he'd never ached before.

So he went to work. It's what he did.

The only way he had to ease the pain.

The whole Bonnie trail. The prison computer hack. Hudson and his team's work. The threatening messages to Jess. Lincoln. Birds of Paradise. None of it had had anything to do with Brooke.

Except that…they knew Clint had to have passed the baby off, or done whatever he'd done with her, before the night he'd spent with Bonnie. So that was one less day on the timeline.

He deleted the fourth day from all of his spreadsheets.

It didn't change much. Gave him no clearer view to the baby's fate.

But at least there was a little less to stare at.

Jessica's meeting with Clint the next day lurked on his shoulder, filling him with a quiet desperation as he forced his mind to see something differently. Something new.

He went back to the clues—homing in on the fourth ones. And on Barneysville in particular. Street names. Business names. All of it.

Maybe the clues weren't biblical references—though Bonnie had mentioned Clint attending Bible study as Brian and Jess had surmised. But maybe they all added up to something else. Something that started in Barneysville or through Clint's meeting with Bonnie. And it could be that the Birds of Paradise clue had just been a dig at Jessica. Clint smearing his affair in her face—on the off chance she'd figure it out.

Running internet searches on several minimized and open windows, each with one of the patterned clues, he brought up screen after screen, reading everything that popped up. In Barneysville and beyond. Opening links

he hadn't seen before. Using less-known search engines and social media apps.

Grasping at straws.

Trying not to think of the woman suffering down the hall.

And he couldn't seem to escape her, either. He knew the feeling so well. Sitting down the hall, helpless…unable to solve his parents' problems. Him being there, them having a son, a family, hadn't been enough.

Love wasn't enough.

That feeling…right there…was why he'd chosen the life he had.

Anderson called. They'd let Bonnie Lichen go. The detective was planning another visit to see Clint in the morning. Talked about charges being filed for the computer hacking, but didn't say what they'd be. And he had his team scouring motels in Barneysville, looking for surveillance cameras, showing Clint's picture around—all the things Brian would be doing if he were a cop.

The detective said he'd send Brian whatever they got, and keep him updated, day or night.

Whatever had happened to Brooke Johnson…the answers would be found.

One way or another.

That left Brian sitting at Jessica's dining table, scrolling on his screen, certain that her baby girl was there someplace, trying to tell him what her mother needed to know.

And…*the rising star.* The biblical reference to a savior…

Sitting forward, Brian read, visions of Clint Johnson rising up to enrage him.

When he'd finished clicking, and learning, he went to find Jessica.

* * *

It was not going to beat her. She was strong. Able-bodied, and there was no way pieces of inanimate wood were going to prevent her from doing what she had to do.

Her daughter needed a bed.

These pieces of wood were it.

She had one side and end of the crib off. Couldn't get one bolt each on the remaining pieces unscrewed. Had to turn the thing to get to leg screws that were mingling with the carpet. She'd remove all the screws she could and then get back to the problem ones.

Except that the solid wood, awkward half piece of put-together furniture wasn't cooperating. With a side and end gone, the piece wasn't weighted in any way she could lower, push or roll, and have it move in the way she wanted it to do.

For a second, she felt the prick of tears. Refused to give in to them.

Her daughter was going to need a bed.

Period.

She tried again, got what was left of the crib up on one of the remaining legs, and the whole thing started to spin. Out of control, it was going to fall and…

It didn't.

It stopped midstream.

Halted by the male hand that grabbed it just in time.

He couldn't have just walked in…

"How long have you been standing there?" she asked.

"Just a few minutes."

"I need to do this myself."

"No, you don't, Jess. What Clint did to you was all targeted at you. For a lot of years. That, you had to do yourself. But this…" He spread his arm wide, as if encompassing the room, or maybe the whole world, her

whole life. "Look around you, at the teams of professionals who are giving their all to help you."

She wanted to argue. To stomp her foot and order him out of her home at the top of her voice.

"I'm here," he told her, his tone soft but with an odd note. "And I'm not leaving until you've got the answers you hired me to find."

He was promising.

And perhaps was determined to show her that she could rely on him not to let her down.

She didn't need his reassurance. She already knew she could trust him.

She needed more from herself. How did she love so completely and have it all go so wrong?

"How could I have let this happen?" she asked him. Not with a whimper or a whine. And not just talking about the crib either.

He seemed to think that's what she meant, though, as he asked for her screwdriver, tipped the crib, and tackled the first of the screws she hadn't been able to get out. With only one of them gone, and the remaining side off, the crib was easier to manage.

At work on the second screw, he said, "You didn't let anything happen. You met someone, opened your heart, and had no way of knowing that the person you were with had a very sick side to him. Clint's not a decent human being, Jess. He showed you what he needed you to see until he had you on the hook, until you were married. And then he made things happen, to suit him, and you did your best to do damage control. Every step of the way, from what I can see."

She got another screw undone. And another. Allowing herself the satisfaction of dropping a crib leg to the floor. Thinking about what Brian had said.

Her life had been all about damage control. Recognizing the truth she'd been unable to see, absorbing it, her heart settled a bit.

It didn't have any of the answers she had to have. Didn't ease the pain. But she…felt a bit better about herself. Could feel smidgeons of trust there. Making her stronger.

And was glad again, even with all that had happened, that she'd hired Brian. That he was there.

"Thank you," she said as he removed the final screw from the crib, freeing all parts to be rearranged, or stored, as necessary.

"I'm guessing we're now going to build this?" he asked, picking up the instruction booklet she'd had open on the floor.

"That's the plan." The new one. Her original intent had been to build it alone.

But he was right. She wasn't alone.

Starting to feel more like herself, it occurred to her that he'd come looking for her…why else would he have been watching her struggle with the crib? Why would he have been there in time to save her?

Again. Visions of flying bullets hit her, followed by another surge of gratitude toward the man in the room with her.

"Did you need me for something?" she asked, getting outside herself to help him if she could. "You were coming to find me…"

"I found the rising star."

Holding a piece of a trundle bed siding, she stared at him. "You…what?" She set the board down, stood there staring at him. He'd…and he was only then telling her?

The shake of his head bothered her. Like he was… what? Irritated with her? Blowing her off?

She was only a job to him, but this was her *life* they were dealing with.

"It has nothing to do with Brooke," he told her, but she wanted to reach that conclusion for herself.

"What is it?"

"The kind of bar you wouldn't get near for all the money in the world. Fifteen miles outside of Little Rock. Its clientele have been busted for prostitution, for allegations of rape, and dealing drugs, from what I could see, comparing names from the prison database. I'm guessing there's cartel money behind it."

Okay, so now he was just fishing. He had to be.

"Clint would never get near a place like that."

And if Brian wanted her to believe there was something else going on there, the selling of…

No. Clint would just not do something like that. Have an affair with a sweet, naïve woman who fell for his neediness and was willing to pander to him? Yeah. She could see that.

But…

"I told you I don't think it has anything to do with Brooke, Jess…"

His tone was too kind. It rubbed her wrong. She waited for him to explain himself. Or not.

She was fine to just let it go.

They'd had a rough night. Nerves were frayed.

Time was passing.

"It was the last clue before I arrived in Fayetteville. I'm guessing that Clint sensed your restlessness. He knew you were reaching breaking point. Maybe he didn't know you'd hire me. He could have just decided that you were going to give up on him. That his money tree was no longer going to produce for him. And he was at least going to get the pleasure out of making you pay for ruining his life. I checked prison records, Jess. It seems too much

of a coincidence that the blue barn and The Rising Star both had people in prison, minimum security, like Clint, at the same time he's been there, and he just happens to put you on to them with the clues."

"What are you saying?"

"I don't know. That he overheard talk. Or that someone's helping him. Either way, if you'd found the place, you'd have gone right in there, showing Clint's picture around..."

Probably.

"I think it was just like the blue barn. His game has turned sick to the point of depraved. He was setting you up to get hurt. Can you imagine what could have happened to you, walking in a place like The Rising Star all alone?"

"I'd have been fine."

Because she'd have stayed by the door. Or...

"Even if a couple of big brutes started to circle around you?"

He was talking movie stuff, not real life.

"Or what if one of them offered to help the pretty lady, just to get close to her...?"

Shivering, she picked up the trundle side. He'd hit a little too close.

Was being paid to think outside the box.

Brian let it go after that. He stayed with her, though. Helping her build Brooke's toddler bed. Even if he believed, as she figured he probably did, as he'd warned, that Brooke might not ever be home to sleep in it.

And as soon as it was done, before she even had the sheets on it, he headed toward the door.

"Thank you." She had to give him that.

He turned.

"I mean it. For...everything."

He nodded. Watched her a second longer and was gone.

Chapter 26

Brian wasn't going to sleep with Jessica that night. He wasn't going to go walking into her room after she'd gone to bed. Not again.

And wasn't sure he could lie with her, in honesty, with the problem of Clint hanging over them.

He didn't want her anywhere near her weekly Clint meeting.

Because he knew in his gut that Clint was going to send her into more danger.

And she'd go running into it, head-on.

Back out at the dining room table, he continued to work. Growing more frantic with the knowledge that if he didn't do what he did, and get the job done, Jess might not be alive for another week.

"I know you think that Clint isn't helping me find Brooke. That he's doing the exact opposite by sending me on wild-goose chases, and wasting valuable investigative resources, so I won't find her."

Her voice startled him. Pulled him out of the deep focus.

She'd spoken from the entry to the dining room. Was wearing the yellow negligee thing again.

Not fair.

She didn't know he'd decided to sleep alone.

"But if not for those clues, we'd still have nothing," she told him. "We wouldn't have found Birds of Paradise, or spoken to Bonnie, wouldn't have known about Clint's burner phone, found in the cell search due to the text messages Bonnie was sending me. We wouldn't have known that he's been hacking the prison computer to message with her the past few months. Or know that he stayed in Barneysville after he took Brooke. We wouldn't have found the Brandywines, or known that Clint was possibly getting information from other prisoners…"

She wasn't wrong.

But…

"He's ramping up, Jess. Like you said, he noticed a difference in you. And by tomorrow afternoon, he'll know that you know about Bonnie. He's out to hurt you, not help you. It needs to stop before he succeeds. You see now what he is, what he does. If you refuse to meet with him tomorrow, cut him off, and with Bonnie cutting him off…he's going to come unglued. That's when we have a chance for someone getting the truth out of him. Especially if he wants to gain any goodwill from you…"

When she stood there, calm, nodding, he had hope. Real hope.

"As you say, he's going to know his gig is up, which is all the more reason for me to meet with him," she said, and his heart sank. "Anytime he gets caught at anything, his response is to talk his way out of it. He'll be eager to explain to me, to get me to understand, to forgive him.

I've got a better-than-average chance that he'll give me something real tomorrow."

"Or he'll get you killed."

"If I don't meet with him, and he comes unglued, he may kill himself."

And take her last hope of finding out what he'd done with Brooke. He didn't need to hear her say it to know that was what she'd been thinking.

"He's threatened suicide before. If he truly believes that everyone is against him, that he can't find a way out..."

Clint had lost her. But Brian wasn't going to win with her either...

He looked up, needing a miracle to happen before the next afternoon. Needing to be better than he was.

"Come to bed with me, please?" She wasn't begging. Or flirting either.

She needed him. For the moment. To get through the night.

And truth be told, he needed her, too.

Brian had no idea what woke him up. Feeling Jess beside him, he lay there, eyes still closed, fully alert as he listened. Was someone in the house?

He'd left his gun on the nightstand, within arm's reach.

But all was silent.

And it hit him. What had woken him.

He'd been dreaming...

He knew where pieces fit.

Feeling as though he had gallons of caffeine rushing through him, he slid carefully from the bed where Jess had ridden him with desperation the night before.

And had cried a little as she'd fallen asleep in his arms.

He didn't want to wake her.

Twenty minutes later, he went out into the garage and called Anderson, completely unapologetic for waking the man in the middle of the night. He immediately sent over the files he'd just compiled and sent to his phone. So he'd have them on the road.

He had no proof. Just a whole mess of puzzle pieces that fit together.

He might never find Brooke. He wasn't inhuman. He was as fallible as the next guy.

He wouldn't quit trying.

But he could fail.

He knew he'd found the way the pieces fit.

And would never be Jess's knight in shining armor, even if he'd managed to find her answers.

"Brian?"

In the flowing yellow robe again, she opened the garage door. Saw him standing there with his phone, and tears in his eyes.

"Yeah."

"I heard the garage door. What are you doing out here?"

"Calling Anderson."

"Why?" She hadn't come any closer.

He didn't want to answer her. The more he thought, the more he told himself he was grasping at straws.

And while his gut told him he was not, that he'd just solved another case, for some reason, he couldn't let himself accept the possibility of victory.

More, he couldn't bear to watch Jess be disappointed again.

"What's going on?"

He had to tell her.

What if he was wrong?

"Brian? You're scaring me. Come inside."

Because he couldn't very well head out in the under-

wear he'd pulled on as he'd left her bed, he did as she asked. Glad to give her something she wanted.

Even while he knew, no matter what did or didn't pan out from his fully put-together puzzle, he was losing her.

She put on coffee in spite of the fact that it was only four in the morning. Four and a half hours before the bell rang, at which time she'd be fully engrossed at her desk.

That would get her through until time for Clint's call.

No matter what Brian thought, life would go on as it had until she had Brooke home.

"What's wrong?" she asked again as Brian, coming back from the hallway pulling on his pants, joined her in the kitchen.

"I just had an idea, needed to run it by Anderson."

"And?" Something was different about him. Not in a good way.

"He's going to check it out."

"In the middle of the night?"

He shrugged.

Had he angered the detective, getting him out of bed in the middle of the night?

She'd woken Anderson a couple of times. The man had always been kind to her about it.

But she was a grieving mother, not an investigator on a payroll.

"Is this because of Clint? Because I don't agree with you about today's call?" He'd been weird ever since they'd left the police station the evening before.

He looked at her, kind of assessing like. Didn't answer.

Took the filled coffee cup she handed him. Turned back toward the dining room. As though he was just going to leave her there.

"I have a right to do what I need to do, Brian. I'm of sound mind and body, and even if what I believe is the

best choice turns out to be wrong, I still have to do what my heart tells me to do." She heard the words.

Was kind of shocked by them.

But couldn't deny their truth.

"I know."

"So...what? This is it? We can't be...we aren't... You're done with me because of it?"

"Ah, Jess, of course not." He sat, so she did, too.

"I'm not *done with you.*" He kind of mimicked the way she said it. Not in an insulting way, but more in understanding. "Not yet. But we both knew that us...you and me...wasn't ever going to be a permanent thing. We've known all along that we'd both be done with it."

"So you are done." Panic filled her. She pushed it back. Knew he wouldn't quit her job.

Like she'd known Clint? The man who'd been having an affair by mail the entire time he'd been swearing he wanted his family back with Jess?

He'd never been going to get that family, she'd have died before she'd ever have let that happen, but she'd believed he wanted it.

"You can't be done," she said. "You wouldn't leave without finding Brooke." Just like her heart was telling her she couldn't not take Clint's call, she knew the truth of what she'd just said.

"No, I wouldn't." He grinned, a sad, tired smile, as he met her gaze.

And she wanted to believe that everything was going to be fine with them.

But knew it wasn't.

He had to tell her. Had to give her time to call for someone else to handle her clients' affairs that last day before the market went on its weekly two-day hiatus.

Just in case.

If there was no news, if he was wrong, it would be better for her to be working. Oblivious.

And that wasn't his choice to make.

Just like Jess wasn't his to love.

The word knocked him blind for a second.

He didn't do love.

It wasn't enough.

He came in to help where love failed.

Not to keep a woman's heart from breaking any further. That was the impossible task.

She was in her room, making the bed. "I put some pieces of the puzzle together." He stood in the doorway, leaning on the jamb, his coffee still in hand.

Turning, she stared at him. Sat on the edge of the partially made bed, her hands in her lap. With her hair all tousled from sleep, and no makeup on, she looked… like an angel.

Something pure and sweet and mighty, too.

"Do they, um, do they fit?" Her voice was froggy. She swallowed.

He had to join her. Didn't even question the why of it. Sitting down next to her, close but not touching, he shrugged. Put his coffee cup on the nightstand next to hers, and met her wide, worried gaze.

"I think they do," he told her. "Anderson is checking things out now."

"In the middle of the night?"

He knew what his nod was going to tell her. He gave it to her.

"And?" He'd worked a lot of cases, some with not good endings, a lot with not good endings, and he'd never seen such stark terror before.

"She might be alive."

There.

He'd given her the hope she'd so desperately needed.

And if he was wrong…

Jessica's head roared so loudly with sound through cotton, she barely heard his words. She stared at him, watching his lips.

Read the same message there that she was hearing.

"'Might be'?" Heart on overdrive, she could feel the blood rushing through her face. Her temples. Pounding in her fingertips.

"If I'm right."

Why wasn't he more excited?

"Tell me."

"It's kind of far-fetched, Jess. Nothing like anything I've ever come up with before. But…considering Clint… his irrational need to have everything his own way, his inability to accept that he can't always have what he wants…and his lack of control over the childish need to lash out…"

Yeah. Yeah. She was there with him. Clint was all those things. And…

She wanted to ask him to get right to the point. Needed what air she had just to stay conscious.

If it had been Clint talking, she'd have her guard up. But with Brian…she trusted every word he was saying.

Didn't care if it was far-fetched.

"I think he took her on the spur of the moment. He'd been there in the house that morning. He had to leave. He knew you were going back to your room to tend to Brooke. To nurse her. An intimacy of which I'm guessing he was jealous, thinking as he did that your body was his…"

She nodded again, captivated by how right he was

about things she'd never spoken of…and by the hope that she wanted him to keep alive as long as he could.

Once she heard his theory, she might know why it wouldn't be right and then…

"And once he had her, he didn't know what to do next. He's not one to have planned it all out. When he's not happy, his thoughts are more in the moment because, for him, only the current moment matters. How he's feeling right then."

Again, pretty accurate.

"So he drives her around, maybe she's awake, crying, but she falls asleep. He ends up in Lincoln that first day, she's asleep in the car seat. He's hungry, needs to eat. To get away from what he's done for a few minutes. Maybe he thinks he'd be better able to figure out what to do if she's not right there. But, as you said, he's not the type to hurt a baby…"

Good. Good. "Go on." The words stuck in her throat and she coughed.

"He sees the Birds of Paradise. The big window. Figures if he parks his truck in front of it, he can leave her in it and keep an eye out to make sure nothing happens to her. The worst thing would be she'd wake up and cry some more, and he wouldn't be having to listen to every minute of it."

He paused. Met her gaze. And didn't let go.

"He meets Bonnie that day," he told her. "She nurtures him. Makes him feel like you used to."

He stopped talking. She didn't look away. Couldn't find a thing off about the picture he was painting.

"She gives him her phone number and now he's got a reason to hang on. To hang around. Her interest buys him some time. He can hide out with the baby, get to know Bonnie, and maybe she'll help him figure it all out. Or,

at least, she made him feel better in the moment while he decided what to do next."

Right. He was right. It's exactly what Clint would do. With absolutely no thought to Jessica at home, dying a little more every moment her baby girl was missing…

"He finds an out-of-the-way motel, probably one that takes cash. He finally gets the baby to sleep—he's fed her before. He knows how to read to her. She knows him. Falls asleep. He calls Bonnie and they talk half the night."

"She…she did know him. He…fed her sometimes, during the day, when I was working. I pumped and there were always bottles in the freezer…"

"One day becomes two and then three. He's been watching the news. He's seen his picture plastered all over the major sources. He's getting desperate, not sure how long he can keep driving in to see Bonnie. And then, on that third day, he knows she's going to be staying in the back, other than when she comes out to tend to him. And because he's paranoid at this point, and doesn't want his face to be recognized, he picks up a newspaper from a table by the door and buries his face in it the whole time he's there."

Brian had her completely captivated. She had to hear what happened next.

"But…why, then, does he take the paper with him?" he asked.

And she tried to find his answer. Had to find his answer.

"Because he'd read something in it that caught his attention," he said.

Relieved that he'd found his own answer, realizing that, of course, he had or he wouldn't have called Anderson and they wouldn't be sitting there…

"This is where it gets dicey, Jess. And why I didn't want to tell you until we know more."

Scared again. Terrified. "Tell me." She trusted him. He didn't come up with harebrained schemes.

Or run out when the going got tough.

"The paper was the *Barneysville Weekly Gazette*. It didn't have anything about the kidnapping because it had been published the night before he took Brooke. What it did have was an article about a car crash somewhere east of Barneysville, near a town called Slader."

"I've never heard of it."

And if the accident had happened before the kidnapping, which it had since it was in that paper, then she didn't have to worry that…

"There'd been a one car crash. A divorced couple and their baby had gone over a guardrail and into a river. They'd been in a custody dispute and, at first, it was believed that they'd been arguing and that that had been the cause of the crash. But when searching only turned up the body of the mother, when they pulled up the car and saw that the windows had been open, that the river's current had been running through the car…"

"The river runs through it." Oh God. "The river runs through it."

His glance dropped. He stared ahead of him as he said, "They figured the other two bodies had been swept away, but after a week of searching, not even finding articles of clothing for either the father or the infant girl, authorities put out a 'be on the lookout' for the father. Theory was that he'd either staged the crash, planning to kidnap his daughter, or the crash happened and he'd seen his opportunity. Then, before they could investigate further—"

"I remember this." Jessica jumped up. Paced to the dresser and back. Twice. Fast. "The baby turned up…in

another town…where the maternal grandmother lived. She was left in a baby drawer at a church…you know, those box things they have if you want to abandon your baby, with a note that had her name and the words 'I'm sorry. I will love Annabelle forever.'"

Reality hadn't caught up with her yet as tears streamed down her face. Her heart was in her throat. Hands on her hips as Brian stood up from the bed and she faced him. "They thought the father left her there. I remember because by the time that all came out, Clint had been arrested for kidnapping and I was so glad to see that at least one father did the right thing. It gave me hope that Clint really would have, too." She stopped. Heart pounding. Stared at him. "Are…you…telling me…you think Clint put our baby, Brooke, in that drawer?"

His nod undid her.

Sobs tore up out of her, cutting off any ability to speak. There was no thought. No burst of joy. No wondering if it made sense. No thought to the possibilities. Just the release of eighteen months of pent-up grief.

She had an answer that she could accept.

And Brian was there, wrapping his arms around her, holding her up.

Chapter 27

Jessica was doing just as he'd feared she'd do. Buzzing around the house, conquering dust bunnies and glass smudges, stopping every few minutes to cry a little. She'd showered, put on what she called her bumblebee outfit—the one she'd been wearing the first day they'd gone clue hunting together. A yellow short-sleeved, button-down shirt with puffy sleeves and her skinny black pants and black tennis shoes. She'd called someone to handle her client base for the day.

Had already cleaned the baby's room from top to bottom.

She was speeding faster than was good for her, all the way up to cloud nine, not that he blamed her, and could only hope that he hadn't just set her up for one hell of a fall.

He'd just come out of the shower. Putting on the dress pants and shirt he'd worn the first day he'd met her—maybe in accordance with a side plan to be ready to head

out to his own life and whatever job needed to be done immediately, no matter how small—he found her in the kitchen, shining her ceramic stovetop.

"I need to get to the store," she told him. "I'll need food. I have nothing in the cupboard for a two-year old, and she's going to need clothes. And bigger diapers..."

"Jess..."

"No. I know. Don't tell me. You could be wrong." She faced him then, looking at him as she had in bed that first night, like he was far more than just a hired hand. "But you could be right, Brian, and I have to be prepared. I should have already taken care of all of this, you know. I need to be ready."

She was the strongest woman he'd ever known. And seemed about as fragile as glass right then. Like, if Anderson called with bad news, she might just shatter.

"Even if I'm right, it's going to take at least twenty-four hours before any kind of DNA test can come back. And that's assuming the grandmother allows one. She hadn't seen the baby since birth, but she's taken on full responsibility for her. Is protective of her. If she doesn't allow the test, they'll need to get a warrant and—"

She was shaking her head, her eyes bright with the sheen of tears. "Brooke was born with a little birthmark on her elbow. It looks more like a freckle, except that, I have one, too."

Turning her arm, she showed him the tiny, kind of oblong spot on the underside of her left elbow. "See? It wasn't enough of an identifier to put on any of the posters when she went missing, but Anderson knows about it. He has a picture of it."

Her hope was contagious. They'd been over all the clues. Every single one of them had fallen into place, which he'd known before he'd called Anderson. Even

the butterflies are free—the baby in the car accident had been wearing a butterfly onesie the day of the crash, and had been wearing an identical-looking one the day she'd been returned. The blanket with her had been identical, too, matching up with "her blankie made it" clue. Photos of both had been publicized during the first frantic week of searching for bodies. So searchers would know if they'd found pertinent items of clothing. And so Clint would have known what to shop for.

And the one about wrinkles…a grandmother's face, an older face.

What if Brian was right? He'd found the missing pieces!

His heart soared for a second. With a lightness he didn't recognize. He smiled at Jess.

And wanted her happiness to last forever.

The second Brian's phone rang, Jessica's heart plummeted.

Staring at his pocket, at the hand pulling the device out of his pocket, she didn't want to know. Didn't want her time, suspended outside of hell, to end.

The house wasn't completely clean yet. She still had the kitchen floor. And the laundry room. The garage could use some work. Maybe the lawn. She hadn't been shopping.

And couldn't suck in air until she knew.

"It's Anderson." That early in the day, she'd figured.

Brian answered with a "Hold on, I'm putting you on speakerphone."

He tapped his phone screen, walking toward her as he did so.

"I can't believe I'm about to say this." The man sounded upset. Overcome with emotion. "I'm in Bloomsdale with the grandmother. And…it's her. It's Brooke."

She sagged. Lost every bit of strength she had. Brian was there. Caught her with an arm around her waist. Supported her weight against him with one arm as he held the phone.

She'd…what…? "Oh my God," she huffed. Dragging in air to ask, "Are you sure?" with another short-of-breath puff.

"The freckle is exactly as the picture shows. Identical to yours."

He'd taken the photo on his search. Duane Anderson had kept the photo. And had taken it with him.

Tears flooded her eyes then. "Thank you," she sort of mumbled. Looking at the phone, at Brian. "Thank both of you sooooo…" There was supposed to have been a "much" there, but she couldn't get it out for the sobs taking over her airways.

Her precious baby girl was alive.

She wasn't losing her mind. She'd been right all along.

Brooke was coming home.

Brian saw Jess fall to the couch. Listened as Anderson talked about finding the house. The grandmother answering the door.

And saw the second when Jess came back to herself. She was a mother. Had a job to do. It was like he could read the resolution in her eyes.

Her own needs would have to wait.

She stood, joined him at the phone.

"When can I see her? Should we come there? How far is Bloomsdale?" The third question, uttered on top of the other two without breath in between, was posed to Brian. He knew because Jess had looked at him as she'd asked it.

"We have to work all that out," Anderson said, his tone sounding more like the detective she'd come to know over

the past year and a half. "I'm outside the home right now. Sonya, one of my detectives is inside with the child. The grandmother is obviously upset, though insistent that you get Brooke back immediately. She goes by the name Annabelle right now."

When the stark expression crossed Jess's face, Brian caught a whole new wave of tough moments ahead for her.

Things she'd mentioned once before. Late at night. After lovemaking one night. About how her own daughter wouldn't know her. And that Jess could walk by her on the street and not even know the baby she'd given birth to.

"It's just momentary blips," he'd reached down to whisper in her ear. Where the words came from, he didn't know, but they seemed to work. She straightened. Nodded.

Held her own weight.

That kept her away from him.

He'd known it would happen. That she'd move away from his body. Stand on her own two feet.

He'd had no idea what a kick it would be when she did.

"What do you want us to do?" she asked then, almost sounding like the woman he'd first met. Take charge. Letting nothing get in her way.

"Should we come there?" she asked again. "It makes sense that we would so she sees me in the house she's known. Sees her grandmother smiling as she's leaving with me. Maybe I could talk to the grandmother, too. I know Brooke isn't the biological granddaughter she lost, but she's spent the last eighteen or so months taking care of her. Loving her. She's family, and I'll be happy to have her be a permanent part of Brooke's life. Not just for the transition, though that would be best for Brooke, probably, if she's willing, but..."

She glanced up at Brian then. He didn't know what she saw as she met his gaze, but her tirade stopped abruptly.

"I, um, apologize, Detective," she said with a shrug at Brian. "What do you want us to do?"

Us. We. She kept using those words.

They weren't an *us*. A *we*.

His job was done. As soon as they were off his phone, he'd put in a call to his team leader at Sierra's Web. Hopefully get a job starting yet that night. Or that weekend at the very least.

"I'd like you to make the trip here, if that's okay with you both. I agree that it would be better for the child if you're the one who takes her out of the house, rather than a stranger she may cling to and then lose in another couple of hours." Right, that made sense. And Brian supposed he should drive her. Jess wasn't in any state to be driving herself. Would be less so during those first hours after she was reunited with her daughter.

And, considering all that he and Jess had…shared… over the past weeks, he kind of wanted to actually see her reunion with her daughter. See her happy and at peace, with Brooke back in her arms.

"I've got something I'd like to discuss with you when you get here, Brian, if you're open to hearing it," Anderson continued.

"Of course." There'd be reports. Follow up. His jobs didn't usually involve such close contact with the police, but he knew procedures.

Had grown up with them.

They were the symbol of job's end.

She had blond hair, wispy curls of it hanging over her neck, forehead and ears. Like it had never been cut.

Jessica filled with gratitude for that choice. It was

something she could hold on to. Something simple like haircuts. A first haircut. Something nonthreatening…

The little girl's chubby, somewhat stumbling legs, chased after a ball an older woman had just rolled for her. With every step Jessica took from the street across the front yard, her heart burst a little more. With some grief for all she'd lost and with incredible joy, too.

Lillie Wilson knew they were there. And Jess's heart broke a little more, not for herself or Brooke, but for the woman who'd lost her daughter and now, possibly, her granddaughter, too.

Brian had pointed out, on the two-hour drive to Bloomsdale, that the woman's ex-son-in-law had probably taken his daughter as had been originally thought until Clint had deposited Brooke in that safe drawer. Maybe Lillie's son-in-law ran with his daughter, maybe not. She had a right to know. With her daughter dead, she had legal right to access to her biological grandchild. And Anderson had assured Lillie that they'd do everything they could to find that little girl, Annabelle.

Still, Lillie was losing day-to-day access to the little girl she'd loved as her own for a year and a half.

Brooke squealed as she raced the last couple of steps to the ball, tripped and rolled over with it. Jessica's eyes welled yet again.

In pink shorts and a matching pink-and-white-striped T-shirt, Brooke looked abundant. Healthy. Well-loved.

Just as Clint had promised. Whether he'd just been guessing, assuming, or had followed Annabelle's story, she didn't know.

He wasn't getting off the hook. He'd never have access to his daughter again. And would be doing more time in jail. Beyond that, she didn't want to know.

Didn't care.

If she had to move, she'd do so, but didn't think it would come to that. Clint was a disturbed, incredibly selfish individual who lacked compassion and had a disturbing mean streak because of it, but he wasn't a physically violent man. Manipulation was his weapon.

One thing she felt certain of, he couldn't hurt her anymore.

"You ready?"

Brian's words reached her where she'd stopped in her tracks, afraid to move forward. What if Brooke didn't like her? Was afraid of her? Wouldn't leave with her?

Tears filled her eyes just watching the little girl. And she ached, so badly she ached, to hold the child, but…a crying, clutching woman was only going to scare her.

"Hey, Annabelle!" Brian called, loudly and with cheer. "Throw me the ball!"

"Throw the ball, Little One," Lillie coached, while Detective Anderson watched from his perch on the front porch.

The precious angel, standing again, bent down, her arms closing around the basketball-sized rubber orb, pulling it into her chest, and heaved with her whole body. She fell, but didn't seem to care as she watched the ball roll down a slight incline toward Brian and… Jessica.

Up again at once, the toddler half ran, half galloped after her toy. It fell short of them, but Brian stepped out, gave it a soft kick aimed right at Jessica.

Giggling, shrieking, her face alight with glee, Brooke ran toward the ball, stumbling just before she reached it and would have fallen, hard, if Jessica hadn't reached out and caught her up to hold her safe and sound against her chest.

It happened so naturally, the save from danger, the

pulling her in, and then there she was, holding her daughter against her heart.

Certain she was never ever going to let her go again.

Brian was quiet on the drive home. Jessica had been hoping for time alone with him, and yet, was finding herself suddenly unsure of what to say.

Back at the house, while Brooke had sat in her high chair, having a snack, Jessica had had a short but deeply emotional talk with Lillie. The woman, Mima, Brooke called her, was going to be coming to Fayetteville for a visit in another week—giving Jessica enough time to get Brooke settled back in at home first—and would be staying for a while, at least, in the apartment Jessica had rented for Brian, to babysit during the day while Jessica worked.

Jessica was going to have to call her ma, too. Jackie Shepherd wouldn't be waiting the week to get to Fayetteville. She'd be catching the first flight out after she heard.

But her life was in California. And it worked better for both her and Jessica to keep it that way.

The whole time Jessica had been talking to Lillie, she'd been waiting for Brian to come inside, to meet the woman face-to-face, not just across a yard, to speak with her.

Instead, he'd stayed outside, in conversation with Detective Anderson. Like an investigator talking shop with a coworker.

And maybe that was it…the reason for his silence. His job was done.

Surely, he wasn't thinking about just…

What? Leaving?

Of course he was.

The job was done.

The thought struck her so hard she almost gasped out loud. He glanced her way. She smiled, pretending that all was fine.

And sat in shock. Her daughter was asleep behind her. A two-year-old child who didn't know her, who was going to need a lot of time and attention.

Her time and attention.

She'd already made a call, as soon as they'd started the drive home and Brooke had fallen asleep in her car seat, to have someone cover for her at work for the next week.

Her life was all falling into place. She had plenty of clothes for Brooke—Lillie had packed them all up. And diapers. Even two grocery bags of toddler food. She had the toys from the Brain Play Toys complete package she'd purchased.

And Brian…he had a life to get back to as well.

She kept repeating the fact to herself all the way home. Afraid to break the silence that had fallen between them.

Not wanting to hear that he'd already booked a flight out yet that night.

But as they turned into her drive and he opened the garage door and pulled inside as he'd done so many times over the past many days, she wasn't just thinking about introducing Brooke back into her home.

The toddler was still sound asleep, for one thing. She opened the back passenger door. Carefully unbuckled a car seat she hadn't used in eighteen months—one that was facing forward instead of backward as it had been…

Emotion started to overwhelm her as she looked at the sleeping child and the enormity of the immediate change in her life hit her. For so many months she'd been alone. Living alone. Doing only for herself…

"Let me get her." Brian's voice came softly from be-

hind her. She stepped back without a lot of thought on the matter. Watched as he carefully lifted her daughter, and followed him in as he managed to lay her in her bed without Brooke waking up.

It felt right. Him doing that.

He did it well.

"How did you know how to do that?" she asked.

He shrugged. "Seemed pretty clear. You don't want her to wake up, you support her body so she won't, and you lay her down the same way."

His words made her grin. She'd been dealing with tragedy for so long, she'd forgotten how to take life on the simple.

How to not worry about every little thing.

Like Brian getting ready to tell her he was leaving?

"What were you and Anderson talking about?" she asked as she flipped on the baby monitor, grabbed up her portable speaker part of it, took a long glance at her daughter, hardly believing Brooke was really there, and followed him out to the dining room and watched him collect up the debris from his investigation. As long as they'd worked at that table together, as many hours as he'd spent there alone, it took no time for him to gather papers in file folders, stack them, unplug his laptop and lay it on top of them.

All ready to be packed.

And he hadn't answered her.

He stood there, hands in his pockets, watching her.

"Love isn't enough."

Whatever she'd been expecting, it wasn't that. "What?"

"It can't keep bad things from happening."

Not at all sure where he was headed, or why, she still

couldn't leave well enough alone. "No, but it sustains you until you get through them," she said.

He looked like he had more to say, like he was about to argue with her, but stopped and then said, "You've been right about a lot of things."

"So have you."

At least they had that settled.

"What was Anderson talking to you about? He'd said he had something to talk to you about."

"He offered me a job, sort of. The department is looking for a full-time investigator, hired as a contractor, not as a member of the force. Contractors aren't under the auspices of department policy. The state police have expressed a desire to have access to this person as well. Starting with finding Lillie's granddaughter and the little girl's father. Apparently, there were questions about the crash. Things that made it look deliberate..."

The way his chin was jutting, and his hands were fisted inside his pockets, scared her. Her heart, though... it was thudding a mile a minute.

And it hit her.

She hadn't just needed to find her daughter. She'd needed to find herself.

To fight for herself.

To ask for what she needed. The first big step she'd taken had been to call Sierra's Web and hire Brian.

She had Brooke back. Had a daughter who had to be able to rely on her mother to set a healthy example for her in life.

"For what it's worth, I'd like you to stay," she said. "I know it's only been a couple of weeks, but what we've been through...the way we fit...and the sex..."

His lips pursed. His eyes narrowed.

She pulled it all out. "I love you, Brian."

Still nothing from him. Just looks that spoke to her soul.

"Do you think there's any chance, even a little one, that you could, maybe, down the road, start to love me back?"

He shook his head. Once. Twice. Studied her intently. Shrugged.

"I suspect I might have already crossed that bridge."

His words burst through her heart, causing an eruption like she'd never known before. Showing her a paradise she hadn't known to hope for.

She wasn't sure what to do with it.

How to even accept the possibility of it.

Was afraid…

"Though it's completely illogical, makes no sense, to spend twenty-nine years certain love wasn't for you, and then think you've fallen in two weeks' time."

Heart still soaring way ahead of her mind, she glommed on what she could handle. "You're only twenty-nine?"

"Yeah, and you're thirty-two. I know, it was in the case file. I'm a little younger than you. You have a problem with that?"

"No." None at all.

That got her another nod.

"What did you tell Anderson?" It should have been her first question. The only question, really, because if he'd already said no, he'd made up his mind.

He looked at her. Those striking hazel eyes seeming to brim with things she wanted to believe.

"What did you tell him?" she asked again.

"That I'd think about it."

"And have you?"

"Some. I didn't think I was done yet."

One word stood out. So loud she didn't let the rest in. "'Didn't'?" she repeated.

"I don't think love can make everything perfect."

"Neither do I. Life isn't about perfection. It's about choices. But here's something I've learned, that I can promise you, Brian. Love, even only after knowing it for a few months, can give you the strength to move mountains if you let it. Whether the one you love is there or not, the love you feel for them can hold you up forever."

Loving Brooke had taught her that.

His glance toward her daughter's room told her he got her point.

"She won't remember her biological father," she said then, softly. "She'll need to know about him someday, but if she's been raised by a good man, if she's secure in his love, the news won't be so devastating to her. And right now, as she transitions in, if you're here, around, you could be as much father in her memory as I am mother. It won't be an easy gig. And I sure as hell don't want to talk you into anything. Just…if you feel it…you know, a need to hang around, there's a position open here for you."

"I can't believe I'm saying this…"

He hadn't said anything.

"What?" she asked.

"I accept."

He changed with those two words. Before her eyes, his expression lit up, his hands came out of his pockets, and his chin…there was no tension there at all. His face softened so much she almost didn't recognize him.

Standing there with more joy than she'd ever imagined flowing through her, feeling weak and strong and afraid she'd wake up and find out that none of it was real, she had no words.

Brian didn't seem to need words. He walked toward her slowly. Holding her gaze. Sliding his arms around her.

"I love you, Jess."

His whispered words were the light in her window.

One that would never burn out.

Not in the tough times.

Not in old age.

Not ever.

* * * * *

COMING NEXT MONTH FROM

HARLEQUIN

ROMANTIC SUSPENSE

#2243 CHASING A COLTON KILLER

The Coltons of New York

by Deborah Fletcher Mello

Stella Maxwell is one story away from Pulitzer gold, but when she becomes the prime suspect in the murder of her ex-boyfriend, those aspirations are put on hold. FBI agent Brennan Colton suspects Stella might be guilty of something, but it isn't murder. Between his concern for Stella's well-being and the notorious Landmark Killer taunting them, Brennan never anticipates fighting for his heart.

#2244 MISSING IN TEXAS

by Karen Whiddon

It's been four brutal years for Jake Cassin, who finally locates the daughter who's been missing all that time. But his little girl is abducted before he can even meet her. Despite his reservations and an unwanted stirring of attraction, he must work with Edie Beswick, her adoptive mother, who is just as frantic as he is. How can they stay rational on this desperate search when they have everything to lose?

#2245 A FIREFIGHTER'S HIDDEN TRUTH

Sierra's Web • by Tara Taylor Quinn

When Luke Dennison wakes up in the hospital with amnesia, he doesn't know why a beautiful woman is glaring down at him. He soon learns he is a firefighter, a father and someone wants them both dead. After engaging the experts of Sierra's Web, Luke and Shelby are whisked into protective custody. Could this proximity bring them to a greater understanding of each other...or finally separate them forever?

#2246 TEXAS LAW: SERIAL MANHUNT

Texas Law • by Jennifer D. Bokal

For more than twenty years, Sage Sauter has been keeping a secret—her daughter's biological father is Dr. Michael O'Brien. Michael has never forgotten about his first love, Sage. So when Sage's daughter shows up at his hospital—presumably after being attacked by a serial killer—he offers to help. Sage knows that Michael's the best forensic pathologist around, but she's terrified that he'll discover her secret if he gets involved with a very deadly investigation.

D1044222